FOR EVERY AMERICAN DREAM, THERE IS A NIGHTMARE . . .

Volume Two of this haunting collection includes ghost stories, old and new, from the darkest corners of America . . .

Nightmare in New Mexico . . .
What was the archaeologist planning to do with those ancient artifacts he stole? Raise the dead?

Mania in Minnesota . . .
John Jeremy had an eerie talent for finding missing corpses. Everyone was dying to know his secret.

Weirdness in Washington . . .
The homeless man eagerly accepted the farmer's offer to use his old log cabin. Even if the cabin had this odd habit of disappearing.

Creepy Crawly in Kentucky . . .
The old Indian legends are not to be believed. But try telling that to an Indian ghost.

AND MUCH MORE!

Also available from Berkley Books

GREAT AMERICAN GHOST STORIES
VOLUME ONE

GREAT AMERICAN GHOST STORIES

VOLUME TWO

Edited by Frank D. McSherry, Jr.,
Charles G. Waugh, and
Martin H. Greenberg

BERKLEY BOOKS, NEW YORK

This volume is an abridged edition of the compilation of stories appearing in *Great American Ghost Stories*.

Additional copyright information appears in the Acknowledgments on page 259.

This Berkley book contains the abridged text of the original hardcover edition. It has been completely reset in a typeface designed for easy reading, and was printed from new film.

GREAT AMERICAN GHOST STORIES
Volume Two

A Berkley Book / published by arrangement with
Rutledge Hill Press

PRINTING HISTORY
Rutledge Hill Press edition published 1991
Berkley edition / February 1993

All rights reserved.
Copyright © 1991 by Frank D. McSherry, Jr.,
Martin Harry Greenberg, and Charles G. Waugh.
This book may not be reproduced in whole or in part,
by mimeograph or any other means, without permission.
For information address: The Berkley Publishing Group,
200 Madison Avenue, New York, New York 10016.

ISBN: 0-425-13623-X

A BERKLEY BOOK ® TM 757,375
Berkley Books are published by The Berkley Publishing Group,
200 Madison Avenue, New York, New York 10016.
The name "BERKLEY" and the "B" logo
are trademarks belonging to Berkley Publishing Corporation.

PRINTED IN THE UNITED STATES OF AMERICA

10 9 8 7 6 5 4 3 2 1

CONTENTS

The Borders
of the Unknown

Here he comes. Right at you.

Nice looking, well dressed, pleasant enough. A complete stranger. But—

Why do you feel you've seen him before—somewhere? Why does an icy shiver run down your spine, like a black spider the size of your palm scurrying down between your shoulder blades? Cold and dead and *moving*—

Ghosts come in many kinds.

Drifting misty white at night over smoking battlefields, strolling real as rock among guests at a harvest ball, a whispered voice warning a ship captain to change course, even a pale image of a skull in a White House mirror warning President Abraham Lincoln of his coming death—

The fascinating and eerie variety of ghosts is reflected in the thirteen tales collected in this volume. All are American ghosts. Each story is set in a state whose territory and history is integral to the story and provides an additional bonus for the reader.

The authors include the prolific writer Joyce Carol Oates, "one of the finest Southern writers that ever came out of the North"; Pulitzer prize-winner Oliver La Farge, author of *Laughing Boy*; master of the detective story, Julius Long;

and Civil War veteran Ambrose Bierce, whose life ended as mysteriously as his classic stories.

Their ghosts gleam and glimmer and sometimes kill—in such places as haunted Massachusetts and a pine-surrounded phantom farmhouse in Maine. And the night court judge and jury in a sleepy southern town are out of this world.

These mysterious beings appear in every time, in every place. Are they all the results of superstition, of terror, misunderstanding, wishful thinking?

It is understandable that a grieving mother, looking at a filthy curtain blowing in the rain from an open window at night, could see a dead child returning. It should cause no surprise that in his last moments of life a wounded soldier might try to see his loved ones again . . . and that he might possibly succeed.

So pay no attention to that person coming down the street. The one you've never met but seems somehow familiar.

Haven't you seen him somewhere?

Him, the one whose face just turned into a skull—

—*Frank D. McSherry*

GREAT AMERICAN GHOST STORIES

VOLUME TWO

Perry Moore was a scientist, an objective researcher into fraudulent psychic mediums—until a voice from his own past spoke out of the darkness.

1

Night-Side

Joyce Carol Oates

6 February 1887. Quincy, Massachusetts. Montague House.
Disturbing experience at Mrs. A——'s home yesterday evening. Few theatrics—comfortable though rather pathetically shabby surroundings—an only mildly sinister atmosphere (especially in contrast to the Walpurgis Night presented by that shameless charlatan in Portsmouth: the Dwarf Eustace who presumed to introduce me to Swedenborg himself, under the erroneous impression that I am a member of the Church of the New Jerusalem—*I!*). Nevertheless I came away disturbed, and my conversation with Dr. Moore afterward, at dinner, though dispassionate and even, at times, a bit flippant, did not settle my mind. Perry Moore is of course a hearty materialist, an Aristotelian-Spencerian with a love of good food and drink, and an appreciation of the more nonsensical vagaries of life; when in his company I tend to support that general view, as I do

1

at the University as well—for there is a terrific pull in my nature toward the gregarious that I cannot resist. (That I do not wish to resist.) Once I am alone with my thoughts, however, I am accursed with doubts about my own position and nothing seems more precarious than my intellectual "convictions."

The more hardened members of our Society, like Perry Moore, are apt to put the issue bluntly: Is Mrs. A—— of Quincy a conscious or unconscious fraud? The conscious frauds are relatively easy to deal with; once discovered, they prefer to erase themselves from further consideration. The unconscious frauds are not, in a sense, "frauds" at all. It would certainly be difficult to prove criminal intention. Mrs. A——, for instance, does not accept money or gifts so far as we have been able to determine, and both Perry Moore and I noted her courteous but firm refusal of the Judge's offer to send her and her husband (presumably ailing?) on holiday to England in the spring. She is a mild, self-effacing, rather stocky woman in her mid-fifties who wears her hair parted in the center, like several of my maiden aunts, and whose sole item of adornment was an old-fashioned cameo brooch; her black dress had the appearance of having been home-made, though it was attractive enough, and freshly ironed. According to the Society's records she has been a practicing medium now for six years. Yet she lives, still, in an undistinguished section of Quincy, in a neighborhood of modest frame dwellings. The A——s' house is in fairly good condition, especially considering the damage routinely done by our winters, and the only room we saw, the parlor, is quite ordinary, with overstuffed chairs and the usual cushions and a monstrous horsehair sofa and, of course, the oaken table; the atmosphere would have been so conventional as to have seemed disappointing had not Mrs. A—— made an attempt to brighten it, or perhaps to give it a glamourously occult air, by hanging certain watercolors about the room. (She claims that the watercolors were "done" by one of her contact spirits, a young Iroquois girl who died in the seventeen seventies of smallpox. They are touchingly garish—mandalas and triangles and stylized eyeballs and even a transparent Cosmic Man with Indian-black hair.)

At last night's sitting there were only three persons in addition to Mrs. A——. Judge T—— of the New York State Supreme Court (now retired); Dr. Moore; and I, Jarvis Williams. Dr. Moore and I came out from Cambridge under the aegis of the Society for Psychical Research in order to make a preliminary study of the kind of mediumship Mrs. A—— affects. We did not bring a stenographer along this time though Mrs. A—— indicated her willingness to have the sitting transcribed; she struck me as being rather warmly cooperative, and even interested in our formal procedures, though Perry Moore remarked afterward at dinner that she had struck him as "noticeably reluctant." She was, however, flustered at the start of the séance and for a while it seemed as if we and the Judge might have made the trip for nothing. (She kept waving her plump hands about like an embarrassed hostess, apologizing for the fact that the spirits were evidently in a "perverse uncommunicative mood tonight.")

She did go into a trance eventually, however. The four of us were seated about the heavy round table from approximately 6:50 P.M. to 9:00 P.M. For nearly forty-five minutes Mrs. A—— made abortive attempts to contact her Chief Communicator and then slipped abruptly into trance (dramatically, in fact: her eyes rolled back in her head in a manner that alarmed me at first), and a personality named Webley appeared. "Webley's" voice appeared to be coming from several directions during the course of the sitting. At all times it was at least three yards from Mrs. A——; despite the semi-dark of the parlor I believe I could see the woman's mouth and throat clearly enough, and I could not detect any obvious signs of ventriloquism. (Perry Moore, who is more experienced than I in physical research, and rather more casual about the whole phenomenon, claims he has witnessed feats of ventriloquism that would make poor Mrs. A—— look quite shabby in comparison.) "Webley's" voice was raw, singsong, peculiarly disturbing. At times it was shrill and at other times so faint as to be nearly inaudible. Something brattish about it. Exasperating. "Webley" took care to pronounce his final *g*'s in a self-conscious manner, quite unlike Mrs. A———. (Which could be, of course, a deliberate ploy.)

This Webley is one of Mrs. A———'s most frequent manifesting spirits, though he is not the most reliable. Her Chief Communicator is a Scots patriarch who lived "in the time of Merlin" and who is evidently very wise; unfortunately he did not choose to appear yesterday evening. Instead, Webley presided. He is supposed to have died some seventy-five years ago at the age of nineteen in a house just up the street from the A———s'. He was either a butcher's helper or an apprentice tailor. He died in a fire—or by a "slow dreadful crippling disease"—or beneath a horse's hooves, in a freakish accident; during the course of the sitting he alluded self-pityingly to his death but seemed to have forgotten the exact details. At the very end of the evening he addressed me directly as Dr. Williams of Harvard University, saying that since I had influential friends in Boston I could help him with his career—it turned out he had written hundreds of songs and poems and parables but none had been published; would I please find a publisher for his work? Life had treated him so unfairly. His talent—his genius—had been lost to humanity. I had it within my power to help him, he claimed, was I not *obliged* to help him . . . ? He then sang one of his songs, which sounded to me like an old ballad; many of the words were so shrill as to be unintelligible, but he sang it just the same, repeating the verses in a haphazard order:

> This ae nighte, this ae nighte,
> 　—Every nighte and alle,
> Fire and fleet and candle-lighte,
> 　And Christe receive thy saule.

> When thou from hence away art past,
> 　—Every nighte and alle,
> To Whinny-muir thou com'st at last:
> 　And Christe receive thy saule.

From Brig o' Dread when thou may'st pass,
  —Every nighte and alle,
The whinnes sall prick thee to the bare bane:
And Christe receive thy saule.

The elderly Judge T—— had come up from New York City in order, as he earnestly put it, to "speak directly to his deceased wife as he was never able to do while she was living"; but Webley treated the old gentleman in a high-handed, cavalier manner, as if the occasion were not at all serious. He kept saying, "Who is there tonight? *Who* is there? Let them introduce themselves again—I don't *like* strangers! I tell you I don't *like* strangers!" Though Mrs. A—— had informed us beforehand that we would witness no physical phenomena, there were, from time to time, glimmerings of light in the darkened room, hardly more than the tiny pulsations of light made by fireflies; and both Perry Moore and I felt the table vibrating beneath our fingers. At about the time when Webley gave way to the spirit of Judge T——'s wife, the temperature in the room seemed to drop suddenly and I remember being gripped by a sensation of panic—but it lasted only an instant and I was soon myself again. (Dr. Moore claimed not to have noticed any drop in temperature and Judge T——was so rattled after the sitting that it would have been pointless to question him.)

The séance proper was similar to others I have attended. A spirit—or voice—laid claim to being the late Mrs. T——; this spirit addressed the survivor in a peculiarly intense, urgent manner, so that it was rather embarrassing to be present. Judge T—— was soon weeping. His deeply creased face glistened with tears like a child's.

"Why Darrie! *Darrie!* Don't cry! Oh, don't cry!" the spirit said. "No one is dead, Darrie. There is no death. No death! . . . Can you hear me, Darrie? Why are you so frightened? So upset? No need, Darrie, no need! Grandfather and Lucy and I are together here—happy together. Darrie, look up! Be brave, my dear! My poor frightened dear! We never knew each other, did we? My poor dear! My love! . . .

I saw you in a great transparent house, a great burning house; poor Darrie, they told me you were ill, you were weak with fever; all the rooms of the house were aflame and the staircase was burnt to cinders, but there were figures walking up and down, Darrie, great numbers of them, and you were among them, dear, stumbling in your fright—so clumsy! Look up, dear, and shade your eyes, and you will see me. Grandfather helped me—did you know? Did I call out his name at the end? My dear, my darling, it all happened so quickly—we never knew each other, did we? Don't be hard on Annie! Don't be cruel! Darrie? Why are you crying?'' And gradually the spirit voice grew fainter; or perhaps something went wrong and the channels of communication were no longer clear. There were repetitions, garbled phrases, meaningless queries of "Dear? Dear?'' that the Judge's replies did not seem to placate. The spirit spoke of her gravesite, and of a trip to Italy taken many years before, and of a dead or unborn baby, and again of Annie—evidently Judge T——'s daughter; but the jumble of words did not always make sense and it was a great relief when Mrs. A—— suddenly woke from her trance.

Judge T—— rose from the table, greatly agitated. He wanted to call the spirit back; he had not asked her certain crucial questions; he had been overcome by emotion and had found it difficult to speak, to interrupt the spirit's monologue. But Mrs. A—— (who looked shockingly tired) told him the spirit would not return again that night and they must not make any attempt to call it back.

"The other world obeys its own laws,'' Mrs. A—— said in her small, rather reedy voice.

We left Mrs. A——'s home shortly after 9:00 P.M. I too was exhausted; I had not realized how absorbed I had been in the proceedings.

Judge T—— is also staying at Montague House, but he was too upset after the sitting to join us for dinner. He assured us, though, that the spirit was authentic—the voice had been his wife's, he was certain of it, he would stake his life on it. She had never called him "Darrie''during her lifetime, wasn't it odd that she called him "Darrie" now?—and was so concerned for him, so loving?—and concerned for their daughter as well? He was very moved. He had a great deal to think about. (Yes, he'd had a fever some weeks ago—a severe attack of bronchitis and a fever; in fact, he had not completely recovered.) What was extraordinary about the entire experience was the wisdom revealed: There is no death.

There is no death.

Dr. Moore and I dined heartily on roast crown of lamb, spring potatoes with peas, and buttered cabbage. We were served two kinds of bread—German rye and sour cream rolls; the hotel's butter was superb; the wine excellent; the dessert—crepes with cream and toasted almonds—looked marvelous, though I had not any appetite for it. Dr. Moore was ravenously hungry. He talked as he ate, often punctuating his remarks with rich bursts of laughter. It was his opinion, of course, that the medium was a fraud—and not a very skillful fraud, either. In his fifteen years of amateur, intermittent investigations he had encountered far more skillful mediums. Even the notorious Eustace with his levitating table and hobgoblin chimes and shrieks was cleverer than Mrs. A——; one knew of course that Eustace was a cheat, but one was hard pressed to explain his method. Whereas Mrs. A—— was quite transparent.

Dr. Moore spoke for some time in his amiable, dogmatic way. He ordered brandy for both of us, though it was nearly midnight when we finished our dinner and I was anxious to get to bed. (I hoped to rise early and work on a lecture dealing with Kant's approach to the problem of Free Will, which I would be delivering in a few days.) But Dr. Moore enjoyed talking and seemed to have been invigorated by our experience at Mrs. A——'s.

At the age of forty-three Perry Moore is only four years my senior, but he has the air, in my presence at least, of being considerably older. He is a second cousin of my mother, a very successful physician with a bachelor's flat and office in Louisburg Square; his failure to marry, or his refusal, is one of Boston's perennial mysteries. Everyone agrees that he is learned, witty, charming, and extraordinarily intelligent. Striking rather than conventionally handsome, with a dark, lustrous beard and darkly bright eyes, he is an excellent amateur violinist, an enthusiastic sailor, and a lover of literature—his favorite writers are Fielding, Shakespeare, Horace, and Dante. He is, of course, the perfect investigator in spiritualist matters since he is detached from the phenomena he observes and yet he is indefatigably curious; he has a positive love, a mania, for facts. Like the true scientist he seeks facts that, assembled, may possibly give rise to hypotheses: he does not set out with a hypothesis in mind, like a sort of basket into which certain facts may be tossed, helter-skelter, while others are conveniently ignored. In all things he is an empiricist who accepts nothing on faith.

"If the woman is a fraud, then," I say hesitantly, "you believe she is a self-deluded fraud? And her spirits' information is gained by means of telepathy?"

"Telepathy indeed. There can be no other explanation," Dr. Moore says emphatically. "By some means not yet known to science—by some uncanny means she suppresses her conscious personality—and thereby releases other, secondary personalities that have the power of seizing upon others' thoughts and memories. It's done in a way not understood by science at the present time. But it will be understood eventually. Our investigations into the unconscious powers of the human mind are just beginning; we're on the threshold, really, of a new era."

"So she simply picks out of her clients' minds whatever they want to hear, " I say slowly. "And from time to time she can even tease them a little—insult them, even: she can unloose a creature like that obnoxious Webley upon a person like Judge T——without fear of being discovered. Telepathy . . . Yes, that would explain a great deal. Very nearly everything we witnessed tonight."

"*Everything*, I should say, " Dr. Moore says.

In the coach returning to Cambridge I set aside Kant and my lecture notes and read Sir Thomas Browne: *Light that makes all things seen, makes some things invisible. The greatest mystery of Religion is expressed by adumbration.*

19 March 1887. Cambridge. 11 P.M.

Walked ten miles this evening; must clear cobwebs from mind.

Unhealthy atmosphere. Claustrophobic. Last night's sitting in Quincy—a most unpleasant experience.

(Did not tell my wife what happened. Why is she so curious about the Spirit World?—about Perry Moore?)

My body craves more violent physical activity. In the summer, thank God, I will be able to swim in the ocean: the most strenuous and challenging of exercises.

Jotting down notes re the Quincy experience:

I. Fraud

Mrs. A——, possibly with accomplices, conspires to deceive: she does research into her clients' lives beforehand, possibly bribes servants. She is either a very skillful ventriloquist or works with someone who is. (Husband? Son? The husband is a retired cabinetmaker said to be in poor health; possibly consumptive. The son, married, lives in Waterbury.)

Her stated wish to avoid publicity and her declining of payment may simply be ploys; she may intend to make a great deal of money at some future time.

(Possibility of blackmail?—might be likely in cases similar to Perry Moore's.)

II. Non-fraud
Naturalistic
1. Telepathy. She reads minds of clients.
2. "Multiple personality" of medium. Aspects of her own buried psyche are released as her conscious personality is suppressed. These secondary beings are in mysterious rapport with the "secondary" personalities of the clients.

Spiritualistic
1. The controls are genuine communicators, intermediaries between our world and the world of the dead. These spirits give way to other spirits, who then speak through the medium; or
2. These spirits *influence* the medium, who relays their messages using her own vocabulary. Their personalities are then filtered through and limited by hers.
3. The spirits are not those of the deceased; they are perverse, willful spirits. (Perhaps demons? But there are no demons.)

III. Alternative hypothesis
Madness: the medium is mad, the clients are mad, even the detached, rationalist investigators are mad.

Yesterday evening at Mrs. A——'s home, the second sitting Perry Moore and I observed together, along with Miss Bradley, a stenographer from the Society, and two legitimate clients—a Brookline widow, Mrs. P——, and her daughter Clara, a handsome young woman in her early twenties. Mrs. A—— exactly as she appeared to us in February; possibly a little stouter. Wore black dress and cameo brooch. Served Lapsang tea, tiny sandwiches, and biscuits when we arrived shortly after 6:00 P.M. Seemed quite friendly to Perry, Miss Bradley, and me; fussed over us, like any hostess, chattered a bit about the cold spell. Mrs. P—— and her daughter arrived at six-thirty and the sitting began shortly thereafter.

Jarring from the very first. A babble of spirit voices. Mrs. A—— in trance, head flung back, mouth gaping, eyes rolled upward. Queer. Unnerving. I glanced at Dr. Moore but he seemed unperturbed, as always. The widow and her daughter, however, looked as frightened as I felt.

Why are we here, sitting around this table?

What do we believe we will discover?

What are the risks we face . . . ?

"Webley" appeared and disappeared in a matter of minutes. His shrill, raw, aggrieved voice was supplanted by that of a creature of indeterminate sex who babbled in Gaelic. This creature in turn was supplanted by a hoarse German, a man who identified himself as Felix; he spoke a curiously ungrammatical German. For some minutes he and two or three other spirits quarreled. (Each declared himself Mrs. A——'s Chief Communicator for the evening.) Small lights flickered in the semi-dark of the parlor and the table quivered beneath my fingers and I felt, or believed I felt, something brushing against me, touching the back of my head. I shuddered violently but regained my composure at once. An unidentified voice proclaimed in English that the Spirit of our Age was Mars: there would be a catastrophic war shortly and most of the world's population would be destroyed. All atheists would be destroyed. Mrs. A—— shook her head from side to side as if trying to wake. Webley appeared, crying "Hello? Hello? I can't see any-one! Who is there? Who has called me?" but was again supplanted by another spirit who shouted long strings of words in a foreign language. [Note: I discovered a few days later that this language was Walachian, a Romanian dialect. Of course Mrs. A——, whose ancestors are English, could not possibly have known Walachian, and I rather doubt that the woman has ever heard of the Walachian people.]

The sitting continued in this chaotic way for some minutes. Mrs. P—— must have been quite disappointed, since she had wanted to be put in contact with her deceased husband. (She needed advice on whether or not to sell certain pieces of property.) Spirits babbled freely in English, German, Gaelic, French, even in Latin, and at one point Dr. Moore queried a spirit in Greek, but the spirit retreated at once as if not equal to Dr. Moore's wit. The atmosphere was alarming but at the same time rather manic; almost jocular. I found myself suppressing laughter. Something touched the back of my head and I shivered violently and broke into perspiration, but the experience was not altogether unpleas-ant; it would be very difficult for me to characterize it.

And then . . .

And then, suddenly, everything changed. There was complete calm. A spirit voice spoke gently out of a corner of the room, addressing Perry Moore by his first name in a slow, tentative, groping way. "Perry? Perry . . . ?" Dr. Moore jerked about in his seat. He was astonished; I could see by his expression that the voice belonged to someone he knew.

"Perry . . . ? This is Brandon. I've waited so long for you, Perry, how could you be so selfish? I forgave you. Long ago. You couldn't help your cruelty and I couldn't help my innocence. Perry? My glasses have been broken . . . I can't see. I've been afraid for so long, Perry, please have mercy on me! I can't bear it any longer. I didn't *know* what it would be like. There are crowds of people here, but we can't see one another, we don't know one another, we're strangers, there is a universe of strangers. . . . I can't see anyone clearly . . . I've been lost for twenty years, Perry. I've been waiting for you for twenty years! You don't dare turn away again, Perry! Not again! Not after so long!"

Dr. Moore stumbled to his feet, knocking his chair aside. "No . . . Is it . . . I don't believe . . ."

"Perry? Perry? Don't abandon me again, Perry! Not again!"

"What is this?" Dr. Moore cried.

He was on his feet now; Mrs. A—— woke from her trance with a groan. The women from Brookline were very upset and I must admit that I was in a mild state of terror, my shirt and my underclothes drenched with perspiration.

The sitting was over. It was only seven-thirty.

"Brandon?" Dr. Moore cried. "Wait. Where are . . . ? Brandon? Can you hear me? Where are you? Why did you do it, Brandon? Wait! Don't leave! Can't anyone call him back— Can't anyone help me . . . ?"

Mrs. A—— rose unsteadily. She tried to take Dr. Moore's hands in hers but he was too agitated.

"I heard only the very last words," she said. "They're always that way . . . so confused, so broken . . . the poor things. . . . Oh, what a pity! It wasn't murder, was it? Not murder! Suicide . . . ? I believe suicide is even worse for them! The poor broken things, they wake in the other world and are utterly, utterly lost—they have no guides, you see—no help in crossing over. . . . They are completely alone for eternity . . ."

"Can't you call him back?" Dr. Moore asked wildly. He was peering into a corner of the parlor, slightly stooped, his face distorted as if he were staring into the sun. "Can't someone help me? . . . Brandon? Are you here? Are you here somewhere? For God's sake can't someone help!"

"Dr. Moore, please, the spirits are gone—the sitting is over for tonight—"

"You foolish old woman, leave me alone! Can't you see I . . . I . . . I must not lose him . . . Call him back, will you? I insist! I insist!"

"Dr. Moore, please . . . You mustn't shout . . ."

"I said call him back! At once! *Call him back!*"

Then he burst into tears. He stumbled against the table and hid his face in his hands and wept like a child; he wept as if his heart had been broken

And so today I have been reliving the séance. Taking notes, trying to determine what happened. A brisk windy walk of ten miles. Head buzzing with ideas. Fraud? Deceit? Telepathy? Madness?

What a spectacle! Dr. Perry Moore calling after a spirit, begging it to return . . . and then crying, afterward, in front of four astonished witnesses.

Dr. Perry Moore of all people.

My dilemma: whether I should report last night's incident to Dr. Rowe, the president of the Society, or whether I should say nothing about it and request that Miss Bradley say nothing. It would be tragic if Perry's professional reputation were to be damaged by a single evening's misadventure; and before long all of Boston would be talking.

In his present state, however, he is likely to tell everyone about it himself.

At Montague House the poor man was unable to sleep. He would have kept me up all night had I had the stamina to endure his excitement.

There *are* spirits! There have always been spirits!

His entire life up to the present time has been misspent!
And of course, most important of all . . . there is no
death!

He paced about my hotel room, pulling at his beard
nervously. At times there were tears in his eyes. He seemed
to want a response of some kind from me but whenever I
started to speak he interrupted; he was not really listening.

"Now at last I know. I can't undo my knowledge," he
said in a queer hoarse voice. "Amazing, isn't it, after so
many years . . . so many wasted years . . . Ignorance
has been my lot, darkness . . . and a hideous compla-
cency. My God, when I consider my deluded smugness! I
am so ashamed, so ashamed. All along people like Mrs.
A—— have been in contact with a world of such
power . . . and people like me have been toiling in
ignorance, accumulating material achievements, expending
our energies in idiotic transient things. . . . But all that is
changed now. Now I know. I *know.* There is no death, as
the Spiritualists have always told us."

"But, Perry, don't you think . . . Isn't it possible
that . . ."

"I *know,*" he said quietly. "It's as clear to me as if I had
crossed over into that other world myself. Poor Brandon!
He's no older now than he was *then.* The poor boy, the poor
tragic soul! To think that he's still living after so many
years . . . Extraordinary . . . It makes my head spin,"
he said slowly. For a moment he stood without speaking.
He pulled at his beard, then absently touched his lips with
his fingers, then wiped at his eyes. He seemed to have
forgotten me. When he spoke again his voice was hollow,
rather ghastly. He sounded drugged. "I . . . I had been
thinking of him as . . . as dead, you know. As dead.
Twenty years. Dead. And now, tonight, to be forced to
realize that . . . that he isn't dead after all . . . It was
laudanum he took. I found him. His rooms on the third floor
of Weld Hall. I found him. I had no real idea, none at all, not
until I read the note . . . and of course I destroyed the
note . . . I had to, you see: for his sake. For his sake
more than mine. It was because he realized there could

be no . . . no hope . . . Yet he called me cruel! You heard him, Jarvis, didn't you? Cruel! I suppose I was. Was I? I don't know what to think. I must talk with him again. I . . . I don't know what to . . . what to think. I . . ."

"You look awfully tired, Perry. It might be a good idea to go to bed," I said weakly.

". . . recognized his voice at once. Oh at once: no doubt. None. What a revelation! And my life so misspent . . . Treating people's *bodies*. Absurd. I know now that nothing matters except that other world . . . nothing matters except our dead, our beloved dead . . . who are *not dead*. What a colossal revelation . . . ! Why, it will change the entire course of history. It will alter men's minds throughout the world. You were there, Jarvis, so you understand. You were a witness . . ."

"But . . ."

"You'll bear witness to the truth of what I am saying?"

He stared at me, smiling. His eyes were bright and threaded with blood.

I tried to explain to him as courteously and sympathetically as possible that his experience at Mrs. A——'s was not substantially different from the experiences many people have had at séances. "And always in the past psychical researchers have taken the position . . ."

"You were *there*," he said angrily. "You heard Brandon's voice as clearly as I did. Don't deny it!"

". . . have taken the position that . . . the phenomenon can be partly explained by the telepathic powers of the medium . . ."

"That was Brandon's *voice*," Perry said. "I felt his presence, I tell you! *His*. Mrs. A—— had nothing to do with it . . . nothing at all. I feel as if . . . as if I could call Brandon back by myself. . . . I feel his presence even now. Close about me. He isn't dead, you see; no one is dead, there's a universe of . . . of people who are not dead . . . Parents, grandparents, sisters, brothers, everyone . . . everyone . . . How can you deny, Jarvis, the evidence of your own senses? You were there with me tonight and you know as well as I do . . ."

"Perry, I don't *know*. I did hear a voice, yes, but we've heard voices before at other sittings, haven't we? There are always voices. There are always 'spirits.' The Society has taken the position that the spirits could be real, of course, but that there are other hypotheses that are perhaps more likely . . ."

"Other hypotheses indeed!" Perry said irritably. "You're like a man with his eyes shut tight who refuses to open them out of sheer cowardice. Like the cardinals refusing to look through Galileo's telescope! And you have pretensions of being a man of learning, of science. . . . Why, we've got to destroy all the records we've made so far; they're a slander on the world of the spirits. Thank God we didn't file a report yet on Mrs. A——! It would be so embarrassing to be forced to call it back . . ."

"Perry, please. Don't be angry. I want only to remind you of the fact that we've been present at other sittings, haven't we? . . . and we've witnessed others responding emotionally to certain phenomena. Judge T——, for instance. He was convinced he'd spoken with his wife. But you must remember, don't you, that you and I were not at all convinced . . . ? It seemed to us more likely that Mrs. A—— is able, through extrasensory powers we don't quite understand, to read the minds of her clients, and then to project certain voices out into the room so that it sounds as if they are coming from other people. . . . You even said, Perry, that she wasn't a very skillful ventriloquist. You said—"

"What does it matter what, in my ignorance, I said?" he cried. "Isn't it enough that I've been humiliated? That my entire life has been turned about? Must you insult me as well . . . sitting there so smugly and insulting *me?* I think I can make claim to being someone whom you might respect."

And so I assured him that I did respect him. And he walked about the room, wiping at his eyes, greatly agitated. He spoke again of his friend, Brandon Gould, and of his own ignorance, and of the important mission we must undertake to inform men and women of the true state of affairs. I tried to talk with him, to reason with him, but it was hopeless. He scarcely listened to me.

". . . must inform the world . . . crucial truth. . . . There is no death, you see. Never was. Changes civilization, changes the course of history. Jarvis?" he said groggily. "You see? *There is no death.*"

25 March 1887. Cambridge.

Disquieting rumors re Perry Moore. Heard today at the University that one of Dr. Moore's patients (a brother-in-law of Dean Barker) was extremely offended by his behavior during a consultation last week. Talk of his having been drunk . . . which I find incredible. If the poor man appeared to be excitable and not his customary self, it was not because he was *drunk*, surely.

Another far-fetched tale told me by my wife, who heard it from her sister Maude: Perry Moore went to church (St. Aidan's Episcopal Church on Mount Street) for the first time in a decade, sat alone, began muttering and laughing during the sermon, and finally got to his feet and walked out, creating quite a stir. *What delusions! What delusions!* . . . he was said to have muttered.

I fear for the poor man's sanity.

31 March 1887. Cambridge. 4 A.M.

Sleepless night. Dreamed of swimming . . . swimming in the ocean . . . enjoying myself as usual when suddenly the water turns thick . . . turns to mud. Hideous! Indescribably awful. I was swimming nude in the ocean, by moonlight, I believe, ecstatically happy, entirely alone, when the water turned to mud. . . . Vile, disgusting mud; faintly warm; sucking at my body. Legs, thighs, torso, arms. Horrible. Woke in terror. Drenched with perspiration: pajamas wet. One of the most frightening nightmares of my adulthood.

A message from Perry Moore came yesterday just before dinner. Would I like to join him in visiting Mrs. A—— sometime soon, in early April perhaps, on a noninvestigative basis . . . ? He is uncertain now of the morality of our "investigating" Mrs. A—— or any other medium.

4 April 1887. Cambridge.

Spent the afternoon from two to five at William James's home on Irving Street, talking with Professor James of the inexplicable phenomenon of consciousness. He is robust as always, rather irreverent, supremely confident in a way I find enviable; rather like Perry Moore before his conversion. (Extraordinary eyes—so piercing, quick, playful; a graying beard liberally threaded with white; close-cropped graying hair; a large, curving, impressive forehead; a manner intelligent and graceful and at the same time rough-edged, as if he anticipates or perhaps even hopes for recalcitration in his listeners.) We both find conclusive the ideas set forth in Binét's *Alterations of Personality*—unsettling as these ideas may be to the rationalist position. James speaks of a *peculiarity* in the constitution of human nature: this is, the fact that we inhabit not only our ego-consciousness but a wide field of psychological experience (most clearly represented by the phenomenon of memory, which no one can adequately explain) over which we have no control whatsoever. In fact, we are not generally aware of this field of consciousness.

We inhabit a lighted sphere, then; and about us is a vast penumbra of memories, reflections, feelings, and stray uncoordinated thoughts that "belong" to us theoretically, but that do not seem to be part of our conscious identity. (I was too timid to ask Professor James whether it might be the case that we do not inevitably own these aspects of the personality . . . that such phenomena belong as much to the objective world as to our subjective selves.) It is quite possible that there is an element of some indeterminate kind: oceanic, timeless, and living, against which the individual being constructs temporary barriers as part of an ongoing process of unique, particularized survival; like the ocean itself, which appears to separate islands that are in fact not "islands" at all, but aspects of the earth firmly joined together below the surface of the water. Our lives,

then, resemble these islands. . . . All this is no more than
a possibility, Professor James and I agreed.

James is acquainted, of course, with Perry Moore. But he
declined to speak on the subject of the poor man's increas-
ingly eccentric behavior when I alluded to it. (It may be that
he knows even more about the situation than I do—he
enjoys a multitude of acquaintances in Cambridge and
Boston.) I brought our conversation round several times to
the possibility of the *naturalness* of the conversion experience in terms of the individual's evolution of self, no matter
how his family, his colleagues, and society in general
viewed it, and Professor James appeared to agree; at least he
did not emphatically disagree. He maintains a healthy
skepticism, of course, regarding Spiritualist claims, and all
evangelical and enthusiastic religious movements, though
he is, at the same time, a highly articulate foe of the
"rationalist" position and he believes that psychical research of the kind some of us are attempting will eventually
unearth riches . . . revealing aspects of the human psyche
otherwise closed to our scrutiny.

"The fearful thing," James said, "is that we are at all
times vulnerable to incursions from the 'other side' of the
personality. . . . We cannot determine the nature of the
total personality simply because much of it, perhaps most, is
hidden from us. . . . When we are invaded, then, we are
overwhelmed and surrender immediately. Emotionally
charged intuitions, hunches, guesses, even ideas may be the
least aggressive of these incursions; but there are visual and
auditory hallucinations, and forms of automatic behavior
not controlled by the conscious mind. . . . Ah, you're
thinking I am simply describing insanity?"

I stared at him, quite surprised.

"No. Not at all. Not at all," I said at once.

Reading through my grandfather's journals, begun in East
Anglia many years before my birth. Another world then.
Another language, now lost to us. *Man is sinful by nature.
God's justice takes precedence over His mercy.* The dogma

of Original Sin: something brutish about the innocence of that belief. And yet consoling. . . .

Fearful of sleep since my dreams are so troubled now. The voices of impudent spirits (Immanuel Kant himself come to chide me for having made too much of his categories!), stray shouts and whispers I cannot decipher, the faces of my own beloved dead hovering near, like carnival masks, insubstantial and possibly fraudulent. Impatient with my wife, who questions me too closely on these personal matters; annoyed from time to time, in the evenings especially, by the silliness of the children. (The eldest is twelve now and should know better.) Dreading to receive another lengthy letter—sermon, really—from Perry Moore re his "new position," and yet perversely hoping one will come soon.

I must know.

(Must know *what?*)

I must know.

10 April 1887. Boston. St. Aidan's Episcopal Church.

Funeral service this morning for Perry Moore; dead at forty-three.

17 April 1887. Seven Hills, New Hampshire.

A weekend retreat. No talk. No need to think.

Visiting with a former associate, author of numerous books. Cartesian specialist. Elderly. Partly deaf. Extraordinarily kind to me. (Did not ask about the Department or about my work.) Intensely interested in animal behavior now, in observation primarily; fascinated with the phenomenon of hibernation.

He leaves me alone for hours. He sees something in my face I cannot see myself.

The old consolations of a cruel but just God: ludicrous today.

In the nineteenth century we live free of God. We live in the illusion of freedom-of-God.

Dozing off in the guest room of this old farmhouse and

then waking abruptly. *Is someone here? Is someone here?* My voice queer, hushed, childlike. *Please: is someone here?*

Silence.

Query: Is the penumbra outside consciousness all that was ever meant by "God"?

Query: Is inevitability all that was ever meant by "God"?

God—the body of fate we inhabit, then; no more and no less.

God pulled Perry down into the body of fate: into Himself. (Or Itself.) As Professor James might say, Dr. Moore was "vulnerable" to an assault from the other side.

At any rate he is dead. They buried him last Saturday.

25 April 1887. Cambridge.

Shelves of books. The sanctity of books. Kant, Plato, Schopenhauer, Descartes, Hume, Hegel, Spinoza. The others. All. Nietzsche, Spencer, Leibnitz (on whom I did a torturous Master's thesis). Plotinus. Swedenborg. *The Transactions of the American Society for Psychical Research.* Voltaire. Locke. Rousseau. And Berkeley: the good Bishop adrift in a dream.

An etching by Halbrech above my desk, "The Thames 1801." Water too black. Inky-black. Thick with mud . . . ? Filthy water in any case.

Perry's essay, forty-five scribbled pages, "The Challenge of the Future." Given to me several weeks ago by Dr. Rowe, who feared rejecting it for the *Transactions* but could not, of course, accept it. I can read only a few pages at a time, then push it aside, too moved to continue. Frightened also.

The man had gone insane.

Died insane.

Personality broken: broken bits of intellect.

His argument passionate and disjointed, with no pretense of objectivity. Where some weeks ago he had taken the stand that it was immoral to investigate the Spirit World, now he took the stand that it was imperative we do so. We are on the brink of a new age . . . new knowledge of the universe . . . comparable to the stormy transitional period between the Ptolemaic and the Copernican theories of the universe. . . . More experiments required. Money. Donations. Subsidies by private institutions. All psychological research must be channeled into a systematic study of the Spirit World and the ways by which we can communicate with that world. Mediums like Mrs. A—— must be brought to centers of learning like Harvard and treated with the respect their genius deserves. Their value to civilization is, after all, beyond estimation. They must be rescued from arduous and routine lives where their genius is drained off into vulgar pursuits . . . they must be rescued from a clientele that is mainly concerned with being put into contact with deceased relatives for utterly trivial, self-serving reasons. Men of learning must realize the gravity of the situation. Otherwise we will fail, we will stagger beneath the burden, we will be defeated, ignobly, and it will remain for the twentieth century to discover the existence of the Spirit Universe that surrounds the Material Universe, and to determine the exact ways by which one world is related to another.

Perry Moore died of a stroke on the eighth of April; died instantaneously on the steps of the Bedford Club shortly after 2:00 P.M. Passers-by saw a very excited, red-faced gentleman with an open collar push his way through a small gathering at the top of the steps . . . and then suddenly fall, as if shot down.

In death he looked like quite another person: his features sharp, the nose especially pointed. Hardly the handsome Perry Moore everyone had known.

He had come to a meeting of the Society, though it was suggested by Dr. Rowe and by others (including myself) that he stay away. Of course he came to argue. To present his "new position." To insult the other members. (He was contemptuous of a rather poorly organized paper on the medium Miss E—— of Salem, a young woman who works with objects like rings, articles of clothing, locks of hair, et cetera; and quite angry with the evidence presented by a young geologist that would seem to discredit, once and for all, the claims of Eustace of Portsmouth. He interrupted a third paper, calling the reader a "bigot" and an "ignorant fool.")

Fortunately the incident did not find its way into any of the papers. The press, misunderstanding (deliberately and maliciously) the Society's attitude toward Spiritualism, delights in ridiculing our efforts.

There were respectful obituaries. A fine eulogy prepared by Reverend Tyler of St. Aidan's. Other tributes. *A tragic loss . . . Mourned by all who knew him . . .* (I stammered and could not speak. I cannot speak of him, of it, even now. Am I mourning, am I aggrieved? Or merely shocked? Terrified?) Relatives and friends and associates glossed over his behavior these past few months and settled upon an earlier Perry Moore, eminently sane, a distinguished physician and man of letters. I did not disagree, I merely acquiesced; I could not make any claim to have really known the man.

And so he has died, and so he is dead. . . .

Shortly after the funeral I went away to New Hampshire for a few days. But I can barely remember that period of time now. I sleep poorly. I yearn for summer, for a drastic change of climate, of scene. It was unwise for me to take up the responsibility of psychical research, fascinated though I am by it; my classes and lectures at the University demand most of my energy.

How quickly he died, and so young: so relatively young. No history of high blood pressure, it is said.

At the end he was arguing with everyone, however. His personality had completely changed. He was rude, impetuous, even rather profane; even poorly groomed. (Rising to challenge the first of the papers, he revealed a shirtfront that appeared to be stained.) Some claimed he had been drinking all along, for years. Was it possible . . . ? (He had clearly enjoyed the wine and brandy in Quincy that evening, but I would not have said he was intemperate.) Rumors, fanciful tales, outright lies, slander. . . . It is painful, the vulnerability death brings.

Bigots, he called us. Ignorant fools. Unbelievers . . . atheists . . . traitors to the Spirit World . . . heretics. Heretics! I believe he looked directly at me as he pushed his way out of the meeting room: his eyes glaring, his face dangerously flushed, no recognition in his stare.

After his death, it is said, books continue to arrive at his home from England and Europe. He spent a small fortune on obscure, out-of-print volumes . . . commentaries on the Kabbala, on Plotinus, medieval alchemical texts, books on astrology, witchcraft, the metaphysics of death. Occult cosmologies. Egyptian, Indian, and Chinese "wisdom." Blake, Swedenborg, Cozad. *The Tibetan Book of the Dead.* Datsky's *Lunar Mysteries.* His estate is in chaos because he left not one but several wills, the most recent made out only a day before his death, merely a few lines scribbled on scrap paper, without witnesses. The family will contest, of course. Since in this will he left his money and property to an obscure woman living in Quincy, Massachusetts, and since he was obviously not in his right mind at the time, they would be foolish indeed not to contest.

Days have passed since his sudden death. Days continue to pass. At times I am seized by a sort of quick, cold panic; at other times I am inclined to think the entire situation has been exaggerated. In one mood I vow to myself that I will never again pursue psychical research because it is simply too dangerous. In another mood I vow I will never again pursue it because it is a waste of time and my own work, my own career, must come first.

Heretics, he called us. Looking straight at me.

Still, he was mad. And is not to be blamed for the vagaries of madness.

19 June 1887. Boston.

Luncheon with Dr. Rowe, Miss Madeleine van der Post, young Lucas Matthewson; turned over my personal records and notes re the mediums Dr. Moore and I visited. (De-

stroyed jottings of a private nature.) Miss van der Post and
Matthewson will be taking over my responsibilities. Both
are young, quickwitted, alert, with a certain ironic play
about their features; rather like Dr. Moore in his prime.
Matthewson is a former seminary student now teaching
physics at the Boston University. They questioned me about
Perry Moore, but I avoided answering frankly. Asked if we
were close, I said *No*. Asked if I had heard a bizarre tale
making the rounds of Boston salons . . . that a spirit
claiming to be Perry Moore has intruded upon a number of
séances in the area. . . . I said honestly that I had not; and
I did not care to hear about it.

Spinoza: *I will analyze the actions and appetites of men as
if it were a question of lines, of planes, and of solids.*
   It is in this direction, I believe, that we must move. Away
from the phantasmal, the vaporous, the unclear; toward
lines, planes, and solids.
   Sanity.

8 July 1887. Mount Desert Island, Maine.
   Very early this morning, before dawn, dreamed of Perry
Moore: a babbling, gesticulating spirit, bearded, bright-
eyed, obviously mad. Jarvis? Jarvis? Don't deny me! he
cried. I am so . . . so bereft. . . .
   Paralyzed, I faced him: neither awake nor asleep. His
words were not really *words* so much as unvoiced thoughts.
I heard them in my own voice; a terrible raw itching at the
back of my throat yearned to articulate the man's grief.
   Perry?
   You don't dare deny me! Not now!
   He drew near and I could not escape. The dream shifted,
lost its clarity. Someone was shouting at me. Very angry, he
was, and baffled . . . as if drunk . . . or ill . . . or injured.
   Perry? I can't hear you—
   . . . our dinner at Montague House, do you remember?
Lamb, it was. And crepes with almond for dessert. You
remember! You remember! You can't deny me! We were

both nonbelievers then, both abysmally ignorant . . . you can't deny me!

(I was mute with fear or with cunning.)

. . . that idiot Rowe, how humiliated he will be! All of them! All of you! The entire rationalist bias, the . . . the conspiracy of . . . of fools . . . bigots . . . In a few years . . . In a few short years . . . Jarvis, where are you? Why can't I see you? Where have you gone? . . . My eyes can't focus: will someone help me? I seem to have lost my way. Who is here? Who am I talking with? You remember me, don't you?

(He brushed near me, blinking helplessly. His mouth was a hole torn into his pale ravaged flesh.)

Where are you? Where is everyone? I thought it would be crowded here but . . . but there's no one . . . I am forgetting so much! My name—what was my name? Can't see. Can't remember. Something very important . . . something very important I must accomplish—can't remember— Why is there no God? No one here? No one in control? We drift this way and that way, we come to no rest, there are no landmarks . . . no way of judging . . . everything is confused . . . disjointed . . . Is someone listening? Would you read to me, please? Would you read to me?— anything!—that speech of Hamlet's—*To be or not*—a sonnet of Shakespeare's—any sonnet, anything—*That time of year thou may in me behold*—is that it?—is that how it begins? *Bare ruin'd choirs where the sweet birds once sang.* How does it go? Won't you tell me? I'm lost—there's nothing here to see, to touch—isn't anyone listening? I thought there was someone nearby, a friend: isn't anyone here?

(I stood paralyzed, mute with caution: he passed by.)

. . . *When in the chronicle of wasted time*—*the wide world dreaming of things to come*—is anyone listening?— can anyone help?—I am forgetting so much . . . my name, my life . . . my life's work . . . to penetrate the mysteries . . . the veil . . . to do justice to the universe of . . . of what . . . what I had intended? . . . am I in my place of repose now, have I come home? Why is it so

empty here? Why is no one in control? My eyes—my
head—mind broken and blown about—slivers—shards—
annihilating all that's made to a . . . a green thought . . .
a green shade—Shakespeare? Plato? Pascal? Will someone
read me Pascal again? I seem to have lost my way. . . . I
am being blown about—Jarvis, was it? My dear young
friend Jarvis? But I've forgotten your last name. . . . I've
forgotten so much . . .

(I wanted to reach out to touch him—but could not move,
could not wake. The back of my throat ached with sorrow.
Silent! Silent! I could not utter a word.)

. . . my papers, my journal—twenty years—a key somewhere hidden—where?—ah yes: the bottom drawer of
my desk—do you hear?—my desk—house—Louisburg
Square—the key is hidden there—wrapped in a linen
handkerchief—the strongbox is—the locked box is—
hidden—my brother Edward's house—attic—trunk—
steamer trunk—initials R.W.M.—Father's trunk, you see—
strongbox hidden inside—my secret journals—life's
work—physical and spiritual wisdom—must not be lost—
are you listening?—is anyone listening? I am forgetting so
much, my mind is in shreds—but if you could locate the
journal and read it to me—if you could salvage it—me—I
would be so very grateful—I would forgive you anything,
all of you—Is anyone there? Jarvis? Brandon? No
one?—My journal, my soul: will you salvage it? Will—

(He stumbled away and I was alone again.)

Perry—?

But it was too late: I awoke drenched with perspiration.

Nightmare.
Must forget.

Best to rise early, before the others. Mount Desert Island
lovely in July. Our lodge on a hill above the beach. No
spirits here: wind from the northeast, perpetual fresh air,
perpetual waves. Best to rise early and run along the beach
and plunge into the chilly water.

Clear the cobwebs from one's mind.

How beautiful the sky, the ocean, the sunrise!

No spirits here on Mount Desert Island. Swimming: skillful exertion of arms and legs. Head turned this way, that way. Eyes half shut. The surprise of the cold rough waves. One yearns almost to slip out of one's human skin at such times . . . ! Crude blatant beauty of Maine. Ocean. Muscular exertion of body. How alive I am, how living, how invulnerable; what a triumph in my every breath . . .

Everything slips from my mind except the present moment. I am living. I am alive, I am immortal. Must not weaken: must not sink. Drowning? No. Impossible. Life is the only reality. It is not extinction that awaits but a hideous dreamlike state, a perpetual groping, blundering—far worse than extinction—incomprehensible: so it is life we must cling to, arm over arm, swimming, conquering the element that sustains us.

Jarvis? someone cried. *Please hear me—*

How exquisite life is, the turbulent joy of life contained in flesh! I heard nothing except the triumphant waves splashing about me. I swam for nearly an hour. Was reluctant to come ashore for breakfast, though our breakfasts are always pleasant rowdy sessions: my wife and my brother's wife and our seven children thrown together for the month of July. Three boys, four girls: noise, bustle, health, no shadows, no spirits. No time to think. Again and again I shall emerge from the surf, face and hair and body streaming water, exhausted but jubilant, triumphant. Again and again the children will call out to me, excited, from the dayside of the world that they inhabit.

I will not investigate Dr. Moore's strongbox and his secret journal; I will not even think about doing so. The wind blows words away. The surf is hypnotic. I will not remember this morning's dream once I sit down to breakfast with the family. I will not clutch my wife's wrist and say *We must not die! We dare not die!*—for that would only frighten and offend her.

Jarvis? she is calling at this very moment.

And I say *Yes—? Yes, I'll be there at once.*

———————

Born in 1938 in New York and educated at Syracuse University and the University of Wisconsin, Joyce Carol Oates is an English teacher, currently at Princeton. Her first book, By the North Gate, *was published in 1963. Strongly influenced by William Faulkner, Oates sets many of her works in her fictional Eden County. She has been called "one of the finest Southern writers that ever came out of the North."*

If the Fourth Witch of Endor was unable to put a good hex on someone, she refused to hex at all. . . .

2

Drawer 14

Talmage Powell

No cracks about my job, please. I've already taken more than enough ribbing from campus cutups. I don't relish being night attendant at the Asheville city morgue, but there are compensations.

For one thing, the job gave me a chance to complete my college work in daytime and do considerable studying at night between catnaps and the light, routine duties.

In their tagged and numbered drawers, the occupants weren't going to disturb me while I was cracking a brain cell on a problem in calculus. Or so I thought.

This particular night I relieved Olaf Daly, like always. Olaf was a man stuck with a job because of his age and a game leg. He lived each day only for the moment when he could flee his profession, as it were. Like always, he grunted a hello and a goodbye in the same breath, the game leg assisting him out of the morgue with surprising alacrity.

Alone in the deep silence of the anteroom, I dropped my thermos, transistor radio, and a couple of textbooks on the desk. I pulled the heavy record book toward me to give it a rundown.

Olaf had made his daily entries in his neat, spidery handwriting. Male victim of drowning. Man and woman dead in auto crash. Wino who didn't wake up when his bed caught fire. Male loser of a knife fight. Woman found dead in river.

Olaf's day had been routine. Nothing had come in like the dilly of last week.

She had been a pitiful, dirty, lonely old woman who had lived in a hovel. Crazy as a scorched moth, she had slipped into a dream world where she wasn't dirty, or old, or forsaken at all. Instead, she had believed she was the Fourth Witch of Endor, with power over the forces of darkness.

The slum section being a breeding ground for ignorance and superstition, some of her neighbors had taken the Fourth Witch of Endor seriously. She had looked the part, with a skull-like face, a beaked nose with a wart on the end, a toothless mouth accenting a long and pointed chin, and strings of dirty hair hanging lank about her sunken cheeks. She had eked out a half-starved living by telling fortunes, performing incantations, predicting winning numbers, and selling love potions and spells. To her credit, she never had gone in for the evil eye, her neighbors reported. If she couldn't put a good hex on a person, she had refused to hex him at all.

On a very hot and humid night, the Fourth Witch of Endor had mounted the roof of her tenement. Nobody knew for sure whether she had slipped or maybe taken a crack at flying to the full moon. Anyhow, she had been scraped off the asphalt six stories below, brought here, and deposited in drawer 14. She had lain in the refrigerated cubicle for four days before an immaculate son had flown in from a distant state to claim the body.

She hadn't departed a moment too soon for Olaf Daly. "I swear," the old man said, "there's a hint of a smell at drawer 14, like you'd figure sulphur and brimstone to smell.''

I hadn't noticed. The only smells assailing my nostrils were those in a chem lab where I was trying hard to keep up with the class.

I turned from the record book for a routine tour of the building.

Lighted brightly, the adjoining room was large, chill, and barren. The floor was spotless gray tile with a faint, antiseptic aroma. Across the room was the double doorway to the outside ramp where the customers were brought in. Near the door was the long, narrow, marble-topped table mounted on casters. Happily, it was empty at the moment, scrubbed clean, waiting for inevitable use. The refrigeration equipment made a low, whispering sound, more felt than heard.

To my right, like an outsized honeycomb, was the bank of drawers where the dead were kept for the claiming, or eventual burial at city expense.

Each occupied drawer was tagged, like with a shipping ticket or baggage check, the tag being attached with thin wire to the proper drawer handle when the body was checked in.

I whistled softly between my teeth, just for the sake of having some sound, as I started checking the tags against my mental tally from the record book.

As I neared drawer 14, I caught myself on the point of sniffing. Instead of sniffing, I snorted. ''That Olaf Daly,'' I muttered. ''He and his smell of sulphur and brimstone!''

A couple steps past drawer 14 I rocked up on my toes, turned my head, then my whole body around.

Olaf had not listed an occupant for drawer 14, but the handle was tagged. I bent forward slightly, reached. The whistle sort of dripped to nothing off my lips.

I turned the tag over casually the first time; then a second and third time, considerably faster.

I straightened and gave my scalp a scratch. Both sides of the tag were blank. Olaf was old, but far from senile. This wasn't like him at all, forgetting to fill in a drawer tag.

Then I half grinned to myself. The old coot was playing a joke on me. I didn't know he had it in him.

The whistle returned to my lips with a wise note, but not exactly appreciative. I took hold of the handle and gave it a yank. The drawer slid open on its rollers. The whistle keened to a thin wail and broke.

The girl in the drawer was young. She was blonde. She was beautiful, even in death.

I stood looking at her with my toes curling away from the soles of my shoes. The features of her face were lovely, the skin like pale tan satin. Her eyes were closed as if she were merely sleeping, her long lashes like dark shadows. She was clothed in a white nylon uniform with a nurse's pin on the collar. The only personal adornment was an I.D. bracelet of delicate golden chain and plaque. The plaque was engraved with initials: Z. L.

I broke my gaze away from the blonde girl and hurried back to the anteroom. At the desk, I jerked the record book toward me. I didn't want to misjudge old man Daly.

I moved my finger down the day's entries. Hesitated. Repeated the process. Went to the previous day by turning a page. Then to the day before that. Nobody, definitely, had been registered in drawer 14.

I puckered, but couldn't find a whistle as I turned again to the door of the morgue room. There was a glass section in the upper portion of the door. I looked through the glass. I didn't have to open the door. I'd left drawer 14 extended, and blonde Z. L. was still there, bigger than life, as big as death.

Carefully, I sat down at the desk, took out my handkerchief, wiped my forehead.

I took a long, deliberate breath, picked up the phone and dialed Olaf Daly's number. While his phone rang, I sneaked a glance in the direction of the morgue room.

Olaf's wife answered sleepily, along about the sixth or seventh ring. No, I couldn't speak to Olaf because he hadn't come home yet.

Then she added suddenly, in a kindlier tone, ''Just a minute. I think I hear him coming now.''

Olaf got on the line with a clearing of his throat. "Yah, what is it?"

"This is Tully Branson, Mr. Daly."

"I ain't available for stand-in duty if some of your college pals have cracked a keg someplace."

"No, sir," I said. "I understand, Mr. Daly. It's just that I need the information on the girl in drawer 14."

"Ain't nobody in drawer 14, Tully."

"Yes, sir. There's a girl in drawer 14. A blonde girl, Mr. Daly, far too young and nice looking to have to die. I'm sure you remember. Only you forgot the record book when she was brought in."

I heard Mrs. Daly asking Olaf what was it. The timber of his voice changed as he spoke in the direction of his wife. "I think young Branson brought straight whisky in his thermos tonight."

"No, sir," I barked at Olaf. "I need it, but I haven't got any whisky. All I've got is a dead blonde girl in drawer 14 that you forgot to make a record of."

"How could I do a thing like that?" Olaf demanded.

"I don't know," I said, "but you did. She's right here. If you don't believe me, come down and have a look."

"I think I'll do just that, son! You're accusing me of a mighty serious thing!"

He slammed the phone down so hard it stabbed me in the eardrum. I hung up with a studied gentleness, lighted a cigarette, poured some coffee from the thermos, lighted a cigarette, took a sip of coffee, and lighted a cigarette.

I had another swallow of coffee, reached for the package, and discovered I already had three cigarettes spiraling smoke from the ashtray. I gave myself a sickly grin and butted out two of the cigarettes to save for later.

With his game leg, Olaf arrived with the motion of a schooner mast on a stormy sea. I returned his glare with a smile that held what smug assurance I was able to muster. Then I bowed him into the morgue room.

He went through the swinging door, with me following closely. Drawer 14 was still extended. He didn't bother to cross all the way to it. Instead, after one look, he whirled on me.

"Branson," he snarled in rage, "if I was twenty years younger I'd bust your nose! You got a nerve, dragging a tired old man back to this stinking place. And just when I'd decided you was one of the nicer members of the younger generation too!"

"But Mr. Daly . . ."

"Don't 'but' me, you young pup! I'll put you on report for this!"

I took another frantic look at drawer 14. She was there, plain as anything. Blonde, and beautiful, and dead.

Olaf started past me, shoving me aside. I caught hold of his arm. I was chicken—and just about ready to moult. "Old man," I yelled, "you see her. I know you do!"

"Get your mitts offa me," he yelled back. "I see exactly what's there. I see an empty drawer. About as empty as your head."

I clutched his arm, not wanting to let go. "I don't know what kind of joke this is . . ."

"And neither do I," he said, shouting me down. "But it's a mighty poor one!"

"Then look at that drawer, old man, and quit horsing around."

"I've looked all I need to. Nothing but an overgrown juvenile delinquent would think up such a shoddy trick to oust a poor old man out of his house!"

He jerked his arm free of my grip, stormed through the door, past the anteroom. At the front door of the building, which was down a short corridor, he stopped, turned, and shook his finger at me.

"You cruel young crumb," he said, "you better start looking for another job tomorrow, if I have anything to do with it!" With that, he was gone.

I'd followed him as far as the anteroom. I turned slowly, looked through the glass pane into the morgue room. A dismal groan came from me. Z. L. still occupied drawer 14.

"Be a good girl," I heard myself mumbling, "and go away. I'll close my eyes, and you just go away."

I closed my eyes, opened them. But she hadn't gone away.

I groped to the desk chair and collapsed. I didn't sit long, on account of a sudden flurry of business which was announced by the buzzer at the service door.

The skirling sound, coming suddenly, lifted me a couple feet off the desk chair. When I came down, I was legging it across the morgue room.

Smith and Macklin, from the meat wagon, were sliding an old guy in tattered clothing from a stretcher to the marble-topped table.

"He walked in front of a truck," Smith said.

"No I.D.," Macklin said. "Ice him as a John Doe."

"Kinda messy, ain't he, Branson?" Smith grinned at me as he pulled the sheet over the John Doe. Smith was always egging me because he knew my stomach wasn't the strongest.

"Yeah," I said. "Kinda." I blew some sweat off my upper lip. "Not like the girl. No marks on her."

"Girl?"

"Sure," a note of eagerness slipped into my voice. "The beautiful blonde. The one in drawer 14."

Smith and Macklin both looked at the open, extended drawer. Then they looked at each other.

"Tully, old boy," Macklin said, "how you feeling these days?"

"Fine," I said, a strip of ice forming where my forehead was wrinkling.

"No trouble sleeping? No recurrent nightmares?"

"Nope," I said. "But the blonde in 14 . . . if you didn't bring her in, then maybe Collins and Snavely can give me the rundown on her."

Smith and Macklin sort of edged from me. Then Smith's guffaw broke the morgue stillness. "Beautiful blonde, drawer 14, where the poor old demented woman was . . . Sure, Branson, I get it."

Macklin looked at his partner uncertainly. "You do?"

"Simple," Smith said, sounding relieved. "Old Tully

here gets bored. Just thought up a little gag to rib us, huh, Tully?''

It was obvious they didn't see the girl and weren't going to see her. If I insisted, I knew suddenly, I was just asking for trouble. So I let out a laugh about as strong as skimmed milk. "Sure," I said. "Got to while away the tedium, you know."

Smith punched me in the ribs with his elbow. "Don't let your corpses get warm, Tully old pal." He departed with another belly laugh. But Macklin was still throwing worried looks over his shoulder at me as he followed Smith out.

I hated to see the outside door close behind them. I sure needed some company. For the first time, being the only living thing in the morgue caused my stomach to shrink to the size of a cold, wrinkled prune.

I skirted drawer 14 like I was crossing a deep gorge on a bridge made of brittle glass.

"Go away," I muttered to Z. L. "You're not real. Not even a dead body. Just a—an *image* that nobody can see but me. So go away!"

My words had no effect whatever on the image. They merely frightened me a little when I caught the tone in which I was conversing with a nonexistent dead body.

Back at the anteroom desk, I sat and shivered for several seconds. Then an idea glimmered encouragingly in my mind. Maybe Olaf Daly, Smith, and Macklin were all in on the gag. Maybe Z. L. had been brought in by Collins and Snavely, who tooled the meat wagon on the dayshift, and everybody had thought it would be a good joke to scare the pants off the bright young college man.

Feeling slightly better, I reached for the phone and called Judd Lawrence. A golfing pal of my father's, Judd was a plainclothes detective attached to homicide. He'd always seemed to think well of me; had, in fact, recommended me for the job here.

Judd wasn't home. He was pulling a three-to-eleven P.M. tour of duty. I placed a second call to police headquarters. Judd had signed out, but they caught him in the locker room.

"Tully Branson, Mr. Lawrence."

"How goes it, Tully?"

"I got a problem."

"Shoot." There was no hesitation in his big, hearty voice.

"Well, uh . . . seems like the record is messed up on one of our transients. A girl. Blonde girl. A nurse. Her initials are Z. L."

"You ought to call Olaf Daly, Tully."

"Yes, sir. But you know how Olaf is when he gets away from here. Anyhow, he's in dreamland by this time and I sure hate to get him riled up. He gets real nasty."

Judd boomed a laugh. "Can't say that I blame him. That all you've got on the girl?"

"Just what I've given you. She's certainly no derelict, furthest thing in the world from that. Girl like her, dead from natural causes, would be in a private funeral home, not here."

"So the fact that she's in the morgue means she died violently," Judd said.

"I guess it has to mean that."

"Murder?"

"Can't think of anything else," I said. "It has to be a death under suspicious circumstances."

"Okay, Tully. I'll see what I can turn up for you."

"Sure hate to put you to the trouble."

"Trouble?" he said. "No trouble. Couple phone calls is all it should take."

"I sure appreciate it, Mr. Lawrence."

I hung up. While I was waiting for Judd Lawrence to call me back, I sneaked to the door of the morgue room and let my gaze creep to the glass pane to make sure the image was still in drawer 14.

It was. I shuffled back to the desk, feeling like I was a tired old man.

When the phone rang finally, I snatched it up. "City morgue. Tully Branson speaking."

"Judd here, Tully."

"Did you . . ."

"Negative from homicide, Tully. No blondes with initials

Z. L., female, have been murdered in the last twenty-four hour period.''

"Oh," I said, gagging, giving vent to a moan of real anguish.

"Checked with nurse's registry," Judd was saying. "There is a nurse answering your description. Young, blonde, just finished training. Her name is Zella Langtry. Lives at 711 Eastland Avenue. She recently went to work at City Hospital. But if any violence occurred to her, it's been in the past half-hour. She just checked off duty when the graveyard shift reported on."

His words, coupled with the image in drawer 14, left one crazy, wild possibility. The inspiration was so weird it turned the hair on my scalp to needles.

"Mr. Lawrence, I have the most terrible feeling Zella Langtry will never reach home alive."

"What is that? What are you saying, Tully?"

"The Fourth Witch of Endor . . ." I gabbled. "She was a kindly soul at heart. Never put a bad hex on anybody. Just good ones."

"What in the blathering world are you carrying on about?" Judd asked sharply. "Tully, you been drinking?"

"No, sir."

"Feel all right?"

"I—uh . . . Yes, sir, and thanks a lot, Mr. Lawrence."

Twenty minutes later, my jalopy rolled to a stop on Eastland Avenue. I got out, started walking along looking for numbers. I knew I was in the right block, and I located number 711 easily enough. It was a small, white cottage with a skimpy yard that attempted to look more wholesome than its lower-class surroundings.

The place was dark, quiet, peaceful.

I was standing there feeling like seventy kinds of fool when the whir of a diesel engine at the street intersection caught my attention. I looked toward the sound, saw a municipal bus lumbering away.

From the shadows of a straggly maple tree, I watched the shadowy figure of a girl coming along Eastland in my direction. But she wasn't the only passenger who had got off the bus. Behind her was a taller, heavier shadow, that of a man. My breathing thinned as I took in the scene.

She realized he was behind her. She started walking faster. So did the man. She looked over her shoulder. She stepped up the pace even more, almost running now.

The man's shoes slapped quick and hard against the sidewalk. The girl's scream was choked off as the man slammed against her.

They were struggling on the sidewalk, the man locking her throat in the crook of his elbow, the girl writhing and kicking.

I went from under the maple tree like invisible trumpets were urging me on with a blood-rousing fanfare. The man heard me coming, released the girl. I piled into him with a shoulder in his midsection.

He brought a knee up hard. It caught me on the point of the chin. I sat down on the sidewalk, and the man turned and ran away.

Firm but gentle hands helped me to my feet. I looked into the eyes of Zella Langtry for the first time. They were very nice, smoky and grateful in the shadowy night.

"You all right?" I asked, getting my breath back.

"I am now, thanks to you. And you?"

"Fine," I said. "Just fine now."

She was regaining her composure. "Lucky thing for me you were around at the right moment!"

"I—uh—just happened to be passing," I said. "Maybe I'd better walk you to your destination. Won't do any good to report that guy now. Didn't get a look at him. Never would catch him."

"I was going home," she said. "I live just down the street."

We walked along, and she told me her name was Zella, and I told her mine was Tully. When we got to her front door, we looked at each other, and I asked if I could call her some time, and she said any time a phone was handy.

I watched her go inside. I was whistling as I returned to the jalopy.

Inside the morgue, I headed straight for drawer 14. If my

theory was correct, the image of Zella Langtry wouldn't be in the drawer, now that she had been rescued from the jaws of death, as it were.

I stood at drawer 14, taking a good, long look. My theory was right as far as it went.

The image of Zella Langtry was no longer in the drawer. The new one was quite a lovely redhead.

The author of more than six hundred short stories, mostly mystery and suspense, Talmage Powell was born in North Carolina in 1920. Except for a short stint as police reporter, he has been a professional writer all his life. His first novel, The Smasher, *appeared in 1959; his Florida private eye, Ed Rivers, stars in five novels, including* The Girl's Number Doesn't Answer *(1959). His fast-moving stories are ingenious and frequently peopled with a large cast of characters.*

Warburg Tantavul had refused to permit his son to marry cousin Arabella. So why did his will promise such a great reward for the birth of their first child?

3

The Jest of Warburg Tantavul

Seabury Quinn

Warburg Tantavul was dying. Little more than skin and bones, he lay propped up with pillows in the big sleigh bed and smiled as though he found the thought of dissolution faintly amusing.

Even in comparatively good health the man was never prepossessing. Now, wasted with disease, that smile of self-sufficient satisfaction on his wrinkled face, he was nothing less than hideous. The eyes, which nature had given him, were small, deep-set and ruthless. The mouth, which his own thoughts had fashioned through the years, was wide and thin-lipped, almost colorless, and even in repose was tightly drawn against his small and curiously perfect teeth. Now, as he smiled, a flickering light, lambent as the quick reflection of an unseen flame, flared in his yellowish eyes, and a hard white line of teeth showed on his lower lip, as if he bit it to hold back a chuckle.

"You're still determined that you'll marry Arabella?" he asked his son, fixing his sardonic, mocking smile on the young man.

"Yes, Father, but—"

"No buts, my boy"—this time the chuckle came, low and muted, but at the same time glassy-hard—"no buts. I've told you I'm against it, and you'll rue it to your dying day if you should marry her; but"—he paused, and breath rasped in his wizened throat—"but go ahead and marry her, if your heart's set on it. I've said my say and warned you—heh, boy, never say your poor old father didn't warn you!"

He lay back on his piled-up pillows for a moment, swallowing convulsively, as if to force the fleeting life-breath back, then, abruptly: "Get out," he ordered. "Get out and stay out, you poor fool; but remember what I've said."

"Father," young Tantavul began, stepping toward the bed, but the look of sudden concentrated fury in the old man's tawny eyes halted him in midstride.

"Get—out—I—said," his father snarled, then, as the door closed softly on his son:

"Nurse—hand—me—that—picture." His breath was coming slowly, now, in shallow labored gasps, but his withered fingers writhed in a gesture of command, pointing to the silver-framed photograph of a woman which stood upon a little table in the bedroom windowbay.

He clutched the portrait as if it were some precious relic, and for a minute let his eyes rove over it. "Lucy," he whispered hoarsely, and now his words were thick and indistinct, "Lucy, they'll be married, 'spite of all that I have said. They'll be married, Lucy, d'ye hear?" Thin and high-pitched as a child's, his voice rose to a piping treble as he grasped the picture's silver frame and held it level with his face. "They'll be married, Lucy dear, and they'll have—"

Abruptly as a penny whistle's note is stilled when no more air is blown in it, old Tantavul's cry hushed. The picture, still grasped in his hands, fell to the tufted coverlet, the man's lean jaw relaxed and he slumped back on his pillows with a shadow of the mocking smile still in his glazing eyes.

Etiquette requires that the nurse await the doctor's confirmation at such times, so, obedient to professional dictates, Miss Williamson stood by the bed until I felt the dead man's pulse and nodded; then with the skill of years of practice she began her offices, bandaging the wrists and jaws and ankles that the body might be ready when the representative of Martin's Funeral Home came for it.

My friend de Grandin was annoyed. Arms akimbo, knuckles on his hips, his black-silk kimono draped round him like a mourning garment, he voiced his plaint in no uncertain terms. In fifteen little so small minutes he must leave for the theatre, and that son and grandson of a filthy swine who was the florist had not delivered his gardenia. And was it not a fact that he could not go forth without a fresh gardenia for his lapel? But certainly. Why did that *sale chameau* procrastinate? Why did he delay delivering that unmentionable flower till this unspeakable time of night? He was Jules de Grandin, he, and not to be oppressed by any species of a goat who called himself a florist. But no. It must not be. It should not be, by blue! He would—

"Axin' yer pardon, sir," Nora McGinnis broke in from the study door, "there's a Miss an' Mr. Tantavul to see ye, an'—"

"Bid them be gone, *ma charmeuse.* Request that they jump in the bay—*Grand Dieu*"—he cut his oratory short—"*les enfants dans le bois!*"

Truly, there was something reminiscent of the Babes in the Wood in the couple who had followed Nora to the study door. Dennis Tantavul looked even younger and more boyish than I remembered him, and the girl beside him was so childish in appearance that I felt a quick, instinctive pity for her. Plainly they were frightened, too, for they clung hand to hand like frightened children going past a graveyard, and in their eyes was that look of sick terror I had seen so often when the X-ray and blood test confirmed preliminary diagnosis of carcinoma.

"Monsieur, Mademoiselle!" The little Frenchman gathered his kimono and his dignity about him in a single sweeping gesture as he struck his heels together and bowed stiffly from the hips. "I apologize for my unseemly words. Were it not that I have been subjected to a terrible, calamitous misfortune, I should not so far have forgotten myself—"

The girl's quick smile cut through his apology. "We understand," she reassured. "We've been through trouble, too, and have come to Dr. Trowbridge—"

"Ah, then I have permission to withdraw?" He bowed again and turned upon his heel, but I called him back.

"Perhaps you can assist us," I remarked as I introduced the callers.

"The honor is entirely mine, Mademoiselle," he told her as he raised her fingers to his lips. "You and Monsieur your brother—"

"He's not my brother," she corrected. "We're cousins. That's why we've called on Dr. Trowbridge."

De Grandin tweaked the already needle-sharp points of his small blond mustache. *"Pardonnez-moi?"* he begged. "I have resided in your country but a little time; perhaps I do not understand the language fluently. It is because you and Monsieur are cousins that you come to see the doctor? Me, I am dull and stupid like a pig; I fear I do not comprehend."

Dennis Tantavul replied: "It's not because of the relationship, Doctor—not entirely, at any rate, but—"

He turned to me: "You were at my father's bedside when he died; you remember what he said about marrying Arabella?"

I nodded.

"There was something—some ghastly, hidden threat concealed in his warning, Doctor. It seemed as if he jeered at me—dared me to marry her, yet—"

"Was there some provision in his will?" I asked.

"Yes, sir," the young man answered. "Here it is." From

his pocket he produced a folded parchment, opened it and indicated a paragraph:

> "To my son Dennis Tantavul I give, devise and bequeath all my property of every kind and sort, real, personal and mixed, of which I may die seized and possessed, or to which I may be entitled, in the event of his marrying Arabella Tantavul, but should he not marry the said Arabella Tantavul, then it is my will that he receive only one half of my estate, and that the residue thereof go to the said Arabella Tantavul, who has made her home with me since childhood and occupied the relationship of daughter to me."

"H'm," I returned the document, "this looks as if he really wanted you to marry your cousin, even though—"

"And see here, sir," Dennis interrupted, "here's an envelope we found in Father's papers."

Sealed with red wax, the packet of heavy, opaque parchment was addressed:

> "To my children, Dennis and Arabella Tantavul, to be opened by them upon the occasion of the birth of their first child."

De Grandin's small blue eyes were snapping with the flickering light they showed when he was interested. "Monsieur Dennis," he took the thick envelope from the caller, "Dr. Trowbridge has told me something of your father's death-bed scene. There is a mystery about this business. My suggestion is you read the message now—"

"No, sir. I won't do that. My father didn't love me— sometimes I think he hated me—but I never disobeyed a wish that he expressed, and I don't feel at liberty to do so now. It would be like breaking faith with the dead. But"—he smiled a trifle shamefacedly—"Father's lawyer Mr. Bainbridge is out of town on business, and it will be his duty to probate the will. In the meantime I'd feel better if the will and this envelope were in other hands than mine. So we came to Dr. Trowbridge to ask him to take charge of them till Mr. Bainbridge gets back, meanwhile—"

"Yes, Monsieur, meanwhile?" de Grandin prompted as the young man paused.

"You know human nature, Doctor," Dennis turned to me; "no one can see farther into hidden meanings than the man who sees humanity with its mask off, the way a doctor does. D'ye think Father might have been delirious when he warned me not to marry Arabella, or—" His voice trailed off, but his troubled eyes were eloquent.

"H'm," I shifted uncomfortably in my chair, "I can't see any reason for hesitating, Dennis. That bequest of all your father's property in the event you marry Arabella seems to indicate his true feelings." I tried to make my words convincing, but the memory of old Tantavul's dying words dinned in my ears. There had been something gloating in his voice as he told the picture that his son and niece would marry.

De Grandin caught the hint of hesitation in my tone. "Monsieur," he asked Dennis, "will not you tell us of the antecedents of your father's warning? Dr. Trowbridge is perhaps too near to see the situation clearly. Me, I have no knowledge of your father or your family. You and Mademoiselle are strangely like. The will describes her as having lived with you since childhood. Will you kindly tell us how it came about?"

The Tantavuls were, as he said, strangely similar. Anyone might easily have taken them for twins. Like as two plaster portraits from the same mold were their small straight noses, sensitive mouths, curling pale-gold hair.

Now, once more hand in hand, they sat before us on the sofa, and as Dennis spoke I saw the frightened, haunted look creep back into their eyes.

"Do you remember us as children, Doctor?" he asked me.

"Yes, it must have been some twenty years ago they called me out to see you youngsters. You'd just moved into the old Stephens house, and there was a deal of gossip about the strange gentleman from the West with his two small children and Chinese cook, who greeted all the neighbors' overtures with churlish rebuffs and never spoke to anyone.''

"What did you think of us, sir?"

"H'm; I thought you and your sister—as I thought her then—had as fine a case of measles as I'd ever seen."

"How old were we then, do you remember?"

"Oh, you were something like three; the little girl was half your age, I'd guess."

"Do you recall the next time you saw us?"

"Yes, you were somewhat older then; eight or ten, I'd say. That time it was the mumps. You were queer, quiet little shavers. I remember asking if you thought you'd like a pickle, and you said, 'No, thank you, sir, it hurts.' "

"It did, too, sir. Every day Father made us eat one; stood over us with a whip till we'd chewed the last morsel."

"What?"

The young folks nodded solemnly as Dennis answered, "Yes, sir; every day. He said he wanted to check up on the progress we were making."

For a moment he was silent, then: "Dr. Trowbridge, if anyone treated you with studied cruelty all your life—if you'd never had a kind word or gracious act from that person in all your memory, then suddenly that person offered you a favor—made it possible for you to gratify your dearest wish, and threatened to penalize you if you failed to do so, wouldn't you be suspicious? Wouldn't you suspect some sort of dreadful practical joke?"

"I don't think I quite understand."

"Then listen: in all my life I can't remember ever having seen my father smile, not really smile with friendliness, humor or affection, I mean. My life—and Arabella's, too—was one long persecution at his hands. I was two years or so old when we came to Harrisonville, I believe, but I still have vague recollections of our Western home, of a house set high on a hill overlooking the ocean, and a wall with climbing vines and purple flowers on it, and a pretty lady who would take me in her arms and cuddle me against her breast and feed me ice cream from a spoon, sometimes. I have a sort of recollection of a little baby sister in that house, too, but these things are so far back in babyhood that possibly they were no more than childish fancies which I built up for myself and which I loved so dearly and so secretly they finally came to have a kind of reality for me.

"My real memories, the things I can recall with certainty, begin with a hurried train trip through hot, dry, uncomfortable country with my father and a strangely silent Chinese servant and a little girl they told me was my cousin Arabella.

"Father treated me and Arabella with impartial harshness. We were beaten for the slightest fault, and we had faults aplenty. If we sat quietly we were accused of sulking and asked why we didn't go and play. If we played and shouted we were whipped for being noisy little brats.

"As we weren't allowed to associate with any of the neighbors' children we made up our own games. I'd be Geraint and Arabella would be Enid of the dovewhite feet, or perhaps I'd be King Arthur in the Castle Perilous, and she'd be the kind Lady of the Lake who gave him back his magic sword. And though we never mentioned it, both of us knew that whatever the adventure was, the false knight or giant I contended with was really my father. But when actual trouble came I wasn't an heroic figure.

"I must have been twelve or thirteen when I had my last thrashing. A little brook ran through the lower part of our land, and the former owners had widened it into a lily pond. The flowers had died out years before, but the outlines of the pool remained, and it was our favorite summer play place. We taught ourselves to swim—not very well, of course, but well enough—and as we had no bathing suits we used to go in our underwear. When we'd finished swimming we'd lie in the sun until our underthings were dry, then slip into our outer clothing. One afternoon as we were splashing in the water, happy as a pair of baby otters, and nearer to shouting with laughter than we'd ever been before, I think, my father suddenly appeared on the bank.

"'Come out o' there!' he shouted to me, and there was a kind of sharp, dry hardness in his voice I'd never heard before. "So this is how you spend your time?' he asked as I climbed up the bank. 'In spite of all I've done to keep you decent, you do a thing like·this!'

" 'Why, Father, we were only swimming—' I began, but he struck me on the mouth.

" 'Shut up, you little rake!' he roared. 'I'll teach you!' He cut a willow switch and thrust my head between his knees; then while he held me tight as in a vice he flogged me with the willow till the blood came through my skin and stained my soaking cotton shorts. Then he kicked me back into the pool as a heartless master might a beaten dog.

"As I said, I wasn't an heroic figure. It was Arabella who came to my rescue. She helped me up the slippery bank and took me in her arms. 'Poor Dennie,' she said. 'Poor, poor Dennie. It was my fault, Dennie, dear, for letting you take me into the water!' Then she kissed me—the first time anyone had kissed me since the pretty lady of my half-remembered dreams. 'We'll be married on the very day that Uncle Warburg dies,' she promised, 'and I'll be so sweet and good to you, and you'll love me so dearly that we'll both forget these dreadful days.'

"We thought my father'd gone, but he must have stayed to see what we would say, for as Arabella finished he stepped from behind a rhododendron bush, and for the first time I heard him laugh. 'You'll be married, will you?' he asked. 'That would be a good joke—the best one of all. All right, go ahead—see what it gets you.'

"That was the last time he ever actually struck me, but from that time on he seemed to go out of his way to invent mental tortures for us. We weren't allowed to go to school, but he had a tutor, a little rat-faced man named Ericson, come in to give us lessons, and in the evening he'd take the book and make us stand before him and recite. If either of us failed a problem in arithmetic or couldn't conjugate a French or Latin verb he'd wither us with sarcasm, and always as a finish to his diatribe he'd jeer at us about our wish to be married, and threaten us with something dreadful if we ever did it.

"So, Dr. Trowbridge, you see why I'm suspicious. It

seems almost as if this provision in the will is part of some horrible practical joke my father prepared deliberately—as if he's waiting to laugh at us from the grave.''

"I can understand your feelings, boy," I answered, "but—''

" 'But' be damned and roasted on the hottest griddle in hell's kitchen!" Jules de Grandin interrupted. "The wicked dead one's funeral is at two tomorrow afternoon, *n'est-ce-pas?*

"*Très bien.* At eight tomorrow evening—or earlier, if it will be convenient—you shall be married. I shall esteem it a favor if you permit that I be best man; Dr. Trowbridge will give the bride away, and we shall have a merry time, by blue! You shall go upon a gorgeous honeymoon and learn how sweet the joys of love can be—sweeter for having been so long denied! And in the meantime we shall keep the papers safely till your lawyer returns.

"You fear the so unpleasant jest? *Mais non,* I think the jest is on the other foot, my friends, and the laugh on the other face!''

Warburg Tantavul was neither widely known nor popular, but the solitude in which he had lived had invested him with mystery; now the bars of reticence were down and the walls of isolation broken, upward of a hundred neighbors, mostly women, gathered in the Martin funeral chapel as the services began. The afternoon sun beat softly through the stained glass windows and glinted on the polished mahogany of the casket. Here and there it touched upon bright spots of color that marked a woman's hat or a man's tie. The solemn hush was broken by occasional whispers: "What'd he die of? Did he leave much? Were the two young folks his only heirs?''

Then the burial office: "Lord, Thou hast been our refuge from one generation to another . . . for a thousand years in Thy sight are but as yesterday . . . Oh teach us to number our days that we may apply our hearts unto wisdom. . . .''

As the final Amen sounded one of Mr. Martin's frock-coated young men glided forward, paused beside the casket, and made the stereotyped announcement: "Those who wish to say goodbye to Mr. Tantavul may do so at this time."

The grisly rite of the passing by the bier dragged on. I would have left the place; I had no wish to look upon the man's dead face and folded hands; but de Grandin took me firmly by the elbow, held me till the final curiosity-impelled female had filed past the body, then steered me quickly toward the casket.

He paused a moment at the bier, and it seemed to me there was a hint of irony in the smile that touched the corners of his mouth as he leant forward. *"Eh bien,* my old one; we know a secret, thou and I, *n'est-ce-pas?"* he asked the silent form before us.

I swallowed back an exclamation of dismay. Perhaps it was a trick of the uncertain light, perhaps one of those ghastly, inexplicable things which every doctor and embalmer meets with sometimes in his practice—the effect of desiccation from formaldehyde, the pressure of some tissue gas within the body, or something of the sort—at any rate, as Jules de Grandin spoke the corpse's upper lids drew back the fraction of an inch, revealing slits of yellow eye which seemed to glare at us with mingled hate and fury.

"Good heavens; come away!" I begged. "It seems as if he *looked* at us, de Grandin!"

"Et puis—and if he did? I damn think I can trade him look for look, my friend. He was clever, that one, I admit it; but do not be mistaken, Jules de Grandin is nobody's imbecile."

The wedding took place in the rectory of St. Chrysostom's. Robed in stole and surplice, Dr. Bentley glanced benignly from Dennis to Arabella, then to de Grandin and me as he began: "Dearly beloved, we are gathered together here in the sight of God and in the face of this company to join together this man and this woman in holy matrimony. . . ." His round and ruddy face grew slightly stern as he admonished, "If any man can show just cause why they should not lawfully be joined together, let him now speak or else hereafter for ever hold his peace."

He paused the customary short, dramatic moment, and I

thought I saw a hard, grim look spread on de Grandin's face. Very faint and far-off seeming, so faint that we could scarcely hear it, but gaining steadily in strength, there came a high, thin, screaming sound. Curiously, it seemed to me to resemble the long-drawn, wailing shriek of a freight train's whistle heard miles away upon a still and sultry summer night, weird, wavering and ghastly. Now it seemed to grow in shrillness, though its volume was no greater.

I saw a look of haunted fright leap into Arabella's eyes, saw Dennis' pale face go paler as the strident whistle sounded shriller and more shrill; then, as it seemed I could endure the stabbing of that needle sound no longer, it ceased abruptly, giving way to the blessed, comforting silence. But through the silence came a burst of chuckling laughter, half breathless, half hysterical, wholly devilish: *Huh—hu-u-uh—hu-u-u-uh!* the final syllable drawn out until it seemed almost a groan.

"The wind, *Monsieur le Curé;* it was nothing but the wind," de Grandin told the clergyman sharply. "Proceed to marry them, if you will be so kind."

"Wind?" Dr. Bentley echoed. "I could have sworn I heard somebody laugh, but—"

"It is the wind, Monsieur; it plays strange tricks at times," the little Frenchman insisted, his small blue eyes as hard as frozen iron. "Proceed, if you will be so kind. We wait on you."

"Forasmuch as Dennis and Arabella have consented to be joined together in holy wedlock, I pronounce them man and wife," concluded Dr. Bentley, and de Grandin, ever gallant, kissed the bride upon the lips, and before we could restrain him, planted kisses on both Dennis' cheeks.

"*Cordieu,* I thought that we might have the trouble, for a time," he told me as we left the rectory.

"What *was* that awful shrieking noise we heard?" I asked.

"It was the wind, my friend," he answered in a hard, flat, toneless voice. "The ten times damned, but wholly ineffectual wind."

"So, then, little sinner, weep and wail for the burden of mortality you have assumed. Weep, wail, cry and breathe, my small and wrinkled one! Ha, you will not? *Pardieu*, I say you shall!"

Gently, but smartly, he spanked the small red infant's small red posterior with the end of a towel wrung out in hot water, and as the smacking impact sounded the tiny toothless mouth opened and a thin, high, piping squall of protest sounded. "Ah, that is better, *mon petit ami*," he chuckled. "One cannot learn too soon that one must do as one is told, not as one wishes, in this world which you have just entered. Look to him, Mademoiselle." He passed the wriggling, bawling morsel of humanity to the nurse and turned to me as I bent over the table where Arabella lay. "How does the little mother, Friend Trowbridge?" he asked.

"U'm'mp," I answered noncommittally. "Bear a hand, here, will you? The perineum's pretty badly torn—have to do a quick repair job—"

"But in the morning she will have forgotten all the pain," laughed de Grandin as Arabella, swathed in blankets, was trundled from the delivery room. "She will gaze upon the little monkey-thing which I just caused to breathe the breath of life and vow it is the loveliest of all God's lovely creatures. She will hold it at her tender breast and smile on it, she will—*Sacré nom d'un rat vert*, what is that?"

From the nursery where, ensconced in wire trays, a score of newborn fragments of humanity slept or squalled, there came a sudden frightened scream—a woman's cry of terror.

We raced along the corridor, reached the glass-walled room and thrust the door back, taking care to open it no wider than was necessary, lest a draft disturb the carefully conditioned air of the place.

Backed against the farther wall, her face gone gray with fright, the nurse in charge was staring at the skylight with terror-widened eyes, and even as we entered she opened her lips to emit another scream.

"Desist, *ma bonne*, you are disturbing your small charges!" De Grandin seized the horrified girl's shoulder and administered a shake. Then: "What is it, Mademoiselle?" he whispered. "Do not be afraid to speak; we shall respect your confidence—but speak softly."

"It—it was up there!" she pointed with a shaking finger toward the black square of the skylight. "They'd just brought Baby Tantavul in, and I had laid him in his crib when I thought I heard somebody laughing. Oh"—she shuddered at the recollection—"it was awful! not really a laugh, but something more like a long-drawn-out hysterical groan. Did you ever hear a child tickled to exhaustion—you know how he moans and gasps for breath, and laughs, all at once? I think the fiends in hell must laugh like that!"

"Yes, yes, we understand," de Grandin nodded, "but tell us what occurred next."

"I looked around the nursery, but I was all alone here with the babies. Then it came again, louder, this time, and seemingly right above me. I looked up at the skylight, and—there it was!

"It was a face, sir—just a face, with no body to it, and it seemed to float above the glass, then dip down to it, like a child's balloon drifting in the wind, and it looked right past me, down at Baby Tantavul, and laughed again."

"A face, you say, Mademoiselle—"

"Yes, sir, yes! The awfullest face I've ever seen. It was thin and wrinkled—all shriveled like a monkey—and as it looked at Baby Tantavul its eyes stretched open till their whites glared all around the irises, and the mouth opened, not widely, but as if it were chewing something it relished—and it gave that dreadful, cackling, jubilating laugh again. That's it! I couldn't think before, but it seemed as if that bodiless head were laughing with a sort of evil triumph, Dr. de Grandin!"

"H'm," he tweaked his tightly waxed mustache, "I should not wonder if it did, Mademoiselle." To me he whispered, "Stay with her, if you will, my friend, I'll see the supervisor and have her send another nurse to keep her company. I shall request a special watch for the small Tantavul. At present I do not think the danger is great, but mice do not play where cats are wakeful."

"Isn't he just lovely?" Arabella looked up from the small bald head that rested on her breast, and ecstasy was in her eyes. "I don't believe I ever saw so beautiful a baby!"

"*Tiens,* Madame, his voice is excellent, at any rate," de Grandin answered with a grin, "and from what one may observe his appetite is excellent, as well."

Arabella smiled and patted the small creature's back. "You know, I never had a doll in my life," she confided. "Now I've got this dear little mite, and I'm going to be so happy with him. Oh, I wish Uncle Warburg were alive. I know this darling baby would soften even his hard heart.

"But I mustn't say such things about him, must I? He really wanted me to marry Dennis, didn't he? His will proved that. You think he wanted us to marry, Doctor?"

"I am persuaded that he did, Madame. Your marriage was his dearest wish, his fondest hope," the Frenchman answered solemnly.

"I felt that way, too. He was harsh and cruel to us when we were growing up, and kept his stony-hearted attitude to the end, but underneath it all there must have been some hidden stratum of kindness, some lingering affection for Dennis and me, or he'd never have put that clause in his will—"

"Nor have left this memorandum for you," de Grandin interrupted, drawing from an inner pocket the parchment envelope Dennis had entrusted to him the day before his father's funeral.

She started back as if he menaced her with a live scorpion, and instinctively her arms closed protectively around the baby at her bosom. "The—that—letter?" she faltered, her breath coming in short, smothered gasps. "I'd forgotten all about it. Oh, Dr. de Grandin, burn it. Don't let me see what's in it. I'm afraid!"

It was a bright May morning, without sufficient breeze to stir the leaflets on the maple trees outside the window, but as de Grandin held the letter out I thought I heard a sudden sweep of wind around the angle of the hospital, not loud, but shrewd and keen, like wind among the graveyard evergreens in autumn, and, curiously, there seemed a note of soft malicious laughter mingled with it.

The little Frenchman heard it, too, and for an instant he looked toward the window, and I thought I saw the flicker of an ugly sneer take form beneath the waxed ends of his mustache.

"Open it, Madame," he bade. "It is for you and Monsieur Dennis, and the little *Monsieur Bébé* here."

"I—I daren't—"

"*Tenez,* then Jules de Grandin does!" With his penknife he slit the heavy envelope, pressed suddenly against its ends so that its sides bulged, and dumped its contents on the counterpane. Ten fifty-dollar bills dropped on the coverlet. And nothing else.

"Five hundred dollars!" Arabella gasped. "Why—"

"A birthday gift for *petit Monsieur Bébé,* one surmises," laughed de Grandin. "*Eh bien,* the old one had a sense of humor underneath his ugly outward shell, it seems. He kept you on the tenterhooks lest the message in this envelope contained dire things, while all the time it was a present of congratulation."

"But such a gift from Uncle Warburg—I can't understand it!"

"Perhaps that is as well, too, Madame. Be happy in the gift and give your ancient uncle credit for at least one act of kindness. *Au 'voir.*"

"Hanged if I can understand it, either," I confessed as we left the hospital. "If that old curmudgeon had left a message berating them for fools for having offspring, or even a new will that disinherited them both, it would have been in character, but such a gift—well, I'm surprised."

Amazingly, he halted in midstep and laughed until the tears rolled down his face. "*You* are surprised!" he told me when he managed to regain his breath, "*Cordieu,* my friend, I do not think that you are half as much surprised as Monsieur Warburg Tantavul!"

• • •

Dennis Tantavul regarded me with misery-haunted eyes. "I just can't understand it," he admitted. "It's all so sudden, so utterly—"

"Pardonnez-moi," de Grandin interrupted from the door of the consulting room, "I could not help but hear your voice, and if it is not an intrusion—"

"Not at all, sir," the young man answered. "I'd like the benefit of your advice. It's Arabella, and I'm terribly afraid she's—"

"Non, do not try it, *mon ami,"* de Grandin warned. "Do you give us the symptoms, let us make the diagnosis. He who acts as his own doctor has a fool for a patient, you know."

"Well, then, here are the facts: this morning Arabella woke me up, crying as if her heart would break. I asked her what the trouble was, and she looked at me as if I were a stranger—no, not exactly that, rather as if I were some dreadful thing she'd suddenly found at her side. Her eyes were positively round with horror, and when I tried to take her in my arms to comfort her she shrank away as if I were infected with the plague.

"'Oh, Dennie, don't!' she begged and positively cringed away from me. Then she sprang out of bed and drew her kimono around her as if she were ashamed to have me see her in her pajamas, and ran out of the room.

"Presently I heard her crying in the nursery, and when I followed her in there—" He paused and tears came to his eyes. "She was standing by the crib where little Dennis lay, and in her hand she held a long sharp steel letter-opener. 'Poor little mite, poor little flower of unpardonable sin,' she said. 'We've got to go, Baby darling; you to limbo, I to hell—oh, God wouldn't, *couldn't* be so cruel as to damn you for our sin!—but we'll all three suffer torment endlessly, because we didn't know!'

"She raised the knife to plunge it in the little fellow's heart, and he stretched out his hands and laughed and cooed as the sunlight shone on the steel. I was on her in an instant, wrenching the knife from her with one hand and holding her against me with the other, but she fought me off.

"'Don't touch me, Dennie, please, *please* don't,' she begged. 'I know it's mortal sin, but I love you so, my dear, that I just can't resist you if I let you put your arms about me.'

"I tried to kiss her, but she hid her face against my shoulder and moaned as if in pain when she felt my lips against her neck. Then she went limp in my arms, and I carried her, unconscious but still moaning piteously, into her sitting room and laid her on the couch. I left Sarah the nursemaid with her, with strict orders not to let her leave the room. Can't you come over right away?"

De Grandin's cigarette had burned down till it threatened his mustache, and in his little round blue eyes there was a look of murderous rage. "*Bête!*" he murmured savagely. "*Sale chameau;* species of a stinking goat! This is his doing, undoubtlessly. Come, my friends, let us rush, hasten, fly. I would talk with Madame Arabella."

"No, sir, she's done gone," the portly nursemaid told us when we asked for Arabella. "The baby started squealing something awful right after Mister Dennis left, and I knew it was time for his breakfast, so Miss Arabella was laying nice and still on the sofa, and I said, 'You lay still there, honey, whilst I see after your baby'; so I went to the nursery, and fixed him all up, and carried him back to the setting room where Miss Arabella was, and she ain't there no more. No, sir."

"I thought I told you—" Dennis began furiously, but de Grandin laid a hand upon his arm.

"Do not upbraid her, *mon ami,* she did wisely, though she knew it not; she was with the small one all the while, so no harm came to him. Was it not better so, after what you witnessed in the morning?"

"Ye-es," the other grudgingly admitted, "I suppose so. But Arabella—"

"Let us see if we can find a trace of her," the Frenchman

interrupted. "Look carefully, do you miss any of her clothing?"

Dennis looked about the pretty chintz-hung room. "Yes," he decided as he finished his inspection, "her dress was on that lounge and her shoes and stockings on the floor beneath it. They're all gone."

"So," de Grandin nodded. "Distracted as she seemed, it is unlikely she would have stopped to dress had she not planned on going out. Friend Trowbridge, will you kindly call police headquarters and inform them of the situation? Ask to have all exits to the city watched."

As I picked up the telephone he and Dennis started on a room-by-room inspection of the house.

"Find anything?" I asked as I hung up the 'phone after talking with the missing persons bureau.

"Corbleu, but I should damn say yes!" de Grandin answered as I joined them in the upstairs living room. "Look yonder, if you please, my friend."

The room was obviously the intimate apartment of the house. Electric lamps under painted shades were placed beside deep leather-covered easy chairs, ivory-enameled bookshelves lined the walls to a height of four feet or so, upon their tops was a litter of gay, unconsidered trifles— cinnabar cigarette boxes, bits of hammered brass. Old china, blue and red and purple, glowed mellowly from open spaces on the shelves, its colors catching up and accenting the muted blues and reds of antique Hamadan carpet. A Paisley shawl was draped scarfwise across the baby grand piano in one corner.

Directly opposite the door a carven crucifix was standing on the bookcase top. It was an exquisite bit of Italian work, the cross of ebony, the corpus of old ivory, and so perfectly executed that though it was a scant six inches high, one could note the tense, tortured muscles of the pendent body, the straining throat which overfilled with groans of agony, the brow all knotted and bedewed with the cold sweat of torment. Upon the statue's thorn-crowned head, where it made a bright iridescent halo, was a band of gem-encrusted platinum, a woman's diamond-studded wedding ring.

"*Hélas,* it is love's crucifixion!" whispered Jules de Grandin.

Three months went by, and though the search kept up unremittingly, no trace of Arabella could be found. Dennis Tantavul installed a fulltime highly-trained and recommended nurse in his desolate house, and spent his time haunting police stations and newspaper offices. He aged a decade in the ninety days since Arabella left; his shoulders stooped, his footsteps lagged, and a look of constant misery lay in his eyes. He was a prematurely old and broken man.

"It's the most uncanny thing I ever saw," I told de Grandin as we walked through West Forty-second Street toward the West Shore Ferry. We had gone over to New York for some surgical supplies, and I do not drive my car in the metropolis. Truck drivers there are far too careless and repair bills for wrecked mudguards far too high. "How a full-grown woman would evaporate this way is something I can't understand. Of course, she may have done away with herself, dropped off a ferry, or—"

"*S-s-st,*" his sibilated admonition cut me short. "That woman there, my friend, observe her, if you please." He nodded toward a female figure twenty feet or so ahead of us.

I looked, and wondered at his sudden interest at the draggled hussy. She was dressed in tawdry finery much the worse for wear. The sleazy silken skirt was much too tight, the cheap fur jaquette far too short and snug, and the high heels of her satin shoes were shockingly run over. Makeup was fairly plastered on her cheeks and lips and eyes, and short black hair bristled untidily beneath the brim of her abbreviated hat. Written unmistakably upon her was the nature of her calling, the oldest and least honorable profession known to womanhood.

"Well," I answered tartly, "what possible interest can you have in a—"

"Do not walk so fast," he whispered as his fingers closed upon my arm, "and do not raise your voice. I would that we should follow her, but I do not wish that she should know."

The neighborhood was far from savory, and I felt

uncomfortably conspicuous as we turned from Forty-second Street into Eleventh Avenue in the wake of the young strumpet, followed her provocatively swaying hips down two malodorous blocks, finally pausing as she slipped furtively into the doorway of a filthy, unkempt "rooming house."

We trailed her through a dimly lighted barren hall and up a flight of shadowy stairs, then up two further flights until we reached a sort of oblong foyer bounded on one end by the stairwell, on the farther extremity by a barred and very dirty window, and on each side by sagging, paint-blistered doors. On each of these was pinned a card, handwritten with the many flourishes dear to the chirography of the professional card-writer who still does business in the poorer quarters of our great cities. The air was heavy with the odor of cheap whiskey, bacon rind and fried onions.

We made a hasty circuit of the hall, studying the cardboard labels. On the farthest door the notice read *Miss Sieglinde.*

"*Mon Dieu,*" he exclaimed as he read it, "*c'est le mot propre!*"

"Eh?" I returned.

"Sieglinde, do not you recall her?"

"No-o, can't say I do. The only Sieglinde I remember is the character in Wagner's *Die Walküre* who unwittingly became her brother's paramour and bore him a son—"

"*Précisément.* Let us enter, if you please." Without pausing to knock he turned the handle of the door and stepped into the squalid room.

The woman sat upon the unkempt bed, her hat pushed back from her brow. In one hand she held a cracked teacup, with the other she poised a whiskey bottle over it. She had kicked her scuffed and broken shoes off; we saw that she was stockingless, and her bare feet were dark with long-accumulated dirt and black-nailed as a miner's hands. "Get out!" she ordered thickly. "Get out o' here. I ain't receivin'—" a gasp broke her utterance, and she turned her head away quickly. Then: "Get out o' here, you lousy

bums!'' she screamed. ''Who d'ye think you are, breakin'
into a lady's room like this? Get out, or—''

De Grandin eyed her steadily, and as her strident command wavered: ''Madame Arabella, we have come to take
you home,'' he announced softly.

''Good God, man, you're crazy!'' I exclaimed. ''Arabella?
This—''

''Precisely, my old one; this is Madame Arabella Tantavul whom we have sought these many months in vain.''
Crossing the room in two quick strides he seized the
cringing woman by the shoulders and turned her face up to
the light. I looked, and felt a sudden swift attack of nausea.

He was right. Thin to emaciation, her face already lined
with the deep-bitten scars of evil living, the woman on the
bed was Arabella Tantavul, though the shocking change
wrought in her features and the black dye in her hair had
disguised her so effectively that I should not have known
her.

''We have come to take you home, *ma pauvre*,'' he
repeated. ''Your husband—''

''My husband!'' her reply was half a scream. ''Dear God,
as if I had a husband—''

''And the little one who needs you,'' he continued. ''You
cannot leave them thus, Madame.''

''I can't? Ah, that's where you're wrong, Doctor, I can
never see my baby again, in this world or the next. Please go
away and forget you've seen me, or I shall have to drown
myself—I've tried it twice already, but the first time I was
rescued, and the second time my courage failed. But if you
try to take me back, or if you tell Dennis you saw me—''

''Tell me, Madame,'' he broke in, ''was not your flight
caused by a visitation from the dead?''

Her faded brown eyes—eyes that had been such a
startling contrast to her pale-gold hair—widened. ''How did
you know?'' she whispered.

''*Tiens,* one may make surmises. Will not you tell us just
what happened? I think there is a way out of your difficul-
ties.''

''No, no, there isn't; there can't be!'' Her head drooped

listlessly. "He planned his work too well; all that's left for me is death—and damnation afterward."

"But if there were a way—if I could show it to you?"

"Can you repeal the laws of God?"

"I am a very clever person, Madame. Perhaps I can accomplish an evasion, if not an absolute repeal. Now tell us, how and when did Monsieur your late but not at all lamented uncle come to you?"

"The night before—before I went away. I woke about midnight, thinking I heard a cry from Dennie's nursery. When I reached the room where he was sleeping I saw my uncle's face glaring at me through the window. It seemed to be illuminated by a sort of inward hellish light, for it stood out against the darkness like a jack-o'-lantern, and it smiled an awful smile at me. 'Arabella,' it said, and I could see its thin dead lips writhe back as if all the teeth were burning-hot, 'I've come to tell you that your marriage is a mockery and a lie. The man you married is your brother, and the child you bore is doubly illegitimate. You can't continue living with them, Arabella. That would be an even greater sin. You must leave them right away, or'—once more his lips crept back until his teeth were bare—'or I shall come to visit you each night, and when the baby has grown old enough to understand I'll tell him who his parents really are. Take your choice, my daughter. Leave them and let me go back to the grave, or stay and see me every night and know that I will tell your son when he is old enough to understand. If I do it he will loathe and hate you; curse the day you bore him.'

" 'And you'll promise never to come near Dennis or the baby if I go?' I asked.

"He promised, and I staggered back to bed, where I fell fainting.

"Next morning when I wakened I was sure it had been a bad dream, but when I looked at Dennis and my own reflection in the glass I knew it was no dream, but a dreadful visitation from the dead.

"Then I went mad. I tried to kill my baby, and when Dennis stopped me I watched my chance to run away, came over to New York and took to this." She looked significantly around the miserable room. "I knew they'd never look for Arabella Tantavul among the city's whores; I was safer from pursuit right here than if I'd been in Europe or China."

"But, Madame," de Grandin's voice was jubilant with shocked reproof, "that which you saw was nothing but a dream; a most unpleasant dream, I grant, but still a dream. Look in my eyes, if you please!"

She raised her eyes to his, and I saw his pupils widen as a cat's do in the dark, saw a line of white outline the cornea, and, responsive to his piercing gaze, beheld her brown eyes in a fixed stare, first as if in fright, then with a glaze almost like that of death.

"Attend me, Madame Arabella," he commanded softly. "You are tired—*grand Dieu,* how tired you are! You have suffered greatly, but you are about to rest. Your memory of that night is gone; so is all memory of the things which have transpired since. You will move and eat and sleep as you are bidden, but of what takes place around you till I bid you wake you will retain no recollection. Do you hear me, Madame Arabella?"

"I hear," she answered softly in a small tired voice.

"*Très bon.* Lie down, my little poor one. Lie down to rest and dreams of love. Sleep, rest, dream and forget.

"Will you be good enough to 'phone to Dr. Wyckoff?" he asked me. "We shall place her in his sanitorium, wash this *sacré* dye from her hair and nurse her back to health; then when all is ready we can bear her home and have her take up life and love where she left off. No one shall be the wiser. This chapter of her life is closed and sealed for ever.

"Each day I'll call upon her and renew hypnotic treatments that she may simulate the mild but curable mental case which we shall tell the good Wyckoff she is. When finally I release her from hypnosis her mind will be entirely cleared of that bad dream that nearly wrecked her happiness."

Arabella Tantavul lay on the sofa in her charming boudoir, an orchid negligée about her slender shoulders, an eiderdown rug tucked around her feet and knees. Her wedding ring was once more on her finger. Pale with a pallor not to be disguised by the most skillfully applied cosmetics, and with deep violet crescents underneath her amber eyes, she lay back listlessly, drinking in the cheerful warmth that emanated from the fire of apple-logs that snapped and crackled on the hearth. Two months of rest at Dr. Wyckoff's sanitorium had cleansed the marks of dissipation from her face, and the ministrations of beauticians had restored the pale-gold luster to her hair, but the listlessness that followed her complete breakdown was still upon her like the weakness from a fever.

"I can't remember anything about my illness, Dr. Trowbridge," she told me with a weary little smile, "but vaguely I connect it with some dreadful dream I had. And"—she wrinkled her smooth forehead in an effort at remembering—"I think I had a rather dreadful dream last night, but—"

"Ah-*ha?*" de Grandin leant abruptly forward in his chair. "What was it that you dreamed, Madame?"

"I—don't—know," she answered slowly. "Odd, isn't it, how you can remember that a dream was so unpleasant, yet not recall its details? Somehow, I connect it with Uncle Warburg; but—"

"*Parbleu,* do you say so? Has he returned? *Ah bah,* he makes me to be so mad, that one!"

"It is time we went, my friend," de Grandin told me as the tall clock in the hall beat out its tenth deliberate stroke; "we have important duties to perform."

"For goodness' sake," I protested, "at this hour o' night?"

"Precisely. At Monsieur Tantavul's I shall expect a visitor tonight, and—we must be ready for him.

"Is Madame Arabella sleeping?" he asked Dennis as he answered our ring at the door.

"Like a baby," answered the young husband. "I've been sitting by her all evening, and I don't believe she even turned in bed."

"And you did keep the window closed, as I requested?"

"Yes, sir; closed and latched."

"*Bien*. Await us here, *mon brave;* we shall rejoin you presently."

He led the way to Arabella's bedroom, removed the wrappings from a bulky parcel he had lugged from our house, and displayed the object thus disclosed with an air of inordinate pride. "Behold him," he commanded gleefully. "Is he not magnificent?"

"Why—what the devil?—it's nothing but an ordinary window screen," I answered.

"A window screen, I grant, my friend; but not an ordinary one. Can not you see it is of copper?"

"Well—"

"*Parbleu*, but I should say it is well," he grinned. "Observe him, how he works."

From his kit bag he produced a roll of insulated wire, an electrical transformer, and some tools. Working quickly he passe-patouted the screen's wooden frame with electrician's tape, then plugged a wire in a nearby lamp socket, connected it with the transformer, and from the latter led a double strand of cotton-wrapped wire to the screen. This he clipped firmly to the copper meshes and led a third strand to the metal grille of the heat register. Last of all he filled a bulb syringe with water and sprayed the screen, repeating the performance till it sparkled like a cobweb in the morning sun. "And now, *Monsieur le Revenant*," he chuckled as he finished, "I damn think all is ready for your warm reception!"

For something like an hour we waited, then he tiptoed to the bed and bent over Arabella.

"Madame!"

The girl stirred slightly, murmuring some half-audible response, and:

"In half an hour you will rise," he told her. "You will put your robe on and stand by the window, but on no account will you go near it or lay hands on it. Should anyone address you from outside you will reply, but you will not remember what you say or what is said to you."

He motioned me to follow, and we left the room, taking station in the hallway just outside.

How long we waited I have no accurate idea. Perhaps it was an hour, perhaps less; at any rate the silent vigil seemed unending, and I raised my hand to stifle back a yawn when:

"Yes, Uncle Warburg, I can hear you," we heard Arabella saying softly in the room beyond the door.

We tiptoed to the entry: Arabella stood before the window, and from beyond it glared the face of Warburg Tantavul.

It was dead, there was no doubt about that. In sunken cheek and pinched-in nose and yellowish-gray skin there showed the evidence of death and early putrefaction, but dead though it was, it was also animated with a dreadful sort of life. The eyes were glaring horribly, the lips were red as though they had been painted with fresh blood.

"You hear me, do you?" it demanded. "Then listen, girl; you broke your bargain with me, now I'm come to keep my threat: every time you kiss your husband"—a shriek of bitter laughter cut his words, and his staring eyes half closed with hellish merriment—"or the child you love so well, my shadow will be on you. You've kept me out thus far, but some night I'll get in, and—"

The lean dead jaw dropped, then snapped up as if lifted by sheer will-power, and the whole expression of the corpse-face changed. Surprise, incredulous delight, anticipation as before a feast were pictured on it. "Why"—its cachinnating laughter sent a chill up my spine—"why your window's open! You've changed the screen and I can enter!"

Slowly, like a child's balloon stirred by a vagrant wind, the awful thing moved closer to the window. Closer to the screen it came, and Arabella gave ground before it and put up her hands to shield her eyes from the sight of its hellish grin of triumph.

"*Sapristi*," swore de Grandin softly. "Come on, my old and evil one, come but a little nearer—"

The dead thing floated nearer. Now its mocking mouth

and shriveled, pointed nose were almost pressed against the copper meshes of the screen; now they began to filter through the meshes like a wisp of fog—

There was a blinding flash of blue-white flame, the sputtering gush of fusing metal, a wild, despairing shriek that ended ere it fairly started in a sob of mortal torment, and the sharp and acrid odor of burned flesh!

"Arabella—darling—is she all right?" Dennis Tantavul came charging up the stairs. "I thought I heard a scream—"

"You did, my friend," de Grandin answered, "but I do not think that you will hear its repetition unless you are unfortunate enough to go to hell when you have died."

"What was it?"

"*Eh bien,* one who thought himself a clever jester pressed his jest too far. Meantime, look to Madame your wife. See how peacefully she lies upon her bed. Her time for evil dreams is past. Be kind to her, *mon jeune.* Do not forget, a woman loves to have a lover, even though he is her husband." He bent and kissed the sleeping girl upon the brow. "*Au 'voir,* my little lovely one," he murmured. Then, to me:

"Come, Trowbridge, my good friend. Our work is finished here. Let us leave them to their happiness."

An hour later in the study he faced me across the fire. "Perhaps you'll deign to tell me what it's all about now?" I asked sarcastically.

"Perhaps I shall," he answered with a grin. "You will recall that this annoying Monsieur Who Was Dead Yet Not Dead appeared and grinned most horrifyingly through windows several times? Always from the outside, please remember. At the hospital, where he nearly caused the *guarde-malade* to have a fit, he laughed and mouthed at her through the glass skylight. When he first appeared and threatened Madame Arabella he spoke to her through the window—"

"But her window was open," I protested.

"Yes, but screened," he answered with a smile. "Screened with iron wire, if you please."

"What difference did that make? Tonight I saw him almost force his features through—"

"A copper screen," he supplied. "Tonight the screen was copper; me, I saw to that."

Then, seeing my bewilderment: "Iron is the most earthy of all metals," he explained. "It and its derivative, steel, are so instinct with the earth's essence that creatures of the spirit cannot stand its nearness. The legends tell us that when Solomon's Temple was constructed no tool of iron was employed, because even the friendly *jinn* whose help he had enlisted could not perform their tasks in close proximity to iron. The witch can be detected by the pricking of an iron pin—never by a pin of brass.

"Very well. When first I thought about the evil dead one's reappearances I noted that each time he stared outside the window. Glass, apparently, he could not pass—and glass contains a modicum of iron. Iron window-wire stopped him. 'He are not a true ghost, then,' I inform me. 'They are things of spirit only, they are thoughts made manifest. This one is a thing of hate, but also of some physical material as well; he is composed in part of emanations from the body which lies putrefying in the grave. *Voilà*, if he have physical properties he can be destroyed by physical means.'

"And so I set my trap. I procured a screen of copper through which he could effect an entrance, but I charged it with electricity. I increased the potential of the current with a step-up transformer to make assurance doubly sure, and then I waited for him like the spider for the fly, waited for him to come through that charged screen and electrocute himself. Yes, certainly."

"But is he really destroyed?" I asked dubiously.

"As the candle flame when one has blown it out. He was—how do you say it?—short-circuited. No malefactor in the chair of execution ever died more thoroughly than that one, I assure you."

"It seems queer, though, that he should come back from the grave to haunt those poor kids and break up their marriage when he really wanted it," I murmured wonder-ingly.

"Wanted it? Yes, as the trapper wants the bird to step within his snare."

"But he gave them such a handsome present when little Dennis was born—"

"*La la,* my good, kind, trusting friend, you are *naïf.* The money I gave Madame Arabella was my own. I put it in that envelope."

"Then what was the real message?"

"It was a dreadful thing, my friend; a dreadful, wicked thing. The night that Monsieur Dennis left that package with me I determined that the old one meant to do him injury, so I steamed the cover open and read what lay within. It made plain the things which Dennis thought that he remembered.

"Long, long ago Monsieur Tantavul lived in San Fran-cisco. His wife was twenty years his junior, and a pretty, joyous thing she was. She bore him two fine children, a boy and a girl, and on them she bestowed the love which he could not appreciate. His surliness, his evil temper, his constant fault-finding drove her to distraction, and finally she sued for divorce.

"But he forestalled her. He spirited the children away, then told his wife the plan of his revenge. He would take them to some far off place and bring them up believing they were cousins. Then when they had attained full growth he would induce them to marry and keep the secret of their relationship until they had a child, then break the dreadful truth to them. Thereafter they would live on, bound together by their fear of censure, or perhaps of criminal prosecution, but their consciences would cause them endless torment, and the very love they had for each other would be like fetters forged of white-hot steel, holding them in odious bondage from which there was no escape. The sight of their children would be a reproach to them, the mere thought of love's sweet communion would cause revulsion to the point of nausea.

"When he had told her this his wife went mad. He thrust her into an asylum and left her there to die while he came with his babies to New Jersey, where he reared them together, and by guile and craftiness nurtured their love, knowing that when finally they married he would have his so vile revenge.''

"But, great heavens, man, they're brother and sister!" I exclaimed in horror.

"Perfectly," he answered coolly. "They are also man and woman, husband and wife, and father and mother."

"But—but—" I stammered, utterly at loss for words.

"But me no buts, good friend. I know what you would say. Their child? *Ah bah*, did not the kings of ancient times repeatedly take their own sisters to wife, and were not their offspring usually sound and healthy? But certainly cross-breeding produces inferior progeny only when defective recessive genes are matched. Look at little Monsieur Dennis. Were you not blinded by your silly, unrealistic training and tradition—did you not know his parents' near relationship—you would not hesitate to pronounce him an unusually fine, healthy child.

"Besides," he added earnestly, "they love each other, not as brother and sister, but as man and woman. He is her happiness, she is his, and little Monsieur Dennis is the happiness of both. Why destroy this joy—*le bon Dieu* knows they earned it by a joyless childhood—when I can preserve it for them by simply keeping silent?"

For a quarter of a century, Seabury Quinn's ghostly tales were almost always ranked first by the readers of Weird Tales, *where nearly all of his more than 160 stories appeared. Born in Washington, D.C., in 1889, Quinn graduated from the Law School of the Washington, D.C. Bar, saw military service in World War I, became the editor of trade journals for mortuary directors, and was an expert on mortuary law and science. He is best known, however, as the creator of Dr. Jules de Grandin, the dapper blond ghosthunter whose best cases are collected in* The Phantom-Fighter. *His best non–de Grandin tales appear in* Is the Devil a Gentleman?

Ted was suspicious when the lot in exclusive Clay Canyon was only $1500. What was the catch?

4

One of the Dead
William Wood

We couldn't have been more pleased. Deep in Clay Canyon we came upon the lot abruptly at a turn in the winding road. There was a crudely lettered board nailed to a dead tree which read, LOT FOR SALE—$1500 OR BEST OFFER, and a phone number.

"Fifteen hundred dollars—in Clay Canyon? I can't believe it," Ellen said.

"Or best offer," I corrected.

"I've heard you can't take a step without bumping into some movie person here."

"We've come three miles already without bumping into one. I haven't seen a soul."

"But there are the houses." Ellen looked about breathlessly.

There indeed were the houses—to our left and our right, to our front and our rear—low, ranch-style houses, unos-

75

tentatious, prosaic, giving no hint of the gay and improbable lives we imagined went on inside them. But as the houses marched up the gradually climbing road there was not a single person to be seen. The cars—the Jaguars and Mercedeses and Cadillacs and Chryslers—were parked unattended in the driveways, their chrome gleaming in the sun; I caught a glimpse of one corner of a pool and a white diving board, but no one swam in the turquoise water. We climbed out of the car, Ellen with her rather large, short-haired head stooped forward as if under a weight. Except for the fiddling of a cicada somewhere on the hill, a profound hush lay over us in the stifling air. Not even a bird moved in the motionless trees.

"There must be something wrong with it," Ellen said.

"It's probably already been sold, and they just didn't bother to take down the sign. . . . There was something here once, though." I had come across several ragged chunks of concrete that lay about randomly as if heaved out of the earth.

"A house, do you think?"

"It's hard to say. If it was a house it's been gone for years."

"Oh, Ted," Ellen cried. "It's perfect! Look at the view!" She pointed up the canyon toward the round, parched hills. Through the heat shimmering on the road they appeared to be melting down like wax.

"Another good thing," I said. "There won't be much to do to get the ground ready except for clearing the brush away. This place has been graded once. We save a thousand dollars right there."

Ellen took both my hands. Her eyes shone in her solemn face. "What do you think, Ted? What do you think?"

Ellen and I had been married four years, having both taken the step relatively late—in our early thirties—and in that time had lived in two different places, first an apartment in Santa Monica, then, when I was promoted to office manager, in a partly furnished house in the Hollywood Hills, always with the idea that when our first child came we would either buy or build a larger house of our own. But the child had not come. It was a source of anxiety and sadness to us both and lay between us like an old scandal for which each of us took on the blame.

Then I made an unexpected killing on the stock market and Ellen suddenly began agitating in her gentle way for the house. As we shopped around she dropped hints along the way—"This place is really too small for us, don't you think?" or "We'd have to fence off the yard, of course"— that let me know that the house had become a talisman for her; she had conceived the notion that perhaps, in some occult way, if we went ahead with our accommodations for a child the child might come. The notion gave her happiness. Her face filled out, the gray circles under her eyes disappeared, the quiet gaiety, which did not seem like gaiety at all but a form of peace, returned.

As Ellen held on to my hands, I hesitated. I am convinced now that there was something behind my hesitation— something I felt then only as a quality of silence, a fleeting twinge of utter desolation. "It's so safe," she said. "There's no traffic at all."

I explained that. "It's not a through street. It ends somewhere up in the hills."

She turned back to me again with her bright, questioning eyes. The happiness that had grown in her during our months of house hunting seemed to have welled into near rapture.

"We'll call the number," I said, "but don't expect too much. It must have been sold long ago."

We walked slowly back to the car. The door handle burned to the touch. Down the canyon the rear end of a panel truck disappeared noiselessly around a bend.

"No," Ellen said, "I have a feeling about this place. I think it was meant to be ours."

And she was right, of course.

Mr. Carswell Deeves, who owned the land, was called upon to do very little except take my check for $1500 and hand over the deed to us, for by the time Ellen and I met him we had already sold ourselves. Mr. Deeves, as we had suspected from the unprofessional sign, was a private citizen. We found his house in a predominantly Mexican section of Santa Monica. He was a chubby, pink man of indeterminate age dressed in white ducks and soft white shoes, as if he had had a tennis court hidden away among the squalid, asphalt-shingled houses and dry kitchen gardens of his neighbors.

"Going to live in Clay Canyon, are you?" he said. "Ros Russell lives up there, or used to." So, we discovered, did Joel McCrea, Jimmy Stewart and Paula Raymond, as well as a cross-section of producers, directors and character actors. "Oh, yes," said Mr. Deeves, "it's an address that will look extremely good on your stationery."

Ellen beamed and squeezed my hand.

Mr. Deeves turned out to know very little about the land other than that a house had been destroyed by fire there years ago and that the land had changed hands many times since. "I myself acquired it in what may strike you as a novel way," he said as we sat in his parlor—a dark, airless box which smelled faintly of camphor and whose walls were obscured with yellowing autographed photographs of movie stars. "I won it in a game of hearts from a makeup man on the set of *Quo Vadis*. Perhaps you remember me. I had a close-up in one of the crowd scenes."

"That was a number of years ago, Mr. Deeves," I said. "Have you been trying to sell it all this time?"

"I've nearly sold it dozens of times," he said, "but something always went wrong somehow."

"What kind of things?"

"Naturally, the fire-insurance rates up there put off a lot of people. I hope you're prepared to pay a high premium—"

"I've already checked into that."

"Good. You'd be surprised how many people will let details like that go till the last minute."

"What other things have gone wrong?"

Ellen touched my arm to discourage my wasting any more time with foolish questions.

Mr. Deeves spread out the deed before me and smoothed

it with this forearm. "Silly things, some of them. One couple found some dead doves . . ."

"Dead doves?" I handed him the signed article. With one pink hand Mr. Deeves waved it back and forth to dry the ink. "Five of them, if I remember correctly. In my opinion they'd sat on a wire and were electrocuted somehow. The husband thought nothing of it, of course, but his wife became so hysterical that we had to call off the transaction."

I made a sign at Mr. Deeves to drop this line of conversation. Ellen loves animals and birds of all kinds with a devotion that turns the loss of a household pet into a major tragedy, which is why, since the death of our cocker spaniel, we had had no more pets. But Ellen appeared not to have heard; she was watching the paper in Mr. Deeves' hand fixedly, as if she were afraid it might vanish.

Mr. Deeves sprang suddenly to his feet. "Well!" he cried. "It's all yours now. I know you'll be happy there."

Ellen flushed with pleasure. "I'm sure we will," she said, and took his pudgy hand in both of hers.

"A prestige address," called Mr. Deeves from his porch as we drove away. "A real prestige address."

Ellen and I are modern people. Our talk in the evenings is generally on issues of the modern world. Ellen paints a little and I do some writing from time to time—mostly on technical subjects. The house that Ellen and I built mirrored our concern with present-day aesthetics. We worked closely with Jack Salmanson, the architect and a friend, who designed a steel module house, low and compact and private, which could be fitted into the irregularities of our patch of land for a maximum of space. The interior *décor* we left largely up to Ellen, who combed the home magazines and made sketches as if she were decorating a dozen homes.

I mention these things to show that there is nothing Gothic about my wife and me: We are as thankful for our common sense as for our sensibilities, and we flattered ourselves that the house we built achieved a balance between the aesthetic and the functional. Its lines were simple and clean; there were no dark corners, and it was surrounded on three sides by houses, none of which were more than eight years old.

There were, however, signs from the very beginning, ominous signs which can be read only in retrospect, though it seems to me now that there were others who suspected but said nothing. One was the Mexican who cut down the tree.

As a money-saving favor to us, Jack Salmanson agreed to supervise the building himself and hire small, independent contractors to do the labor, many of whom were Mexicans or Negroes with dilapidated equipment that appeared to run only by some mechanical miracle. The Mexican, a small, forlorn workman with a stringy moustache, had already burned out two chain-saw blades and still had not cut halfway through the tree. It was inexplicable. The tree, the same one on which Ellen and I had seen the original For Sale sign, had obviously been dead for years, and the branches that already lay scattered on the ground were rotted through.

"You must have run into a batch of knots," Jack said. "Try it again. If the saw gets too hot, quit and we'll pull it down with the bulldozer." As if answering to its name, the bulldozer turned at the back of the lot and lumbered toward us in a cloud of dust, the black shoulders of the Negro operator gleaming in the sun.

The Mexican need not have feared for his saw. He had scarcely touched it to the tree when it started to topple of its own accord. Startled, he backed away a few steps. The tree had begun to fall toward the back of the lot, in the direction of his cut, but now it appeared to arrest itself, its naked branches trembling as if in agitation; then with an awful rending sound it writhed upright and fell back on itself, gaining momentum and plunging directly at the bulldozer. My voice died in my throat, but Jack and the Mexican shouted, and the operator jumped and rolled on the ground just as the tree fell high on the hood, shattering the windshield to bits. The bulldozer, out of control and knocked off course, came directly at us, gears whining and gouging a deep trough in the earth. Jack and I jumped one way, the Mexican the other; the bulldozer lurched between us and ground on toward the street, the Negro sprinting after it.

"The car!" Jack shouted. "The car!"

Parked in front of the house across the street was a car, a car which was certainly brand-new. The bulldozer headed straight for it, its blade striking clusters of sparks from the pavement. The Mexican waved his chain saw over his head like a toy and shouted in Spanish. I covered my eyes with my hands and heard Jack grunt softly, as if he had been struck in the mid-section, just before the crash.

Two women stood on the porch of the house across the street and gaped. The car had caved in at the center, its steel roof wrinkled like tissue paper; its front and rear ends were folded around the bulldozer as if embracing it. Then with a low whoosh, both vehicles were enveloped in creeping blue flame.

"Rotten luck," Jack muttered under his breath as we ran into the street. From the corner of my eye I caught the curious sight of the Mexican on the ground, praying, his chain saw lying by his knees.

In the evening Ellen and I paid a visit to the Sheffits', Sondra and Jeff, our neighbors across the canyon road, where we met the owner of the ruined car, Joyce Castle, a striking blonde in lemon-colored pants. The shock of the accident itself wore off with the passing of time and cocktails, and the three of them treated it as a tremendous joke.

Mrs. Castle was particularly hilarious. "I'm doing better," she rejoiced. "The Alfa-Romeo only lasted two days, but I held on to this one a whole six weeks. I even had the permanent plates on."

"But you mustn't be without a car, Mrs. Castle," Ellen said in her serious way. "We'd be glad to loan you our Plymouth until you can—"

"I'm having a new car delivered tomorrow afternoon. Don't worry about me. A Daimler, Jeff, you'll be interested to know. I couldn't resist after riding in yours. What about the poor bulldozer man? Is he absolutely wiped out?"

"I think he'll survive," I said. "In any case he has two other 'dozers."

"Then you won't be held up," Jeff said.

"I wouldn't think so."

Sondra chuckled softly. "I just happened to look out the window," she said. "It was just like a Rube Goldberg cartoon. A chain reaction."

"And there was my poor old Cadillac at the end of it," Mrs. Castle sighed.

Suey, Mrs. Castle's dog, who had been lying on the floor beside his mistress glaring dourly at us between dozes, suddenly ran to the front door barking ferociously, his red mane standing straight up.

"Suey!" Mrs. Castle slapped her knee. "Suey! Come here!"

The dog merely flattened its ears and looked from his mistress toward the door again as if measuring a decision. He growled deep in his throat.

"It's the ghost," Sondra said lightly. "He's behind the whole thing." Sondra sat curled up in one corner of the sofa and tilted her head to one side as she spoke, like a very clever child.

Jeff laughed sharply. "Oh, they tell some very good stories."

With a sigh Mrs. Castle rose and dragged Suey back by his collar. "If I didn't feel so self-conscious about it I'd take him to an analyst," she said. "Sit, Suey! Here's a cashew nut for you."

"I'm very fond of ghost stories," I said, smiling.

"Oh, well," Jeff murmured, mildly disparaging.

"Go ahead, Jeff," Sondra urged him over the rim of her glass. "They'd like to hear it."

Jeff was a literary agent, a tall, sallow man with dark oily hair that he was continually pushing out of his eyes with his fingers. As he spoke he smiled lopsidedly as if defending against the probability of being taken seriously. "All I know is that back in the late seventeenth century the Spanish used to have hangings here. The victims are supposed to float around at night and make noises."

"Criminals?" I asked.

"Of the worst sort," said Sondra. "What was the story Guy Relling told you, Joyce?" She smiled with a curious inward relish that suggested she knew the story perfectly well herself.

"Is that Guy Relling, the director?" I asked.

"Yes," Jeff said. "He owns those stables down the canyon."

"I've seen them," Ellen said. "Such lovely horses."

Joyce Castle hoisted her empty glass into the air. "Jeff, love, will you find me another?"

"We keep straying from the subject," said Sondra gently. "Fetch me another too, darling"—she handed her glass to Jeff as he went by—"like a good boy. . . . I didn't mean to interrupt, Joyce. Go on." She gestured toward us as the intended audience. Ellen stiffened slightly in her chair.

"It seems that there was one *hombre* of outstanding depravity," Joyce Castle said languidly. "I forgot the name. He murdered, stole, raped . . . one of those endless Spanish names with a 'Luis' in it, a nobleman I think Guy said. A charming sort. Mad, of course, and completely unpredictable. They hanged him at last for some unsavory escapade in a nunnery. You two are moving into a neighborhood rich with tradition."

We all laughed.

"What about the noises?" Ellen asked Sondra. "Have you heard anything?"

"Of course," Sondra said, tipping her head prettily. Every inch of her skin was tanned to the color of coffee from afternoons by the pool. It was a form of leisure that her husband, with his bilious coloring and lank hair, apparently did not enjoy.

"Everywhere I've ever lived," he said, his grin growing crookeder and more apologetic, "there were noises in the night that you couldn't explain. Here there are all kinds of wildlife—foxes, coons, possums—even coyotes up on the ridge. They're all active after sundown."

Ellen's smile of pleasure at this news turned to distress as Sondra remarked in her offhand way, "We found our poor kitty-cat positively torn to pieces one morning. He was all blood. We never did find his head.''

"A fox," Jeff put in quickly. Everything he said seemed hollow. Something came from him like a vapor. I thought it was grief.

Sondra gazed smugly into her lap as if hugging a secret to herself. She seemed enormously pleased. It occurred to me that Sondra was trying to frighten us. In a way it relieved me. She was enjoying herself too much, I thought, looking at her spoiled, brown face, to be frightened herself.

After the incident of the tree everything went well for some weeks. The house went up rapidly. Ellen and I visited it as often as we could, walking over the raw ground and making our home in our mind's eye. The fireplace would go here, the refrigerator here, our Picasso print there. "Ted," Ellen said timidly, "I've been thinking. Why don't we fix up the extra bedroom as a children's room?"

I waited.

"Now that we'll be living out here our friends will have to stay overnight more often. Most of them have young children. It would be nice for them."

I slipped my arm around her shoulders. She knew I understood. It was a delicate matter. She raised her face and I kissed her between her brows. Signal and counter-signal, the keystones of our life together—a life of sensibility and tact.

"Hey, you two!" Sondra Sheffits called from across the street. She stood on her front porch in a pink bathing suit, her skin brown, her hair nearly white. "How about a swim?"

"No suits!"

"Come on, we've got plenty."

Ellen and I debated the question with a glance, settled it with a nod.

As I came out onto the patio in one of Jeff's suits, Sondra said, "Ted, you're pale as a ghost. Don't you get any sun where you are?" She lay in a chaise lounge behind huge elliptical sunglasses encrusted with glass gems.

"I stay inside too much, writing articles," I said.

"You're welcome to come here any time you like"—she smiled suddenly, showing me a row of small, perfect teeth—"and swim."

Ellen appeared in her borrowed suit, a red one with a short, limp ruffle. She shaded her eyes as the sun, glittering metallically on the water, struck her full in the face.

Sondra ushered her forward as if to introduce my wife to me. "You look much better in that suit than I ever did." Her red nails flashed on Ellen's arm. Ellen smiled guardedly. The two women were about the same height, but Ellen was narrower in the shoulders, thicker through the waist and hips. As they came toward me it seemed to me that Ellen was the one I did not know. Her familiar body became strange. It looked out of proportion. Hairs that on Sondra were all but invisible except when the sun turned them to silver, lay flat and dark on Ellen's pallid arm.

As if sensing the sudden distance between us, Ellen took my hand. "Let's jump in together," she said gaily. "No hanging back."

Sondra retreated to the chaise lounge to watch us, her eyes invisible behind her outrageous glasses, her head on one side.

Incidents began again and continued at intervals. Guy Relling, whom I never met but whose pronouncements on the supernatural reached me through others from time to time like messages from an oracle, claims that the existence of the living dead is a particularly excruciating one as they hover between two states of being. Their memories keep the passions of life forever fresh and sharp, but they are able to relieve them only at a monstrous expense of will and energy which leaves them literally helpless for months or sometimes even years afterward. This was why materializations and other forms of tangible action are relatively rare. There are of course exceptions, Sondra, our most frequent translator of Relling's theories, pointed out one evening with the odd joy that accompanied all of her remarks on the subject; some ghosts are terrifically active—particularly the insane ones who, ignorant of the limitations of death as they were of the impossibilities of life, transcend them with the dynamism that is exclusively the property of madness. Generally, however, it was Relling's opinion that a ghost was more to be pitied than feared. Sondra quoted him as having said, "The notion of a haunted house is a misconception semantically. It is not the house but the soul itself that is haunted."

On Saturday, August 6, a workman laying pipe was blinded in one eye by an acetylene torch.

On Thursday, September 1, a rockslide on the hill behind us dumped four tons of dirt and rock on the half-finished house and halted work for two weeks.

On Sunday, October 9—my birthday, oddly enough—while visiting the house alone, I slipped on a stray screw and struck my head on a can of latex paint which opened up a gash requiring ten stitches. I rushed across to the Sheffits'. Sondra answered the door in her bathing suit and a magazine in her hand. "Ted?" She peered at me. "I scarcely recognized you through the blood. Come in. I'll call the doctor. Try not to drip on the furniture, will you?"

I told the doctor of the screw on the floor, the big can of paint. I did not tell him that my foot had slipped because I had turned too quickly and that I had turned too quickly because the sensation had grown on me that there was someone behind me, close enough to touch me, perhaps, because something hovered there, fetid and damp and cold and almost palpable in its nearness; I remember shivering violently as I turned, as if the sun of this burning summer's day had been replaced by a mysterious star without warmth. I did not tell the doctor this nor anyone else.

In November Los Angeles burns. After the long drought of summer the sap goes underground and the baked hills seem to gasp in pain for the merciful release of either life or death—rain or fire. Invariably fire comes first, spreading through the outlying parts of the country like an epidemic, till the sky is livid and starless at night and overhung with dun-colored smoke during the day.

There was a huge fire in Tujunga, north of us, the day Ellen and I moved into our new house—handsome, severe, aggressively new on its dry hillside—under a choked sky

the color of earth and a muffled, flyspeck sun. Sondra and
Jeff came over to help, and in the evening Joyce Castle
stopped by with Suey and a magnum of champagne.

Ellen clasped her hands under her chin. "What a lovely
surprise!"

"I hope it's cold enough. I've had it in my refrigerator
since four o'clock. Welcome to the canyon. You're nice
people. You remind me of my parents. God, it's hot. I've
been weeping all day on account of the smoke. You'll have
air conditioning I suppose?"

Jeff was sprawled in a chair with his long legs straight in
front of him in the way a cripple might put aside a pair of
crutches. "Joyce, you're an angel. Excuse me if I don't get
up. I'm recuperating."

"You're excused, doll, you're excused."

"Ted," Ellen said softly. "Why don't you get some
glasses?"

Jeff hauled in his legs. "Can I give you a hand?"

"Sit still, Jeff."

He sighed. "I hadn't realized I was so out of shape." He
looked more cadaverous than ever after our afternoon of
lifting and shoving. Sweat had collected in the hollows
under his eyes.

"Shall I show you the house, Joyce? While Ted is in the
kitchen?"

"I love you, Ellen," Joyce said. "Take me on the whole
tour."

Sondra followed me into the kitchen. She leaned against
the wall and smoked, supporting her left elbow in the palm
of her right hand. She didn't say a word. Through the open
door I could see Jeff's outstretched legs from the calves
down.

"Thanks for all the help today," I said to Sondra in a
voice unaccountably close to a whisper. I could hear Joyce
and Ellen as they moved from room to room, their voices
swelling and dying: "It's all steel? You mean everything?
Walls and all? Aren't you afraid of lightning?"

"Oh, we're all safely grounded, I think."

Jeff yawned noisily in the living room. Wordlessly

Sondra put a tray on the kitchen table as I rummaged in an unpacked carton for the glasses. She watched me steadily and coolly, as if she expected me to entertain her. I wanted to say something further to break a silence which was becoming unnatural and oppressive. The sounds around us seemed only to isolate us in a ring of intimacy. With her head on one side Sondra smiled at me. I could hear her rapid breathing.

"What's this, a nursery? Ellen, love!"

"No, no! It's only for our friends' children."

Sondra's eyes were blue, the color of shallow water. She seemed faintly amused, as if we were sharing in a conspiracy—a conspiracy I was anxious to repudiate by making some prosaic remark in a loud voice for all to hear, but a kind of pain developed in my chest as the words seemed dammed there, and I only smiled at her foolishly. With every passing minute of silence, the more impossible it became to break through and the more I felt drawn into the intrigue of which, though I was ignorant, I was surely guilty. Without so much as a touch she had made us lovers.

Ellen stood in the doorway, half turned away as if her first impulse had been to run. She appeared to be deep in thought, her eyes fixed on the steel, cream-colored door-jamb.

Sondra began to talk to Ellen in her dry, satirical voice. It was chatter of the idlest sort, but she was destroying, as I had wished to destroy, the absurd notion that there was something between us. I could see Ellen's confusion. She hung on Sondra's words, watching her lips attentively, as if this elegant, tanned woman, calmly smoking and talking of trifles, were her savior.

As for myself, I felt as if I had lost the power of speech entirely. If I joined in with Sondra's carefully innocent chatter I would only be joining in the deception against my wife; if I proclaimed the truth and ended everything by bringing it into the open . . . but what truth? What was there in fact to bring into the open? What was there to end? A feeling in the air? An intimation? The answer was nothing, of course. I did not even like Sondra very much.

There was something cold and unpleasant about her. There was nothing to proclaim because nothing had happened. "Where's Joyce?" I asked finally, out of a dry mouth. "Doesn't she want to see the kitchen?"

Ellen turned slowly toward me, as if it cost her a great effort. "She'll be here in a minute," she said tonelessly, and I became aware of Joyce's and Jeff's voices from the living room. Ellen studied my face, her pupils oddly dilated under the pinkish fluorescent light, as if she were trying to penetrate to the bottom of a great darkness that lay beneath my chance remark. Was it a code of some kind, a new signal for her that I would shortly make clear? What did it mean? I smiled at her and she responded with a smile of her own, a tentative and formal upturning of her mouth, as if I were a familiar face whose name escaped her for the moment.

Joyce came in behind Ellen. "I hate kitchens. I never go into mine." She looked from one to the other of us. "Am I interrupting something?"

At two o'clock in the morning I sat up in bed, wide awake. The bedroom was bathed in the dark red glow of the fire which had come closer in the night. A thin, autumnal veil of smoke hung in the room. Ellen lay on her side, asleep, one hand cupped on the pillow next to her face as if waiting for something to be put in it. I had no idea why I was so fully awake, but I threw off the covers and went to the window to check on the fire. I could see no flame, but the hills stood out blackly against a turgid sky that belled and sagged as the wind blew and relented.

Then I heard the sound.

I am a person who sets store by precision in the use of words—in the field of technical writing this is a necessity. But I can think of no word to describe that sound. The closest I can come with a word of my own invention is "vlump." It came erratically, neither loud nor soft. It was, rather, pervasive and without location. It was not a *solid* sound. There was something vague and whispering about it, and from time to time it began with the suggestion of a sigh—a shuffling dissipation in the air that seemed to take form and die in the same instant. In a way I cannot define, it was mindless, without will or reason, yet implacable. Because I could not explain it immediately I went to seek an explanation.

I stepped into the hall and switched on the light, pressing the noiseless button. The light came down out of a fixture set flush into the ceilings and diffused through a milky plastic-like Japanese rice paper. The clean, indestructible walls rose perpendicularly around me. Through the slight haze of smoke came the smell of the newness, sweet and metallic—more like a car than a house. And still the sound went on. It seemed to be coming from the room at the end of the hall, the room we had designed for our friend's children. The door was open and I could see a gray patch that was a west window. Vlump . . . vlump . . . vlumpvlump. . . .

Fixing on the gray patch, I moved down the hall while my legs made themselves heavy as logs, and all the while I repeated to myself, "The house is settling. All new houses settle and make strange noises." And so lucid was I that I believed I was not afraid. I was walking down the bright new hall of my new steel house to investigate a noise, for the house might be settling unevenly, or an animal might be up to some mischief—raccoons regularly raided the garbage cans, I had been told. There might be something wrong with the plumbing or with the radiant-heating system that warmed our steel and vinyl floors. And now, like the responsible master of the house, I had located the apparent center of the sound and was going responsibly toward it. In a second or two, very likely, I would know. Vlump vlump. The gray of the window turned rosy as I came near enough to see the hillside beyond it. That black was underbrush and that pink the dusty swath cut by the bulldozer before it had run amok. I had watched the accident from just about the spot where I stood now, and the obliterated hole where the tree had been, laid firmly over with the prefabricated floor of the room whose darkness I would eradicate by touching with my right hand the light switch inside the door.

"Ted?"

Blood boomed in my ears. I had the impression that my heart had burst. I clutched at the wall for support. Yet of course I knew it was Ellen's voice, and I answered her calmly. "Yes, it's me."

"What's the matter?" I heard the bedclothes rustle.

"Don't get up, I'm coming right in." The noise had stopped. There was nothing. Only the almost inaudible hum of the refrigerator, the stirring of the wind.

Ellen was sitting up in bed. "I was just checking on the fire," I said. She patted my side of the bed and in the instant before I turned out the hall light I saw her smile.

"I was just dreaming about you," she said softly, as I climbed under the sheets. She rolled against me. "Why, you're trembling."

"I should have worn my robe."

"You'll be warm in a minute." Her fragrant body lay against mine, but I remained rigid as stone and just as cold, staring at the ceiling, my mind a furious blank. After a moment she said, "Ted?" It was her signal, always hesitant, always tremulous, that meant I was to roll over and take her in my arms.

Instead I answered, "What?" just as if I had not understood.

For a few seconds I sensed her struggling against her reserve to give me a further sign that would pierce my peculiar distraction and tell me she wanted love. But it was too much for her—too alien. My coldness had created a vacuum she was too unpracticed to fill—a coldness sudden and inexplicable, unless . . .

She withdrew slowly and pulled the covers up under her chin. Finally she asked, "Ted, is there something happening that I should know about?" She had remembered Sondra and the curious scene in the kitchen. It took, I knew, great courage for Ellen to ask that question, though she must have known my answer.

"No, I'm just tired. We've had a busy day. Good-night, dear." I kissed her on the cheek and sensed her eyes, in the shadow of the fire, searching mine, asking the question she could not give voice to. I turned away, somehow ashamed because I could not supply the answer that would fulfill her need. Because there was no answer at all.

The fire was brought under control after burning some eight hundred acres and several homes, and three weeks later the rains came. Jack Salmanson came out one Sunday to see how the house was holding up, checked the foundation, the roof and all the seams and pronounced it tight as a drum. We sat looking moodily out the glass doors onto the patio—a flatland of grayish mud which threatened to swamp with a thin ooze of silt and gravel the few flagstones I had set in the ground. Ellen was in the bedroom lying down; she had got into the habit of taking a nap after lunch, though it was I, not she, who lay stark awake night after night explaining away sounds that became more and more impossible to explain away. The gagging sound that sometimes accompanied the vlump and the strangled expulsion of air that followed it were surely the result of some disturbance in the water pipes; the footsteps that came slowly down the hall and stopped outside our closed door and then went away again with something like a low chuckle were merely the night contracting of our metal house after the heat of the day. Through all this Ellen slept as if in a stupor; she seemed to have become addicted to sleep. She went to bed at nine and got up at ten the next morning; she napped in the afternoon and moved about lethargically the rest of the time with a Mexican shawl around her shoulders, complaining of the cold. The doctor examined her for mononucleosis but found nothing. He said perhaps it was her sinuses and that she should rest as much as she wanted.

After a protracted silence Jack put aside his drink and stood up. "I guess I'll go along."

"I'll tell Ellen."

"What the hell for? Let her sleep. Tell her I hope she feels better." He turned to frown at the room of the house he had designed and built. "Are you happy here?" he asked suddenly.

"Happy?" I repeated the word awkwardly. "Of course we're happy. We love the house. It's . . . just a little noisy at night, that's all.'' I stammered it out, like the first word of a monstrous confession, but Jack seemed hardly to hear it. He waved a hand. ''House settling.'' He squinted from one side of the room to the other. ''I don't know. There's something about it. . . . It's not right. Maybe it's just the weather . . . the light. . . . It could be friendlier, you know what I mean? It seems cheerless.''

I watched him with a kind of wild hope, as if he might magically fathom my terror—do for me what I could not do for myself, and permit it to be discussed calmly between two men of temperate mind. But Jack was not looking for the cause of the gloom but the cure for it.

''Why don't you try putting down a couple of orange rugs in this room?'' he said.

I stared at the floor as if two orange rugs were an infallible charm. ''Yes,'' I said, ''I think we'll try that.''

Ellen scuffed in, pushing back her hair, her face puffy with sleep. ''Jack,'' she said, ''when the weather clears and I'm feeling livelier, you and Anne and the children must come and spend the night.''

''We'd like that. After the noises die down,'' he added satirically to me.

''Noises? What noises?'' A certain blankness came over Ellen's face when she looked at me now. The expression was the same, but what had been open in it before was now merely empty. She had put up her guard against me; she suspected me of keeping things from her.

''At night,'' I said. ''The house is settling. You don't hear them.''

When Jack had gone, Ellen sat with a cup of tea in the chair where Jack had sat, looking out at the mud. Her long purple shawl hung all the way to her knees and made her look armless. There seemed no explanation for the two white hands that curled around the teacup in her lap. ''It's a sad thing,'' she said tonelessly. ''I can't help but feel sorry for Sondra.''

''Why is that?'' I asked guardedly.

''Joyce was here yesterday. She told me that she and Jeff

have been having an affair off and on for six years.'' She turned to see how I would receive this news.

"Well, that explains the way Joyce and Sondra behave toward each other,'' I said, with a pleasant glance straight into Ellen's eyes; there I encountered only the reflection of the glass doors, even to the rain trickling down them, and I had the eerie sensation of having been shown a picture of the truth, as if she were weeping secretly in the depths of a soul I could no longer touch. For Ellen did not believe my innocence; I'm not sure I still believed in it myself; very likely Jeff and Joyce didn't either. It is impossible to say what Sondra believed. She behaved as if our infidelity were an accomplished fact. In its way it was a performance of genius, for Sondra never touched me except in the most accidental or impersonal way; even her glances, the foundation on which she built the myth of our liaison, had nothing soft in them; they were probing and sly and were always accompanied by a furtive smile, as if we merely shared some private joke. Yet there was something in the way she did it—in the tilt of her head perhaps—that plainly implied that the joke was at everyone's expense. And she had taken to calling me ''darling.''

"Sondra and Jeff have a feebleminded child off in an institution somewhere,'' Ellen said. ''That set them against each other, apparently.''

"Joyce told you all this?''

"She just mentioned it casually as if it were the most natural thing in the world—she assumed we must have known. . . . But I don't want to know things like that about my friends.''

"That's show biz, I guess. You and I are just provincials at heart.''

"Sondra must be a very unhappy girl.''

"It's hard to tell with Sondra.''

"I wonder what she tries to do with her life. . . . If she looks for anything—outside.''

I waited.

"Probably not,'' Ellen answered her own question. ''She seems very self-contained. Almost cold . . .''

I was treated to the spectacle of my wife fighting with herself to delay a wound that she was convinced would come home to her sooner or later. She did not want to believe in my infidelity. I might have comforted her with lies. I might have told her that Sondra and I rendezvoused downtown in a cafeteria and made love in a second-rate hotel on the evenings when I called to say I was working late. Then the wound would be open and could be cleaned and cured. It would be painful of course, but I would have confided in her again and our old system would be restored. Watching Ellen torture herself with doubt, I was tempted to tell her those lies. The truth never tempted me: To have admitted that I knew what she was thinking would have been tantamount to an admission of guilt. How could I suspect such a thing unless it were true? And was I to explain my coldness by terrifying her with vague stories of indescribable sounds which she never heard?

And so the two of us sat on, dumb and chilled, in our watertight house as the daylight began to go. And then a sort of exultation seized me. What if my terror were no more real than Ellen's? What if both our ghosts were only ghosts of the mind which needed only a little common sense to drive them away? And I saw that if I could drive away my ghost, Ellen's would soon follow, for the secret that shut me away from her would be gone. It was a revelation, a triumph of reason.

"What's that up there?" Ellen pointed to something that looked like a leaf blowing at the top of the glass doors. "It's a tail, Ted. There must be some animal on the roof."

Only the bushy tip was visible. As I drew close to it I could see raindrops clinging as if by a geometrical system to each black hair. "It looks like a raccoon tail. What would a coon be doing out so early?" I put on a coat and went outside. The tail hung limply over the edge, ringed with white and swaying phlegmatically in the breeze. The animal itself was hidden behind the low parapet. Using the ship's ladder at the back of the house I climbed up to look at it.

The human mind, just like other parts of the anatomy, is an organ of habit. Its capabilities are bounded by the limits of precedent; it thinks what it is used to thinking. Faced with a phenomenon beyond its range it rebels, it rejects, sometimes it collapses. My mind, which for weeks had steadfastly refused to honor the evidence of my senses that there was Something Else living in the house with Ellen and me, something unearthly and evil, largely on the basis of insufficient evidence, was now forced to the subsequent denial by saying, as Jeff had said, "fox." It was, of course, ridiculous. The chances of a fox's winning a battle with a raccoon were very slight at best, let alone what had been done to this raccoon. The body lay on the far side of the roof. I didn't see the head at all until I had stumbled against it and it had rolled over and over to come to rest against the parapet where it pointed its masked, ferret face at me.

Only because my beleaguered mind kept repeating, like a voice, "Ellen mustn't know, Ellen mustn't know," was I able to take up the dismembered parts and hurl them with all my strength onto the hillside and answer when Ellen called out, "What is it, Ted?" "Must have been a coon. It's gone now," in a perfectly level voice before I went to the back of the roof and vomited.

I recalled Sondra's mention of their mutilated cat and phoned Jeff at his agency. "We will discuss it over lunch," I told myself. I had a great need to talk, an action impossible within my own home, where every day the silence became denser and more intractable. Once or twice Ellen ventured to ask, "What's the matter, Ted?" but I always answered, "Nothing." And there our talk ended. I could see it in her wary eyes; I was not the man she had married; I was cold, secretive. The children's room, furnished with double bunks and wallpaper figured with toys, stood like a rebuke. Ellen kept the door closed most of the time though once or twice, in the late afternoon, I had found her in there moving about aimlessly, touching objects as if half in wonder that they should still linger on after so many long, sterile months; a foolish hope had failed. Neither did our friends bring their children to stay. They did not because we did not ask them. The silence had brought with it a profound and debilitating inertia. Ellen's face seemed perpetually swollen, the fea-

tures cloudy and amorphous, the eyes dull; her whole body
had become bloated, as if an enormous cache of pain had
backed up inside her. We moved through the house in our
orbits like two sleepwalkers, going about our business out of
habit. Our friends called at first, puzzled, a little hurt, but
soon stopped and left us to ourselves. Occasionally we saw
the Sheffitses. Jeff was looking seedier and seedier, told bad
jokes, drank too much and seemed always ill at east. Sondra
did most of the talking, chattering blandly on indifferent
subjects and always hinting by gesture, word or glance at
our underground affair.

Jeff and I had lunch at the Brown Derby on Vine Street
under charcoal caricatures of show folk. At a table next to
ours an agent was eulogizing an actor in a voice hoarse with
trumped-up enthusiasm to a large, purple-faced man who
was devoting his entire attention to a bowl of vichyssoise.

"It's a crazy business," Jeff said to me. "Be glad you're
not in it."

"I see what you mean," I replied. Jeff had not the faintest
idea of why I had brought him there, nor had I given him
any clue. We were "breaking the ice." Jeff grinned at me
with that crooked trick of his mouth, and I grinned back.
"We are friends"—presumably that is the message we
were grinning at each other. Was he my friend? Was I his
friend? He lived across the street; our paths crossed perhaps
once a week; we joked together; he sat always in the same
chair in our living room twisting from one sprawl to
another; there was a straight white chair in his living room
that I preferred. Friendships have been founded on less, I
suppose. Yet he had an idiot child locked off in an asylum
somewhere and a wife who amused herself with infidelity
by suggestion; I had a demon loose in my house and a wife
gnawed with suspicion and growing remote and old because
of it. And I had said, "I see what you mean." It seemed
insufferable. I caught Jeff's eye. "You remember we talked
once abut a ghost?" My tone was bantering; perhaps I
meant to make a joke.

"I remember."

"Sondra said something about a cat of yours that was killed."

"The one the fox got."

"That's what you said. That's not what Sondra said."

Jeff shrugged. "What about it?"

"I found a dead raccoon on our roof."

"Your roof!"

"Yes. It was pretty awful."

Jeff toyed with his fork. All pretense of levity was at an end. "No head?"

"Worse."

For a few moments he was silent. I felt him struggle with himself before he spoke. "Maybe you'd better move out, Ted," he said.

He was trying to help—I knew it. With a single swipe he had tried to push through the restraint that hung between us. He was my friend; he was putting out his hand to me. And I suppose I must have known what he'd suggest. But I could not accept it. It was not what I wanted to hear. "Jeff, I can't do that," I said tolerantly, as if he had missed my point. "We've only been living there five months. It cost me twenty-two thousand to build that place. We have to live in it at least a year under the GI loan."

"Well, you know best, Ted." The smile dipped at me again.

"I just wanted to talk," I said, irritated at the ease with which he had given in. "I wanted to find out what you knew about this ghost business."

"Not very much. Sondra knows more than I do."

"I doubt that you would advise me to leave a house I had just built for no reason at all."

"There seems to be some sort of jinx on the property, that's all. Whether there's a ghost or not I couldn't tell you," he replied, annoyed in his turn at the line the conversation was taking. "How does Ellen feel about this?"

"She doesn't know."

"About the raccoon?"

"About anything."

"You mean there's more?"

"There are noises—at night. . . ."

"I'd speak to Sondra if I were you. She's gone into this business much more deeply than I. When we first moved in, she used to hang around your land a good deal . . . just snooping . . . particularly after that cat was killed . . ." He was having some difficulty with his words. It struck me that the conversation was causing him pain. He was showing his teeth now in a smiling grimace. Dangling an arm over the back of his chair he seemed loose to the point of collapse. We circled warily about his wife's name.

"Look, Jeff," I said, and took a breath, "about Sondra . . ."

Jeff cut me off with a wave of his hand. "Don't worry, I know Sondra."

"Then you know there's nothing between us?"

"It's just her way of amusing herself. Sondra's a strange girl. She does the same thing with me. She flirts with me but we don't sleep together." He picked up his spoon and stared at it unseeingly. "It started when she became pregnant. After she had the boy, everything between us stopped. You know we had a son? He's in a sanitarium in the Valley."

"Can't you do anything?"

"Sure. Joyce Castle. I don't know what I'd have done without her."

"I mean divorce."

"Sondra won't divorce me. And I can't divorce her. No grounds." He shrugged as if the whole thing were of no concern at all to him. "What could I say? I want to divorce my wife because of the way she looks at other men? She's scrupulously faithful."

"To whom, Jeff? To you? To whom?"

"I don't know—to herself, maybe," he mumbled.

Whether with encouragement he might have gone on I don't know, for I cut him off. I sensed that with the enigmatic remark he was giving me my cue and that if I had chosen to respond to it he would have told me what I had asked him to lunch to find out—and all at once I was terrified; I did not want to hear it; I did not want to hear it at all. And so I laughed in a quiet way and said, "Undoubtedly, undoubtedly,'' and pushed it behind the closed door of my mind where I had stored all the impossibilities of the last months—the footsteps, the sounds in the night, the mutilated raccoon—or else, by recognizing them, go mad.

Jeff suddenly looked me full in the face; his cheeks were flushed, his teeth clamped together. "Look, Ted,'' he said, "can you take the afternoon off? I've got to go to the sanitarium and sign some papers. They're going to transfer the boy. He has fits of violence and does . . . awful things. He's finally gotten out of hand.''

"What about Sondra?''

"Sondra's signed already. She likes to go alone to visit him. She seems to like to have him to herself. I'd appreciate it, Ted—the moral support. . . . You don't have to come in. You can wait in the car. It's only about thirty miles from here, you'd be back by dinnertime. . . .'' His voice shook, tears clouded the yellow-stained whites of his eyes. He looked like a man with fever. I noticed how shrunken his neck had become as it revolved in his collar, how his head caved in sharply at the temples. He fastened one hand on my arm, like a claw. "Of course I'll go, Jeff,'' I said. "I'll call the office. They can get along without me for one afternoon.''

He collected himself in an instant. "I'd appreciate it, Ted. I promise you it won't be so bad.''

The sanitarium was in the San Fernando Valley, a complex of new stucco buildings on a newly seeded lawn. Everywhere there were signs that read, PLEASE KEEP OFF, FOLKS. Midget saplings stood in discs of powdery earth along the cement walks angling white and hot through the grass. On these walks, faithfully observing the signs, the inmates strolled. Their traffic, as it flowed somnolently from one avenue to another, was controlled by attendants stationed at intersections, conspicuous in white uniforms and pith helmets.

After a time it became unbearably hot in the car, and I climbed out. Unless I wished to pace in the parking lot among the cars, I had no choice but to join the inmates and their visitors on the walks. I chose a nearly deserted walk

and went slowly toward a building that had a yard attached
to it surrounded by a wire fence. From the slide and the
jungle gym in it I judged it to be for the children. Then I saw
Jeff come into it. With him was a nurse pushing a kind of
cart railed around like an oversized toddler. Strapped into it
was "the boy."

He was human, I suppose, for he had all the equipment
assigned to humans, yet I had the feeling that if it were not
for the cart the creature would have crawled on his belly like
an alligator. He had the eyes of an alligator too—sleepy,
cold and soulless—set in a swarthy face and a head that
seemed to run in a horizontal direction rather than the
vertical, like an egg lying on its side. The features were
devoid of any vestige of intelligence; the mouth hung open
and the chin shone with saliva. While Jeff and the nurse
talked, he sat under the sun, inert and repulsive.

I turned on my heel and bolted, feeling that I had intruded
on a disgrace. I imagined that I had been given a glimpse of
a diseased universe, the mere existence of which constituted
a threat to my life; the sight of that monstrous boy with his
cold, bestial eyes made me feel as if by stumbling on this
shame, I somehow shared in it with Jeff. Yet I told myself
that the greatest service I could do him was to pretend that
I had seen nothing, knew nothing, and not place on him the
hardship of talking about something which obviously
caused him pain.

He returned to the car pale and shaky and wanting a
drink. We stopped first at a place called Joey's on Hollywood Way. After that it was Cherry Lane on Vine Street,
where a couple of girls propositioned us, and then a stop at
the Brown Derby again, where I had left my car. Jeff
downed the liquor in a joyless, businesslike way and talked
to me in a rapid, confidential voice about a book he had just
sold to Warner Brothers Studio for an exorbitant sum of
money—trash in his opinion, but that was always the
way—the parasites made it. Pretty soon there wouldn't be
any good writers left: "There'll only be competent parasites
and incompetent parasites." This was perhaps the third time
we had had this conversation. Now Jeff repeated it mechan-

ically, all the time looking down at the table where he was painstakingly breaking a red swizzle stick into ever tinier pieces.

When we left the restaurant, the sun had gone down, and the evening chill of the desert on which the city had been built had settled in. A faint pink glow from the vanished sun still lingered on the top of the Broadway Building. Jeff took a deep breath, then fell into a fit of coughing. "Goddamn smog," he said. "Goddamn city. I can't think of a single reason why I live here." He started toward his Daimler, tottering slightly.

"How about driving home with me?" I said. "You can pick up your car tomorrow."

He fumbled in the glove compartment and drew out a packet of small cigars. He stuck one between his teeth where it jutted unlit toward the end of his nose. "I'm not going home tonight, Ted friend," he said. "If you'll just drop me up the street at the Cherry Lane I'll remember you for life."

"Are you sure? I'll go with you if you want."

Jeff shook a forefinger at me archly. "Ted, you're a gentleman and a scholar. But my advice to you is to go home and take care of your wife. No, seriously. Take care of her, Ted. As for myself I shall go quietly to seed in the Cherry Lane Café." I had started toward my car when Jeff called out to me again. "I just wanted to tell you, Ted friend. . . . My wife was once just as nice as your wife. . . ."

I had gone no more than a mile when the last glimmer of light left the sky and night fell like a shutter. The sky above the neon of Sunset Boulevard turned jet black, and a sickly half-moon rose and was immediately obscured by thick fog that lowered itself steadily as I traveled west, till at the foot of Clay Canyon it began to pat my windshield with little smears of moisture.

The house was dark, and at first I thought Ellen must have gone out, but then seeing her old Plymouth in the driveway I felt the grip of a cold and unreasoning fear. The events of the day seemed to crowd around and hover at my head in the fog; and the commonplace sight of that car, together with the blackness and silence of the house, sent me into a panic as I ran for the door. I pushed at it with my shoulder as if expecting it to be locked, but it swung open easily and I found myself in the darkened living room with no light anywhere and the only sound the rhythm of my own short breathing. "Ellen!" I called in a high, querulous voice I hardly recognized. "Ellen!" I seemed to lose my balance; my head swam; it was as if this darkness and silence were the one last iota that the chamber of horrors in my mind could not hold, and the door snapped open a crack, emitting a cloudy light that stank of corruption, and I saw the landscape of my denial, like a tomb. It was the children's room. Rats nested in the double bunks, mold caked the red wallpaper, and in it an insane Spanish don hung by his neck from a dead tree, his heels vlumping against the wall, his foppish clothes rubbing as he revolved slowly in invisible currents of bad air. And as he swung toward me, I saw his familiar reptile eyes open and stare at me with loathing and contempt.

I conceded: It is here and It is evil, and I have left my wife alone in the house with It, and now she has been sucked into that cold eternity where the dumb shades store their plasms against an anguished centenary of speech—a single word issuing from the petrified throat, a scream or a sigh or a groan, syllables dredged up from a lifetime of eloquence to slake the bottomless thirst of living death.

And then a light went on over my head, and I found myself in the hall outside the children's room. Ellen was in her nightgown, smiling at me. "Ted? Why on earth are you standing here in the dark? I was just taking a nap. Do you want some dinner? Why don't you say something? Are you all right?" She came toward me; she seemed extraordinarily lovely; her eyes, a deeper blue than Sondra's, looked almost purple; she seemed young and slender again; her old serenity shone through like a restored beacon.

"I'm all right," I said hoarsely. "Are you sure you are?"

"Of course I am," she laughed. "Why shouldn't I be? I'm feeling much, much better." She took my hand and kissed it gaily. "I'll put on some clothes and then we'll have our dinner." She turned and went down the hall to our bedroom, leaving me with a clear view into the children's room. Though the room itself was dark, I could see by the hall light that the covers on the lower bunk had been turned back and that the bed had been slept in. "Ellen," I said. "Ellen, were you sleeping in the children's room?"

"Yes," she said, and I heard the rustle of a dress as she carried it from the closet. "I was in there mooning around, waiting for you to come home. I got sleepy and lay down on the bunk. What were *you* doing, by the way? Working late?"

"And nothing happened?"

"Why? What should have happened?"

I could not answer; my head throbbed with joy. It was over—whatever it was, it was over. All unknowing Ellen had faced the very heart of the evil and had slept through it like a child, and now she was herself again without having been tainted by the knowledge of what she had defeated; I had protected her by my silence, by my refusal to share my terror with this woman whom I loved. I reached inside and touched the light button; there was the brave red wallpaper scattered over with toys, the red-and-white curtains, the blue-and-red bedspreads. It was a fine room. A fine, gay room fit for children.

Ellen came down the hall in her slip. "Is anything wrong, Ted? You seem so distraught. Is everything all right at the office?"

"Yes, yes," I said. "I was with Jeff Sheffits. We went to see his boy in the asylum. Poor Jeff; he leads a rotten life." I told Ellen the whole story of our afternoon, speaking freely in my house for the first time since we had moved there. Ellen listened carefully as she always did, and wanted to know, when I had finished, what the boy was like.

"Like an alligator," I said with disgust. "Just like an alligator."

Ellen's face took on an unaccountable expression of private glee. She seemed to be looking past me into the children's room, as if the source of her amusement lay there.

At the same moment I shivered in a breath of profound cold, the same clammy draft that might have warned me on my last birthday had I been other than what I am. I had a sense of sudden dehydration, as if all the blood had vanished from my veins. I felt as if I were shrinking. When I spoke, my voice seemed to come from a throat rusty and dry with disuse. "Is that funny?" I whispered.

And my wife replied, "Funny? Oh, no, it's just that I'm feeling so much better. I think I'm pregnant, Ted." She tipped her head to one side and smiled at me.

———

All the editors know about William Wood is that he is the author of a fine story of dark, ghostly horrors invading a house in the rainswept California hills.

*Everyone knows cats have nine lives, but what if each
one is a little bigger and meaner than the one before?*

5

Emmett

Dahlov Ipcar

Some of the things that happen in this world can be so crazy
that you hate even to think about them. That's the way I feel
about this business I've just been through with Artie. I'm
just an ordinary guy with a wife and three kids and a nice,
quiet desk job, and I'm the last person in the world you'd
expect to get mixed up in anything really weird.

But there I was in as deep as all hell, right up to my
ears—and all I'd wanted was a nice quiet week of hunting
in the Maine woods, same as I've had every year since I
went to work for Eastern Bio Supplies. You see, I'm willing
to stick around in August, when everyone else wants out of
the city, so they give me this extra week in November or
whenever the deer season opens up there in Sagadahoc
County. Artie had this little old rundown farm way off in the
woods, and he throws me a standing invitation. So every
November that's where I'd head for. I just liked to get in a

week away from the wife and kids, beating the brush, and boozing a little, and yacking with my old pal. Usually I'd come back with a whitetail tied to my fender—the Great Maine Hunter bit—playing it to the hilt for the kids. But it's not really the Call of the Wild with me, not really the Old Blood Lust and all that, I just like the chance to get out of the city and tramp around in the woods where it's nice and peaceful and smells good.

Artie always gave me a big welcome. I'd tell him all the off-color stories I'd picked up during the year, and he'd come up with a few good ones he'd collected, mostly from the vet who doctored his cows; because, believe it or not, Artie really farmed. He had about twelve of these cows and a few hens and this little ol' beagle called Lady Anne, and he lived there in his old house by himself as happy as a clam at high water. I won't swear he lived a virtuous life. He boozed some, and he entertained lady friends; but he never let any of them move in on him. He'd always been a queer egg, sort of an odd-ball, a real hermit type. Didn't want to get tied down to a woman's apron strings, he said; though he sure was tied to those cows' tails, and that's a helluva lot worse. He couldn't go anywhere, even for a day. He always had to be back to milk those four-legged bosses of his—now I know why they call all cows "boss."

But old Artie, he thrived on the life; always looked healthy as an ox, made me feel like I was pale and flabby and going to pot sitting at a desk, though I jog eight blocks to work every morning. I guess it's a good thing I get that much exercise or a week in the woods would kill me. Sometimes I envied Artie; sometimes I thought he was nuts—the way he lived. But he had a good thing going for him there. Not that those twelve cows brought in much income, but they gave Artie something to write about. He wrote a lot of articles for magazines on "How to Be Happy with a Manure Pile and a Fly Swatter" and stuff like that, and it sold like hot cakes. So it seems he was doing okay. He sure always seemed brimming over with health and good spirits—that is until this November.

We'd been bosom pals ever since we were kids. We'd both been sent to this Manumassett School in New Jersey, a progressive-type boarding school. They had this beat-up farm set up—lots of lambkins sporting on the green, cocks treading hens, and cows producing milk and calves and manure like mad. The idea was to take us city kids and introduce us to Nature, elevate our minds by rubbing our noses in the dirt, teach us about the flowers and the bees so we wouldn't get stung, and all that hokum.

Most of it went over with me like a ton of lead, but Artie just ate it up, especially the farm bit. He was the kind of kid who'd follow around behind a cow and admire the beautiful plops she made. He used to tell me all kinds of weird stuff about what the animals were thinking, how they felt about us humans and all. He told me once when he was about nine that everything had a soul and feelings, even trees and vegetables. He claimed it hurt a tree to get chopped down, and that the sap that flowed out of it was just like tears. He had quite an imagination, that kid. I didn't put much stock in the crying vegetables, but sometimes it made kitchen duty a lot pleasanter if I just *pretended* that the carrots and potatoes were suffering as much as I was suffering at having to peel them. Because we all had to pitch in and work as well as keep up on our studies; that was part of the big deal.

But some of the Nature gimmick I really liked, and that was the times we took to the woods on biology walks, collecting specimens. There was this real mucky swamp nearby, where we used to go wading around, coming home with jars full of salamanders and centipedes as long as your arm, and snakes and tree toads and the worst cases of poison ivy on record. I guess that's where I learned to like tramping around in the woods, same as Artie got the rage to go live on a farm for the rest of his life. I know some of that stuff was supposed to rub off on us kids, but I kind of doubt if they expected us to apply it as literally as Artie did. I think they expected us to *sublimate our experience,* like me sitting here writing out orders for frogs in formaldehyde.

Artie and I roomed together for all of six years, and we

got so damn close, we could just about read one another's minds. But the most important thing that happened to us there, I never even thought was important at all—until this business came up.

You see, there was this one teacher, Old Hoyle, who used to entertain us with stories on Friday nights. He'd hold a real session around the big fireplace in the main hall. All the lights would be out, just the fire flickering away, and he'd usually tell these real spooky ghost stories. We really ate it up, though sometimes he just about scared the pants off us. I never forgot one night when he got going on a series of tales about cats. One of them was Edgar Allan Poe's story "The Black Cat"—that one where the cat gets walled up in the cellar with the corpse and wails like crazy. That story really gave me the willies, and Artie got the willies worse than I did. He was so shook up he wouldn't let me turn out the light in our room that night. And for a whole month at least, he made me keep the light burning, though I'd got over the effects long before that.

We were just little kids about ten; but while I got over it, like I said—Artie never did get over it. He never went back to listen to any more storytelling—and he developed this real thing about cats. He never could stand to have a cat near him again. When he got older he told people he was allergic to them, but I knew better; I knew he was plain scared to death of them. I admit that black-cat story got me too, but it didn't make me hate cats. It just made me avoid reading any more Poe for about ten years.

After he grew up, Artie bummed around a while. He never could stick at any city job for long. Finally he bought this little farm in Maine. And then the guy was happy, just living there with his cows and his chickens and his beagle—and *no cats*. I guess he encouraged that beagle to be a cat-killer, because no stray cats ever moved in on him, that is—I never heard of any—before this November when I showed up for the opening of deer season.

The first thing that struck me as I got out of my car was how lousy Artie looked. He really looked sick, sort of nervous and haggard and run-down, his hands shaking and his eyes kind of haunted-looking. I really felt worried about him, but he swore he was in the best of health. He seemed awful glad to see me. We broke open a bottle of the bourbon I'd brought, and I told him a couple of my best stories that I'd been saving, and he seemed to cheer up.

But at four that afternoon he got up to go milk his cows. This struck me as peculiar; because always, ever since I could remember, he'd milked the cows after supper—sometimes as late as ten or eleven at night. That way he didn't have to get up early to milk them again in the morning. That's the kind of farmer he was—casual.

"What's the idea?" I asked. "We going somewhere tonight or something?"

"No," he said. "No. I'm not going anywhere. *Not at night!*" He said this with such emphasis that it took me kind of aback. "I've just started milking the cows early lately, that's all," he said, sort of irritable. "I've reformed."

I didn't quite buy it, but anyhow, he had the cows all milked by five-thirty. We ate supper and sat around and jawed and drank more bourbon, and then around nine o'clock I decided I'd turn in. I wanted to get an early start on the opening day of the season.

I'd left my gear in the car, so I went out to get it. I was standing alongside the car, just getting out the rifle and the shells, when I heard this peculiar noise, sort of a long hiss with a snarl in it. It seemed to come from the darkness not too far off, so I reached in and flicked on the headlights. And there in the lights was the biggest damn Canada lynx—a great big white long-legged bastard—sort of snarling at me. He seemed blinded by the headlights and just stood there for a full minute, and I stood there too, just as stupefied. Then, suddenly I realized I had the rifle in my hand, and I slammed back the bolt and rammed in a shell. The cat seemed to recover himself too. He turned and leapt off into the darkness; but I could see him plain, a white shape bounding away, and I blasted him. He tumbled head over heels and lay there a while kicking.

Boy! I had never felt so excited in my life! I yelled for Artie, but he didn't come out. So I walked up on the cat cautiously, and when I was sure he was really dead, I dragged him back into the headlights and laid him out to admire. He was sure a helluva big one, all white and sort of freckled brownish all over—with long, tufted ears. As handsome an animal as I ever saw.

I ran back in the house, all excited. Artie was sitting there, his head in his hands. He looked up at me real wild-eyed. "You didn't kill him?" he asked. "Oh, God, you didn't, did you?"

"If you mean that lynx, I sure as hell did. Come look at him!" I tried to drag him up on his feet, but he was sort of shaking all over and moaning something about cats and a bigger one coming—none of which made any sense to me.

"Was that what had you so worried?" I asked, kind of beginning to catch on. "You mean that cat's been hanging around, and you've been scared to go out at night?" Hell, I didn't blame him, for a guy that was scared of cats this one was just the ticket. But what baffled me was why he seemed so upset that I had shot the damn thing. You'd think he'd be tickled pink.

But no, he kept moaning. "You shouldn't have shot him. You shouldn't have killed him." Sometimes he'd say something like, "I can't stay here. I've got to get away before the next one comes—" and he'd start shaking like a leaf again.

I got some more bourbon into him and calmed him down some, and he began to make sense after a fashion. Finally he told me the whole story about what was bothering him. It came out sort of bit by bit, but it seemed it had all started about a month before.

He'd been delivering milk to this house on his route, when this little boy had come out holding a little fuzzy white kitten. He shoved it right in Artie's face and said, "This is my kitten. His name is Emmett."

Well, Artie had been upset as hell and yelled at the kid to get the damn thing away from him, and the kid had cried, and he'd had to apologize to the kid's mother, and all that had really gotten him stirred up. Then just as he was ready to drive off, there was the damn kitten sitting right in the driveway. He said he could have blown his horn or waited until it ran off, but he was sore and he hated cats anyhow. So he just stepped on the gas and ran the kitten over, squashed it flat. He didn't even feel guilty doing it, he said. But the kid screamed and carried on, and he had to apologize some more. He said he remembered the little kid yelling at him, "You're a murderer! You murdered Emmett!" That had bothered him, because he may have hated cats, but he kind of liked kids.

Anyhow, that was the beginning. The next thing that happened was a small gray kitten showed up in his barn a few days later, and he didn't hesitate to bait it with milk and poison it. Then about three days after that another kitten appeared, a half-grown one. This one was more wary, but Artie laid for it and got it with his shotgun. Then another cat turned up. He heard this commotion among his hens, and there was this yellow cat running off with a half-grown chick in its mouth. He sicked the beagle on it, and the dog caught up with it halfway to the woods and broke its back.

That was four cats down, but it seems there were more to come. Artie had never been so plagued with cats before, but he didn't really put two and two together yet. He was beginning to get the feeling though, and he wasn't too surprised when a big black-and-white tom cat started hanging around his hen yard. This one was big enough to have a real scrap with the beagle and come out alive. But Artie and his shotgun caught up with him too.

There was about a week, Artie said, when everything seemed to be back to normal. And then one night he put Lady Anne out before he went to bed, and he heard this terrific row out in the yard, the dog yelping like mad and howling, and a snarling and spitting like all the cats of hell. He got out there with his shotgun as fast as he could, and there was this big brown bobcat tangling with old Lady Anne and getting much the best of it. Artie let him have it with both barrels. He killed the bobcat all right; but he wounded the beagle, who was pretty torn up anyhow, and she died at the vet's that night.

Artie was pretty shook up. He felt bad at losing his dog, and he was just beginning to think the thing through—about all those cats coming, one after the other, and each one bigger than the last. The real clincher was when he got back from the vet's that same night. As he pulled up in front of his house, there, sitting by the side of the road in the full glare of the headlights, was this big white Canada lynx—the same one I had killed.

That had really got through to him. He said he sat in his car all night with that animal prowling around in the darkness, letting out earsplitting yells. He didn't dare leave the car until morning when the big cat had gone. That had been two weeks ago, he told me, and that damn lynx had hung around all the time. He didn't dare step out of his door at night. It had raided his hen house and cleaned out all his hens, and he didn't dare let his cows out of the barn. Even in the daytime he walked around looking over his shoulder and getting back under cover as fast as he could.

"But why in hell didn't you try to shoot it?" I asked.

He looked at me pretty funny. "Don't you get it?" he asked. "Don't you understand? That damn cat has nine lives. There's always a bigger cat comes back! I didn't *want* to kill the lynx. I was scared to death of what would show up next. But now you've gone and done it. I've got to get out of here, that's all. I've got to get away—far away— before the next *bigger* cat comes. It may be out there now," he said, shivering as he stared at the black night outside the window.

I tried to reason with him. I thought it all sounded pretty damn silly. I told him it was probably just a coincidence, the lynx following the bobcat like that. "Maybe there's some condition up in the North woods," I told him. "Something that's making the big cats move down this way." But that wasn't exactly the right thing to say.

"Oh, there's a *condition*, all right," he said; and he

started giggling hysterically, sort of choking and shivering all over. It really got me to see him in such a state.

"Look," I said, as reasonably as I could. "There just isn't any bigger cat that can come now. You know damn well there isn't anything bigger than a Canada lynx around here. You know that!"

"It's got to come," he said. "It's got to come. I've counted them all up; there were only seven—there are still two more lives—still two more bigger cats."

"Oh for chrissake!" I said. I was getting kind of fed up with all the argument. "What you need is a real rest. Maybe you ought to see a doctor, get away from this place. You've been alone here too damn much."

"You bet your sweet life I'm getting away," he said. "The first thing in the morning!"

"Well, let's get some sleep," I said, "so we can get an early start."

An early start deer hunting, I meant. I wasn't going along with any of this midnight raving. So he turned in. And so did I, but first I went out and hung my big lynx up in the shed. It was the biggest and handsomest trophy I'd ever shot, and I wasn't going to let it get messed up no matter how nuts Artie was on the subject of cats.

I set the alarm for five to give me plenty of time to get dressed and out in the woods before sunup. But around 3:00 A.M. I woke up and remembered something I'd completely forgotten—one of those spooky cat tales that Old Hoyle had told us kids the night Artie got so bugged on the subject of cats. Before this I'd always thought it was that tale of Poe's that had got to him, same as it got me; but now I remembered another tale Hoyle had told that same night.

As a matter of fact, it wasn't much of a story. It was kind of a foolish thing without even much point. But, of course, Hoyle was a darn good storyteller, and to even a half-baked yarn, he'd given a lot of atmosphere and built up the suspense. As near as I can remember the story went something like this:

There was this young fellow walking alone through the

hills at night, and it gets real dark, and a storm comes up, blowing a gale, and the boy starts looking for some shelter. Up on a high hill he sees this big old house, all dark and deserted-looking. He goes up there and knocks on the door, and nobody answers. But the door isn't locked, so he goes inside, and here is this big spooky old mansion, all full of cobwebs and stuff, and one big room with a huge fireplace in it. He's cold and wet, so he gathers some wood together and builds himself a fire. He's sitting there warming up and enjoying the blaze, when he hears a door creak on its hinges, and in walks this black cat. It walks up to the fire and sits down and looks at him. Then it yawns and sort of blinks its eyes and licks its chops, and it says, "Well, I'll just wait 'til Emmett comes."

He gets up and he says to the cat, "Good evening. I hope you don't mind me warming myself a little here by the fire."

But the cat just looks at him poisonous-like and sits there watching him. The boy sits down again and is sort of dozing off, when he hears the door creak again, and another bigger black cat walks in and sits down alongside the first one. And it too yawns and kind of licks its chops hungry-like, and it says, "Well, I'll just wait 'til Emmett comes."

Then one cat after another comes in and sits down alongside the others, and each one is bigger and blacker than the one before. And each one says in the same kind of ominous way, "Well, I'll just wait 'til Emmett comes."

Finally, a cat walks in, and even sitting down, it's all of six feet tall. It just sits there looking down at him with big green ferocious eyes, with a hungry look in them; and when that cat yawns at him, it's like looking into the mouth of a cave, and it, too, says, "Well, I'll just wait 'til Emmett comes."

But at this, the boy gets up, and he bows with great dignity, and he says to all the cats lined up there watching him, "When Emmett comes, will you all please tell him that I done set, and I done rested myself, and I done left!" And he grabs his hat and lights out of there at a dead run.

Well, that's all there was to the story, and you can see it was pretty damn silly, not even real spooky. Heck, you'd think whoever made it up could've come up with a real spooky name instead of something as common-sounding as "Emmett."

But I figured, lying there half awake, that it was that little kid calling his kitten "Emmett" that had started poor old Artie off on this whole crazy bat. I figured I'd tell him in the morning, show him what had made him flip, and maybe he'd see there was nothing supernatural about it all. I was determined I was going to get in a week of deer hunting or else. So I turned over and went to sleep.

I slept so sound that I never heard the alarm; what woke me up was a whole barrage of rifle fire that sounded like it was right under my window. I jumped out of bed with the daylights scared out of me. The first thing that crossed my mind was that Artie had really gone berserk and was starting the day with some kind of crazy mayhem. But when I barged out into the hall in my pajamas, there was Artie coming out of his room looking as startled as I was.

"They've got their damn nerve," he said right off. "It's not even sunup. If they've shot any of *my* deer on *my* place, I'll have the game warden on the whole lot of them!"

I was relieved, I'll tell you. He sounded like his old self. We looked out all the windows, but the shots must have come from the nearby woods, because no hunters were in sight. We neither of us mentioned cats, but got dressed and were just heating up some coffee, when there comes this knock at the door, and these two hunters are standing there all excited.

"Can we use your phone?" one of them asks. "You guys won't believe it, but we just shot the biggest damn mountain lion—right out here in your woods!"

And then Artie really went all to pieces. He started screaming at them, and at me, and practically frothing at the mouth.

I rushed those two guys outside as fast as I could. They must have thought he was nuts, and I'm not sure he wasn't.

But anyway, I went with these two guys, and they showed me this cat they had killed. It was a mountain lion all right, big and gray with a black tip on his tail, and these two sad black stripes running down his muzzle. There'd always been rumors of mountain lions in Maine; but it was like UFOs, only nuts believed in them. Even standing there, looking down at that big cat, I didn't believe it.

"Listen," I said to those two guys, "I don't care what you do with this cat—take him off and get your pictures in the paper, or bury him right here, but for chrissake get him out of sight, and don't bring him around where my friend is!"

They really thought I was crazy. They tried to argue with me. Their car was parked four miles down the road, they said; all they wanted was to phone and have someone pick them up. They tried to persuade me to drive them down to their car, but I was in a hurry to get back to Artie.

"You get that cat out of here, if you have to drag it all the way!"

"Have a heart, Mac," they begged. "It must weigh three hundred pounds. We had a helluva time lugging it this far."

I didn't waste any more time with them; I just beat it back to the house. I found Artie busy packing, tearing open drawers and grabbing stuff and tossing it in suitcases.

He looked up real wild-eyed when I came in. "Don't try to talk me out of leaving!" he said. "I'm not waiting for any bigger cats!"

"Oh," I said. "You remember that story too."

"What story?" he said and went on throwing stuff around.

But I didn't think it would do any good to go over all that business about the story, not now. I made one last attempt. "You can't just walk out like this, Artie. What about your cows?"

"To hell with the cows," he said. Then he picked up the phone.

He really got pretty efficient there for a while. First he phoned a cattle dealer. "Come pick up the whole herd," he said. "Today. It's got to be today. Sixteen head, counting calves. No, I haven't got time to tell you about them! I'm getting out of here right now. I haven't fed or milked them this morning, so you better get down here today. You can send me a check, whatever the market price is. I'm not going to argue."

He hung up and phoned a real estate agent. "I want to sell my place," he said. "Sell or rent, I don't care. Yeh, lock, stock, and barrel, the works. I'll mail you the keys." That was that.

He phoned the power company and the phone company. Then he went back to packing, gathering up papers and stuff. He may have left something undone, but I don't know what. He even had me down in the cellar with a pipe wrench, draining the water system. It was the fastest house-closing I ever saw. Then we piled all our bags into my car—I wasn't trusting him to drive his own—and we got off, well inside of an hour.

We were tooling down the road, and damned if we didn't pass those two guys, sweating and staggering along, carrying that big lion slung on a pole between them. Here I'd wanted to keep Artie from seeing that cat, but it was too late now. He stared at it, his eyes bugging out, as we sailed by. And those two guys stared back, all grins until they saw who it was, then they looked like they really hated our guts.

Artie started shaking like a leaf. "You see the size of that thing?" he asked me in this queer dead voice. He turned and looked at me, just about as hateful as those two hunters. "You're the guy said there wasn't any bigger cat than that lynx!" He sucked in his breath, and I could hear his teeth chattering. The tears started running down his cheeks.

"Take it easy," I said. "Take it easy, Artie. We're getting out of here. You'll be all right." I went on talking to him like you talk to a kid that's had a nightmare, and after a while, he began to calm down again. I sure felt sorry for him, but I wasn't feeling any too good about it all myself. Things had been happening too fast. I'd even forgotten all about my own trophy I'd left hanging in the shed, but somehow, it didn't seem as wonderful as it had—I wished I'd never shot the damn thing.

We went along okay for about three hours, and I thought Artie was starting to relax at last. Then just outside Boston on the by-pass this cat dashes across the road in front of us.

It was just an ordinary cat. Hell, it wasn't even *black*—and we missed it by a mile. But right away Artie goes all to pieces again. I mean he threw a real fit: he moaned and thrashed around, and spit ran out of his mouth, and he started breathing in this ghastly kind of way, and scared the living daylights out of me.

I pulled up alongside the road and tried to get some bourbon down him—he looked as gray as a corpse—but he just seemed to get more excited when I stopped the car. "Keep going," he managed to gasp. "Just keep going! Please—please keep going!"

So then I figured he was more than I could handle, and I decided to get him to a doctor as fast as I could. I left the turnpike at the next exit and stopped at the first house I came to. By then Artie had passed out on me.

"Where's the nearest doctor?" I asked this dame.

"Well," she says, real slow, and I could have booted her, "the *nearest* doctor is Dr. Vorbrichten, but he's retired!"

"I don't want no doctors of divinity or doctors of philosophy," I said. "If he's a medical doctor just tell me where he is."

"Oh, he's a *medical* doctor. He lives about three miles down the road. But he doesn't *practice*. He's *retired*."

"I don't care how retired he is," I said, feeling real desperate. "This is an emergency!"

I finally got the directions out of her and went on down that road like a bat out of hell, with old Artie all slumped over and passed out beside me.

I found the house and ran up the steps and pounded on the door. This old lady answers it.

"I've got an awful sick friend out in the car," I tell her. "Please, I've got to have the doctor look at him. It's a matter of life or death!" Boy, was I right!

"Come in," she says. "The doctor is in his study. I'll ask him."

Well, she sounded so doubtful that as soon as she opened this study door, I barged right on in determined to convince this guy to get out there and help Artie. I stopped dead in my tracks.

There, standing in the middle of the Persian rug, was the biggest damn African lion I'd ever seen!

I dropped. I dropped like I was sandbagged, keeled right over, passed out cold.

When I came to, I was on this couch; and the doctor, a red-faced, white-haired old guy, was waving smelling salts under my nose and feeling my pulse and all.

"The lion!" I gasped. I tried to sit up. He pushed me back down.

"The lion is nothing to be afraid of, young man," he said. "It's an old, old pet, as gentle as a lamb. There's nothing to be afraid of."

And the damn lion was still there, sitting on his haunches now, looking at me with these mild, gold-colored eyes, very sad-like. But the end of his tail with that big black tassel on it kept sort of twitching, and then he opened his mouth and yawned—and brother!—you never saw such teeth. You could have made a powder horn out of any one of them.

I kind of grabbed onto the doctor and begged him please to take care of Artie out in the car. "But don't let him see that lion!" I almost screamed this. "For chrissake, Doc, I don't care how tame he is. Just don't let Artie see him!"

"Please calm yourself," the doctor said, like I was being unreasonable. "I will put the lion away in his den. You understand, I don't practice medicine any more, otherwise, I would not have such a pet. But there is really nothing, absolutely nothing, to fear."

"Just don't let my friend see him!" I begged, still clutching at his arm.

He managed to pry my fingers loose; and then, holding that lion by a hunk of his shaggy mane, he led him out of the room.

He was back in a few seconds with a pill and a glass of water, which he made me swallow. "That will calm you down," he said. "I'm sorry to have to tell you this, but your friend was beyond my help. I'm afraid he died of heart failure. Of course, it will be just as well to have him examined thoroughly—I have already phoned the hospital—but I'm sure you will find my diagnosis is correct."

"That lion!" I cried sitting up. "He saw that damn lion!"

"No," said the doctor. "No, that is impossible. It was not the lion. I'm afraid he was dead *before* you ever reached my house."

"You mean he died *without* seeing the lion?" I couldn't believe it.

"Please," the doctor protested. "Why do you keep concerning yourself about the lion? I keep telling you: he is a family pet, as gentle as a kitten—Old Emmett wouldn't hurt a fly."

I wasn't so sure about that. There had been a kind of look in those dreamy gold eyes, and I didn't like that yawn—it was kind of a warning.

But the thing that really struck me then—the thing that really got me—was that like the guy in the story—Artie had gone *without waiting until Emmett came.*

Of course, I feel bad about Artie, but otherwise I'm not too sure how I feel about the whole crazy business. I kept thinking about all those cats until I began to get almost as psyched out as Artie. Finally, a couple of days after I got back, I phoned this Curator of Mammals up at the Museum of Natural History, and I asked him if there'd ever been any real proof that there were mountain lions in Maine. He said yes there had been, which made me feel a little better. But I didn't much like the evidence he cited. He said that as a matter of fact just ten days before, two men in southwest Maine had shot a big two hundred and twenty pound male lion *felis concolor.*

As far as I'm concerned that doesn't prove a damn thing!

Author and self-taught illustrator of children's books, Dahlov Ipcar was born in Vermont in 1917. Her parents gave her no training, hoping to keep her style free and fresh. She had the first of many one-woman shows in 1939 at the Museum of Modern Art. Later shows were at the Corcoran Gallery and the Carnegie Institute. She specializes in children's books, mostly self-illustrated, such as The Marvelous Merry-Go-Round. *She also writes adult fiction for such magazines as* Argosy *and* Yankee, *and adult fantasy novels like* A Dark Wind Blowing.

Until Robert Trask realized whose face he had seen, it looked as if he never would learn. . . .

6

Night Court

Mary Elizabeth Counselman

Bob waited, humming to himself in the stifling telephone booth, his collar and tie loosened for comfort in the late August heat, his Panama tilted rakishly over one ear to make room for the instrument. Through it he could hear a succession of female voices: "Garyville calling Oak Grove thuh-ree, tew, niyun, six . . . collect . . ." "Oak Grove. What was that number . . . ?" "Thuh-ree, tew . . ."

He stiffened as a low, sweetly familiar voice joined the chorus:

"Yes, yes! I—I accept the charges . . . Hello? Bob . . . ?"

Instinctively he pressed the phone closer to his mouth, the touch of it conjuring up the feel of cool lips, soft blond hair, and eyes that could melt a steel girder.

"Marian? Sure it's me! . . . Jail? No! No, honey, that's all over. I'm free! Free as a bird, yeah! The judge said it was

125

unavoidable. Told you, didn't I?'' He mugged into the phone as though somehow, in this age of speed, she could see as well as hear him across the twenty-odd miles that separated them. ''It was the postponement that did it. Then they got this new judge—and guess what? He used to go to school with Dad and Uncle Harry! It was a cinch after that . . . Huh?''

He frowned slightly, listening to the soft voice coming over the wire; the voice he could not wait to hear congratulating him. Only, she wasn't. She was talking to him—he grinned sheepishly—the way Mom talked to Dad sometimes, when he came swooping into the driveway. One drink too many at the country club after his Saturday golf . . .

''Say!'' he snorted. ''Aren't you *glad* I don't have to serve ten to twenty years for manslaughter . . . ?''

''Oh, Bob.'' There was a sadness in his fiancee's voice, a troubled note. ''I . . . I'm glad. Of course I'm glad about it. But . . . it's just that you sound so smug, so . . . That poor old Negro . . .''

''Smug!'' He stiffened, holding the phone away slightly as if it had stung him. ''Honey . . . how can you say a thing like that! Why, I've done everything I could for his family. Paid his mortgage on that little farm! Carted one of his kids to the hospital every week for two months, like . . .'' His voice wavered, laden with a genuine regret. ''Like the old guy would do himself, I guess, if he was still . . . *Marian!* You think I'm not *sorry* enough; is that it?'' he demanded.

There was a little silence over the wire. He could picture her, sitting there quietly in the Marshalls' cheery-chintz living room. Maybe she had her hair pinned back in one of those ridiculous, but oddly attractive, ''horse-tails'' the teen-agers were wearing this year. Her little cat-face would be tilted up to the lamp, eyes closed, the long fringe of lashes curling up over shadowy lids. Bob fidgeted, wanting miserably to see her expression at that moment.

''Well? Say something!''

The silence was broken by a faint sigh.

"Darling . . . What is there to say? You're so thoughtless! Not callous; I don't mean that. Just . . . *careless!* Bob, you've got to unlearn what they taught you in Korea. You're . . . you're home again, and this is what you've been fighting for, isn't it? For . . . for the people around us to be safe? For life not to be cheap, something to be thrown away just to save a little *time* . . ."

"Say, listen!" He was scowling now, anger hardening his mouth into ugly lines. "I've had enough lectures these past two months—from Dad, from the sheriff, from Uncle Harry. You'd think a guy twenty-two years old, in combat three years and got his feet almost frozen off, didn't know the score! What's the matter with everybody?" Bob's anger was mounting. "Listen! I got a medal last year for killing fourteen North Koreans. For gunning 'em down! Deliberately! But now, just because I'm driving a little too fast and some old creep can't get his wagon across the highway . . ."

"Bob!"

". . . now, all at once, I'm not a hero, I'm a murderer! I don't know the value of human life! I don't give a hoot how many people I . . ."

"Darling!"

A strangled sob came over the long miles. That stopped him. He gripped the phone, uncertainty in his oddly tiptilted eyes that had earned him, in service, the nickname of "Gook."

"Darling, you're all mixed up. Bob . . . ? Bob dear, are you listening? If I could just *talk* to you tonight . . . ! What time is it? Oh, it's after *six!* I . . . I don't suppose you could drive over here tonight . . ."

The hard line of his mouth wavered, broke. He grinned.

"No? Who says I can't?" His laughter, young, winged and exultant, floated up. "Baby, I'll burn the road . . . Oops! I mean . . ." He broke off, sheepishly. "No, no; I'll keep 'er under fifty. Honest!" Laughing, he crossed his heart—knowing Marian so well that he knew she would sense the gesture left over from their school days.

"There's so much to talk over now," he added eagerly. "Uncle Harry's taking me into the firm. I start peddling real estate for him next week. No kiddin'! And . . . and that little house we looked at . . . It's for sale, all right! Nine hundred down, and . . ."

"Bob . . . Hurry! Please!" The voice over the wire held, again, the tone he loved, laughing and tender. "But drive carefully. Promise!"

"Sure, sure! Twenty miles, twenty minutes!"

He hung up, chuckling, and strode out into the street. Dusk was falling, the slow Southern dusk that takes its time about folding its dark quilt over the Blue Ridge foothills. With a light, springy step Bob walked to where his blue convertible was parked outside the drugstore, sandwiched between a pickup truck and a sedan full of people. As he climbed under the steering wheel, he heard a boy's piping voice, followed by the shushing monotone of an elder:

"Look! That's Bob Trask! He killed that old Negro last Fourth-o-July . . ."

"Danny, hush! Don't talk so loud! He can hear . . ."

"Benny Olsen told me it's his second bad wreck . . ."

"Danny!"

". . . and that's the third car he's tore up in two years. Boy, you oughta seen that roadster he had! Sideswiped a truck and tore off the whole . . ."

"Hmph! License was never revoked, either! Politics! If his uncle wasn't city commissioner . . ."

Bob's scowl returned, cloudy with anger. People! They made up their own version of how an accident happened. That business with the truck, for instance. Swinging out into the highway just as he had tried to pass! Who could blame him for *that?* Or the fact that weeks later, the burly driver had happened to die? From a ruptured appendix! The damage suit had been thrown out of court, because nobody could prove the collision had been what caused it to burst.

Backing out of the parking space in a bitter rush, Bob drove the convertible south, out of Gareyville on 31, headed for Oak Grove. Accidents! Anybody could be involved in an accident! Was a guy supposed to be lucky all the time? Or a mind-reader, always clairvoyant about the other driver?

As the white ribbon of the highway unreeled before him, Bob's anger cooled. He smiled a little, settling behind the steering wheel and switching on the radio. Music poured out softly. He leaned back, soothed by its sound and the rush of wind tousling his dark hair.

The law had cleared him of reckless driving; and that was all that counted. The landscape blurred as the sun sank. Bob switched on his headlights, dimmed. There was, at this hour, not much traffic on the Chattanooga Road.

Glancing at his watch, Bob pressed his foot more heavily on the accelerator. Six-fifteen already? Better get to Marian's before that parent of hers insisted on dragging her off to a movie. He chuckled. His only real problem now was to win over Marian's mother, who made no bones of her disapproval of him, ever since his second wreck. *"Show me the way a man drives a car, and I'll tell you what he's like inside . . ."* Bob had laughed when Marian had repeated those words. A man could drive, he had pointed out, like an old-maid schoolteacher and still be involved in an accident that was not legally his fault. All right, *two* accidents! A guy could have lousy luck twice, couldn't he? Look at the statistics! Fatal accidents happened every day . . .

Yawning, at peace with himself and the lazy countryside sliding past his car window, Bob let the speedometer climb another ten miles an hour. Sixty-five? He smiled, amused. Marian was such an old grandma about driving fast! After they were married, he would have to teach her, show her. Why, he had had this old boat up to ninety on this same tree-shaded stretch of highway! A driver like himself, a good driver with a good car, had perfect control over his vehicle at any . . .

The child seemed to appear out of nowhere, standing in the center of the road. A little girl in a frilly pink dress, her white face turned up in sudden horror, picked out by the headlights' glare.

Bob's cry was instinctive as he stamped on the brakes, and wrenched at the steering wheel. The car careened wildly, skidding sidewise and striking the child broadside. Then, in a tangle of wheels and canvas top, it rolled into a shallow ditch, miraculously rightside up. Bob felt his head strike something hard—the windshield. It starred out with tiny shimmering cracks, but did not shatter. Darkness rushed over him; the sick black darkness of the unconscious; but through it, sharp as a knifethrust, bringing him back to hazy awareness, was the sound of a child screaming.

"Oh, no ohmygodohgod . . ." Someone was sobbing, whimpering the words aloud. Himself.

Shaking his head blurrily, Bob stumbled from the tilted vehicle and looked about. Blood was running from a cut in his forehead, and his head throbbed with a surging nausea. But, ignoring the pain, he sank to his knee and peered under the car.

She was there. A little girl perhaps five years old. Ditch water matted the soft blond hair and trickled into the half-closed eyes, tip-tilted at a pixie-like angle and fringed with long silky lashes. Bob groaned aloud, cramming his knuckles into his squared mouth to check the sob that burst out of him like a gust of desperate wind. She was pinned under a front wheel. Such a lovely little girl, appearing out here, miles from town, dressed as for a party. A sudden thought struck him that he knew this child, that he had seen her somewhere, sometime. On a bus? In a movie lobby . . . ? Where?

He crawled under the car afraid to touch her, afraid not to. She did not stir. Was she dead? Weren't those frilly little organdy ruffles on her small chest moving, ever so faintly . . . ? If he could only get her out from under that wheel! Get the car moving, rush her to a hospital . . . ! Surely, surely there was some spark of life left in that small body . . . !

Bob stood up, reeling, rubbing his eyes furiously as unconsciousness threatened to engulf him again. It was at that moment that he heard the muffled roar of a motorcycle. He whirled. Half in eagerness, half in dread, he saw a shadowy figure approaching down the twilight-misted highway.

The figure on the motorcycle, goggled and uniformed as a state highway patrolman, braked slowly a few feet away. With maddening deliberateness of movement, he dismounted, flipped out a small report-pad, and peered at the convertible, jotting down its license number. Bob beckoned frantically, pointing at the child pinned under the car. But the officer made no move to help him free her; took no notice of her beyond a cursory glance and a curt nod.

Instead, tipping back his cap from an oddly pale face, he rested one booted foot on the rear bumper and beckoned Bob to his side.

"All right, buddy . . ." His voice, Bob noted crazily, was so low that he could scarcely hear it; a whisper, a lip-movement pronouncing sounds that might have been part of the wind soughing in the roadside trees. "Name: Robert Trask? I had orders to be on the lookout for you . . ."

"Orders?" Bob bristled abruptly, caught between anxiety for the child under his car and an instinct for self-preservation. "Now, wait! I've got no record of reckless driving. I . . . I was involved in a couple of accidents; but the charges were dropped . . . Look!" he burst out. "While you're standing here yapping, this child may be . . . Get on that scooter of yours and go phone an ambulance, you! I'll report you for dereliction of duty! . . . Say!" he yelled, as the officer did not move, but went on scribbling in his book. "What kind of man *are* you, anyway? Wasting time booking me, when there still may be time to save this . . . this poor little . . . !"

The white, goggle-obscured face lifted briefly, expressionless as a mask. Bob squirmed under the scrutiny of eyes hidden behind the green glass; saw the lips move . . . and noticed, for the first time, how queerly the traffic officer held his head. His pointed chin was twisted sidewise, meeting the left shoulder. When he looked up, his whole body turned, like a man with a crick in his neck . . .

"What kind of man are *you?*" said the whispering lips. "That's what we have to find out . . . And that's why I got orders to bring you in. *Now!*"

"Bring me in . . . ?" Bob nodded dully. "Oh, you mean I'm under arrest? Sure, sure . . . But the little girl!" He glared, suddenly enraged by the officer's stolid indifference to the crushed form under the car. "Listen, if you don't get on that motorbike and go for help, I . . . I'll knock you out and go myself! Resisting arrest; leaving the scene of an accident . . . Charge me with anything you like! But if there's still time to save her . . ."

The goggled eyes regarded him steadily for a moment. Then, nodding, the officer scribbled something else in his book.

"Time?" the windy whisper said, edged with irony. "Don't waste time, eh? . . . Why don't you speed-demons think about other people *before* you kill them off? Why? *Why?* That's what we want to find out, what we *have* to find out . . . *Come on!*" The whisper lashed out, sibilant as a striking snake. "Let's go, buddy! *Walk!*"

Bob blinked, swayed. The highway patrolman, completely ignoring the small body pinned under the convertible, had strode across the paved road with a peremptory beckoning gesture. He seemed headed for a little byroad that branched off the highway, losing itself among a thick grove of pine trees. It must, Bob decided eagerly, lead to some farmhouse where the officer meant to phone for an ambulance. Staggering, he followed, with a last anxious glance at the tiny form spread-eagled under his car wheel. Where had he seen that little face? *Where* . . . ? Some neighbor's child, visiting out here in the country . . . ?

"You . . . you think she's . . . dead?" he blurted, stumbling after the shadowy figure ahead of him. "Is it too late . . . ?"

The officer with the twisted neck half-turned, swiveling his whole body to look back at him.

"That," the whispering voice said, "all depends. Come on, you—snap it up! We got all night, but there's no sense wastin' time! Eh, buddy?" The thin lips curled ironically. "Time! That's the most important thing in the world . . . to them as still have it!"

Swaying dizzily, Bob hurried after him up the winding

little byroad. It led, he saw with a growing sense of unease, through a country cemetery . . . Abruptly, he brought up short, peering ahead at a gray gleam through the pines. Why, there was no farmhouse ahead! A fieldstone chapel with a high peaked roof loomed against the dusk, its arched windows gleaming redly in the last glow of the sunset.

"Hey!" he snapped. "What *is* this? Where the hell are you taking me?"

The highway patrolman turned again, swiveling his body instead of his stiff, twisted neck.

"Night court," his whisper trailed back on a thread of wind.

"*Night* court!" Bob halted completely, anger stiffening his resolve not to be railroaded into anything, no matter what he had done to that lovely little girl back there in the ditch. "Say! Is this some kind of a gag? A kangaroo court, is it? You figure on lynching me after you've . . . ?"

He glanced about the lonely graveyard in swift panic, wondering if he could make a dash for it. This was no orderly minion of the law, this crazy deformed figure stalking ahead of him! A crank, maybe? Some joker dressed up as a highway patrolman . . . ? Bob backed away a few steps, glancing left and right. A crazy man, a crackpot . . . ?

He froze. The officer held a gun leveled at his heart.

"Don't try it!" The whisper cracked like a whiplash. "Come on, bud. You'll get a fair trial in this court—fairer than the likes of you deserve!"

Bob moved forward, helpless to resist. The officer turned his back, almost insolently, and stalked on up the narrow road. At the steps of the chapel he stood aside, however, waving his gun for Bob to open the heavy doors. Swallowing on a dry throat, he obeyed—and started violently as the rusty hinges made a sound like a hollow groan.

Then, hesitantly, his heart beginning to hammer with apprehension, Bob stepped inside. Groping his way into the darker interior of the chapel, he paused for a moment to let his eyes become accustomed to the gloom. Row on row of hardwood benches faced a raised dais, on which was a pulpit. Here, Bob realized with a chill coursing down his spine, local funeral services were held for those to be buried in the churchyard outside. As he moved forward, his footsteps echoed eerily among the beamed rafters overhead . . .

Then he saw them. People in those long rows of benches! Why, there must be over a hundred of them, seated in silent bunches of twos and threes, facing the pulpit. In a little alcove, set aside for the choir, Bob saw another, smaller group—and found himself suddenly counting them with a surge of panic. There were twelve in the choir box. Twelve, the number of a jury! Dimly he could see their white faces, with dark hollows for eyes, turning to follow his halting progress down the aisle.

Then, like an echo of a voice, deep and reverberating, someone called his name.

"The defendant will please take the stand . . . !"

Bob stumbled forward, his scalp prickling at the ghostly resemblance of this mock-trial to the one in which he had been acquitted only that morning. As though propelled by unseen hands, he found himself hurrying to a seat beside the pulpit, obviously reserved for one of the elders, but now serving as a witness-stand. He sank into the chair, peering through the half-darkness in an effort to make out some of the faces around him . . .

Then, abruptly, as the "bailiff" stepped forward to "swear him in," he stifled a cry of horror.

The man had no face. Where his features had been there was a raw, reddish mass. From this horror, somehow, a nightmare slit of mouth formed the words: ". . . to tell the truth, the whole truth, and nothing but the truth, so help you God?"

"I . . . I do," Bob murmured; and compared to the whispered tones of the bailiff, his own voice shocked him with its loudness.

"State your name."

"R-robert Trask . . ."

"Your third offense, isn't it, Mr. Trask?" the judge whispered drily. "A habitual reckless-driver . . ."

Bob was shaking now, caught in the grip of a nameless terror. What was this? Who were all these people, and why had they had him brought here by a motorcycle cop with a twisted . . . ?

He caught his breath again sharply, stifling another cry as the figure of a dignified elderly man became visible behind the pulpit, where before he had been half-shrouded in shadow. Bob blinked at him, sure that his stern white face was familiar—very familiar, not in the haunting way in which that child had seemed known to him, lying there crushed under his car. This man . . .

His head reeled all at once. Of course! Judge Abernathy! Humorous, lenient old Judge Ab. His father's friend, who had served in the Gareyville circuit court . . . Bob gulped. In 1932! Why, he had been only a youngster then! Twenty years would make this man all of ninety-eight years old, if . . . And it was suddenly that *"if"* which made Bob's scalp prickle with uneasiness. *If he were alive.* Judge Ab was *dead!* Wasn't he? Hadn't he heard his mother and dad talking about the old man, years ago; talking in hushed, sorrowful tones about the way he had been killed by a hit-and-run driver who had never been caught?

Bob shook his head, fighting off the wave of dizziness and nausea that was creeping over him again. It was crazy, the way his imagination was running away with him! Either this was not Judge Ab, but some old fellow who vaguely resembled him in this half-light . . . Or it *was* Judge Ab, alive, looking no older than he had twenty-odd years ago, at which time he was supposed to have been killed.

Squinting out across the rows of onlookers, Bob felt a growing sense of unreality. He could just make out, dimly, the features of the people seated in the first two rows of benches. Other faces, pale blurs against the blackness, moved restlessly as he peered at them . . . Bob gasped. His eyes made out things in the semi-gloom that he wished he had not seen. Faces mashed and cut beyond the semblance of a face! Bodies without arms! One girl . . . He swayed in his chair sickly; her shapely form was without a head!

He got a grip on his nerves with a tremendous effort. Of course! It wasn't real; it was all a horrible, perverted sort of practical joke! All these people were tricked up like corpses in a Chamber-of-Commerce "horror" parade. He tried to laugh, but his lips jerked with the effort . . . Then they quivered, sucking in breath.

The "prosecuting attorney" had stepped forward to question him—as, hours ago, he had been questioned by the attorney for Limestone County. Only . . . Bob shut his eyes quickly. It couldn't be! They wouldn't, whoever these people in this lonely chapel might be, they *wouldn't* make up some old Negro to look like the one whose wagon he had . . . had . . .

The figure moved forward, soundlessly. Only someone who had seen him on the morgue slab, where they had taken him after the accident, could have dreamed up that wooly white wig, that wrinkled old black face, and . . . And that gash at his temple, on which now the blood seemed to have dried forever . . .

"Hidy, Cap'm," the figure said in a diffident whisper. "I got to ast you a few questions. Don't lie, now! Dat's de *wust* thing you could do—tell a lie in dis-*yeah* court! . . . 'Bout how fast you figger you was goin' when you run over de girl-baby?"

"I . . . Pretty fast," he blurted. "Sixty-five, maybe seventy an hour."

The man he had killed nodded, frowning. "Yassuh. Dat's about right, sixty-five accordin' to de officer here." He glanced at the patrolman with the twisted neck, who gave a brief, grotesque nod of agreement.

Bob waited sickly. The old Negro—or whoever was dressed up as a dead man—moved toward him, resting his hand on the ornate rail of the chapel pulpit.

"Cap'm . . ." His soft whisper seemed to come from everywhere, rather than from the moving lips in that black face. "Cap'm . . . *why?* How come you was drivin' fifteen miles over the speed limit on this-yeah road? Same road where you run into my wagon . . ."

The listeners in the tiers of pews began to sway all at

once, like reeds in the wind. *"Why?"* someone in the rear took up the word, and then another echoed it, until a faint, rhythmic chant rose and fell over the crowded chapel:

"Why? Why? Why? . . . Why? Why? Why?"

"Order!" The "judge," the man who looked like a judge long dead, banged softly with his gavel; or it could have been a shutter banging at one of those arched chapel windows, Bob thought strangely.

The chanting died away. Bob swallowed nervously. For the old Negro was looking up at him expectantly, waiting for an answer to his simple question—the question echoed by those looking and listening from that eery "courtroom." *Why?* Why was he driving so fast? If he could only make up something, some good reason . . .

"I . . . I had a date with my girl," Bob heard his own voice, startling in its volume compared to the whispers around him.

"Yassuh?" The black prosecutor nodded gently. "She was gwine off someplace, so's you had to hurry to catch up wid her? Or else, was she bad-off sick and callin' for you . . . ?"

"I . . . No," Bob said, miserably honest. "No. There wasn't any hurry. I just . . . didn't want to . . ." He gestured futilely. "I wanted to be with her as quick as I could! Be-because I love her . . ." He paused, waiting to hear a titter of mirth ripple over the listeners.

There was no laughter. Only silence, sombre and accusing.

"Yassuh." Again the old Negro nodded his graying head, the head with the gashed temple. "All of us wants to be wid the ones we love. We don't want to waste no time doin' it . . . Only, you got to remember de Lawd give each of us a certain po'tion of time to use. And he don't aim for us to cut off de supply dat belong to somebody else. They got a right to live and love and be happy, too!"

The grave words hit Bob like a hammer blow—or like, he thought oddly, words he had been forming in his own mind, but holding off, not letting himself think because they might hurt. He fidgeted in the massive chair, twisting his hands together in sudden grim realization. Remorse had not, up to this moment, touched him deeply. But now it brought tears welling up, acid-like, to burn his eyes.

"Oh . . . please!" he burst out. "Can't we get this over with, this . . . this crazy mock-trial? I don't know who you are, all you people here. But I know you've . . . you've been incensed because my . . . my folks pulled some wires and got me out of two traffic-accidents that I . . . I should have been punished for! Now I've . . . I've run over a little girl, and you're afraid if I go to regular court-trial, my uncle will get me free again; is that it? That's it, isn't it . . . ?" he lashed out, half-rising. "All this . . . masquerade! Getting yourselves up like . . . like people who are dead . . . ! You're doing it to scare me!" He laughed harshly. "But it doesn't scare me, kid tricks like . . . like . . ."

He broke off, aware of another figure that had moved forward, rising from one of the forward benches. A burly man in overalls, wearing a trucker's cap . . . One big square hand was pressed to his side, and he walked as though in pain. Bob recognized those rugged features with a new shock.

"Kid . . . listen!" His rasping whisper sounded patient, tired. "We ain't here to scare anybody . . . Hell, that's for Hallowe'en parties! The reason we hold court here, night after night, tryin' some thick-skinned jerk who thinks he owns the road . . . Look, we just want t' know *why;* see? Why we had to be killed. Why some nice joe like you, with a girl and a happy future ahead of 'im, can't understand that . . . that *we* had a right to live, too! Me! Just a dumb-lug of a truck jockey, maybe . . . But I was doin' all right. I was gettin' by, raisin' my kids right . . ." The square hand moved from the man's side, gestured briefly and pressed back again.

"I figured to have my fool appendix out, soon as I made my run and got back home that Sunday. Only, you . . . Well, gee! Couldn't you have spared me ten seconds, Mac?" the hoarse whisper accused. "Wouldn't you loan me that much of your . . . your precious time, instead of takin' away all of mine? Mine, and this ole darkey's? And tonight . . .''

An angry murmur swept over the onlookers, like a rising wind.

''Order!'' The gavel banged again, like a muffled heart beat. ''The accused is not on trial for previous offenses. Remarks of the defense attorney—who is distinctly out of order—will be stricken from the record. Does the prosecution wish to ask the defendant any more questions to determine the *reason* for the accident?''

The old Negro shook his head, shrugging. ''Nawsuh, Jedge. Reckon not.''

Bob glanced sidewise at the old man who looked so like Judge Ab. He sucked in a quick breath as the white head turned, revealing a hideously crushed skull matted with some dark brown substance. Hadn't his father said something, years ago, about that hit-and-run driver running a wheel over his old friend's head? Were those . . . were those tire-tread marks on this man's white collar . . . ? Bob ground his teeth. How far would these Hallowe'en mummers go to make their macabre little show realistic . . . ?

But now, to his amazement, the burly man in trucker's garb moved forward, shrugging.

''Okay, Your Honor,'' his hoarse whisper apologized. ''I . . . I know it's too late for justice, not for us here. And if the court appoints me to defend this guy, I'll try . . . Look buddy,'' his whisper softened. ''You have reason to believe your girl was steppin' out on you? That why you was hurryin', jumpin' the speed-limit, to get there before she . . . ? You were out of your head, crazy-jealous?''

Bob glared. ''Say!'' he snapped. ''This is going too far, dragging my fiancée's name into this . . . this fake trial . . . Go ahead! I'm guilty of reckless driving—three times! I admit it! There was no reason on this earth for me to be speeding, no excuse for running over that . . . that poor little kid! It's . . . it's just that I . . .'' His voice broke, ''I didn't *see* her! Out here in the middle of nowhere—a child! How was I to know? The highway was clear, and then all at once, there she was right in front of my car . . . But . . . but I *was* going too fast. I deserve to be lynched! Nothing you do to me would be enough . . ."

He crumpled in the chair, stricken with dry sobs of remorse. But fear, terror of this weirdly-made-up congregation, left him slowly, as, looking from the judge to the highway patrolman, from the old Negro to the trucker, he saw only pity in their faces, a kind of sad bewilderment.

"But—why? Why need it happen?" the elderly judge asked softly, in a stern voice Bob thought he could remember from childhood. "Why does it go on and on? This senseless slaughter! If we could only *understand* . . . ! If we could only make the living understand, and stop and think, before it's too late for . . . another such as we. There is no such thing as an accidental death! Accidents are murders—because someone could have prevented them!"

The white-haired man sighed, like a soft wind blowing through the chapel. The sigh was caught up by others, until it rose and fell like a wailing gust echoing among the rafters.

Bob shivered, hunched in his chair. The hollow eyes of the judge fixed themselves on him, stern but pitying. He hung his head, and buried his face in his hands, smearing blood from the cut on his forehead.

"I . . . I . . . Please! Please don't say any more!" he sobbed. "I guess I just didn't realize, I was too wrapped up in my own selfish . . ." His voice broke. "And now it's too late . . ."

As one, the shadowy figures of the old Negro and the burly truck driver moved together in a kind of grim comradeship. They looked at the judge mutely as though awaiting his decision. The gaunt figure with the crushed skull cleared his throat in a way Bob thought he remembered . . .

"Too late? Yes . . . for these two standing before you. But the dead," his sombre whisper rose like a gust of wind in the dark chapel, "the dead can not punish the living.

They are part of the past, and have no control over the present . . . or the future."

"Yet, sometimes," the dark holes of eyes bored into Bob's head sternly, "the dead can guide the living, by giving them a glimpse into the future. The future as it will be . . . unless the living use their power to change it! Do you understand, Robert Trask? Do you understand that you are on trial in this night court, not for the past but for the future . . . ?"

Bob shook his head, bewildered. "The . . . future? I don't understand. I . . ." He glanced up eagerly. "The little girl! You . . . you mean, she's all right? She isn't dead . . . ?" he pressed, hardly daring to hope.

"She is not yet born," the old man whispered quietly. "But one day you will see her, just as you saw her to-night, lying crushed under your careless wheels . . . unless . . ." The whisper changed abruptly; became the dry official voice of a magistrate addressing his prisoner. "It is therefore the judgment of this court that, in view of the defendant's plea of guilty and in view of his extreme youth and of his war record, sentence shall be suspended pending new evidence of criminal behavior in the driver's seat of a motor vehicle. If such new evidence should be brought to the attention of this court, sentence shall be pronounced and the extreme penalty carried out . . . Do you understand, Mr. Trask?" the grave voice repeated. "*The extreme penalty!* . . . Case dismissed."

The gavel banged. Bob nodded dazedly, again burying his face in his hands and shaking with dry sobs. A wave of dizziness swept over him. He felt the big chair tilt, it seemed, and suddenly he was falling, falling forward into a great black vortex that swirled and eddied . . .

Light snatched him back to consciousness, a bright dazzling light that pierced his eyeballs and made him gag with nausea. Hands were pulling at him, lifting him. Then, slowly, he became aware of two figures bending over him: a gnome-like little man with a lantern, and a tall, sunburned young man in the uniform of a highway patrolman. It was not, Bob noted blurrily, the same one, the one with the twisted neck . . . He sat up, blinking.

"My, my, young feller!" The gnome with the lantern was trying to help him up from where he lay on the chapel floor in front of the pulpit. "Nasty lump on your head there! I'm the sexton: live up the road a piece. I heard your car hit the ditch a while ago, and called the highway patrol. Figgered you was drunk . . ." He sniffed suspiciously, then shrugged. "Don't smell drunk. What happened? You fall asleep at the wheel?"

Bob shut his eyes, groaning. He let himself be helped to one of the front pews and leaned back against it heavily before answering. Better tell the truth now. Get it over with . . .

"The . . . little girl. Pinned under my car—you found her?" He forced out the words sickly. "I . . . didn't see her, but . . . It was my fault. I was . . . driving too fast. Too fast to stop when she stepped out right in front of my . . ."

He broke off, aware that the tall tanned officer was regarding him with marked suspicion.

"What little girl?" he snapped. "There's nobody pinned under your car, buddy! I looked. Your footprints were the only ones leading away from the accident . . . and I traced them here! Besides, you were dripping blood from that cut on you . . . Say! You trying to kid somebody?"

"No, no!" Bob gestured wildly. "Who'd kid about a thing like . . . ? Maybe the other highway patrolman took her away on his motorcycle! He . . . All of them . . . There didn't seem any doubt that she'd been killed instantly. But then, the judge said she . . . she wasn't even born yet! They made me come here, to . . . to try me! In . . . night court, they called it! All of them pretending to be . . . dead people, accident victims. Blood all over them! Mangled . . ." He checked himself, realizing how irrational he sounded. "I fainted," his voice trailed uncertainly. "I guess when they . . . they heard you coming, they all ran away . . ."

"*Night* court?" The officer arched one eyebrow, tipped

back his cap, and eyed Bob dubiously. "Say, you *sure* you're sober, buddy? Or maybe you got a concussion . . . There's been nobody here. Not a soul; has there, Pop?"

"Nope." The sexton lifted his lamp positively, causing shadows to dance weirdly over the otherwise empty chapel. A film of dust covered the pews, undisturbed save where Bob himself now sat. "Ain't been nary a soul here since the Wilkins funeral; that was Monday three weeks ago. My, you never saw the like o' flowers . . ."

The highway patrolman gestured him to silence, peering at Bob once more. "What was that you said about another speed cop? There was no report tonight. What was his badge number? You happen to notice?"

Bob shook his head vaguely; then dimly recalled numbers he had seen on a tarnished shield pinned to that shadowy uniform.

"Eight something . . . 84! That was it! And . . . and he had a kind of twisted set to his head . . ."

The officer scowled suddenly, hands on hips. "Sa-ay!" he said in a cold voice. "What're you tryin' to pull? Nobody's worn Badge No. 84 since Sam Lacy got killed two years ago. Chasin' a speed-crazy high school kid, who swerved and made him fall off his motor. Broke his neck!" He compressed his lips grimly. "You're tryin' to pull some kind of gag about *that?*"

"No! N-no . . . !" Bob rose shakily to his feet. "I . . . I . . . Maybe I just dreamed it all! That clonk on the head . . ." He laughed all at once, a wild sound, full of hysterical relief. "You're positive there was no little girl pinned under my wheel? No . . . no signs of . . . ?"

He started toward the wide-flung doors of the chapel, reeling with laughter. But it had all seemed so real! Those nightmare faces, the whispering voices: that macabre trial for a traffic fatality that had never happened anywhere but in his own overwrought imagination . . . !

Still laughing, he climbed into his convertible, found it undamaged by its dive into the ditch, and backed out onto the road again. He waved. Shrugging, grinning, the highway officer and the old sexton waved back, visible in a yellow circle of lanterlight.

Bob gunned his motor and roared away. A lone tourist, rounding a curve, swung sharply off the pavement to give him room as he swooped over on the wrong side of the yellow line. Bob blew his horn mockingly, and trod impatiently on the accelerator. Marian must be tired of waiting! And the thought of holding her in his arms, laughing with her, telling her about that crazy, dream-trial . . . Dead men! Trying him, the living, for the traffic-death of a child yet to be born! "The extreme penalty!" If not lynching, what would that be? He smiled, amused. Was anything that could happen to a man really "a fate worse than death . . . ?"

Bob's smile froze.

Quite suddenly his foot eased up on the accelerator. His eyes widened, staring ahead at the dark highway illuminated by the twin glare of his headlights. Sweat popped out on his cool forehead all at once. Jerkily his hands yanked at the smooth plastic of the steering-wheel, pulling the convertible well over to the right side of the highway . . .

In that instant, Bob thought he knew where he had seen the hauntingly familiar features of that lovely little girl lying dead, crushed, under the wheel of his car. "The extreme penalty?" He shuddered, and slowed down, driving more carefully into the darkness ahead. The darkness of the future . . .

For, the child's blond hair and long lashes, he knew with a swift chill of dread, had been a tiny replica of Marian's . . . and the tip-tilted pixy eyes, closed in violent death, had borne a startling resemblance to his own.

A descendant of John Rolfe, who was among the original settlers of the Jamestown Colony in 1607, Mary Elizabeth Counselman was born in Georgia in 1911 and grew up on an honest-to-Scarlett-O'Hara plantation. Educated at the University of Alabama and Montevallo University, she began selling fiction and poetry to such diverse publications as the Saturday Evening Post and Jungle Stories. Her "The Three Marked Pennies" became the most popular story ever to appear in Weird Tales. The best of her supernatural writing, including "Night Court," is collected in Half in Shadow (Arkham House, 1978).

Murlock's wife died from a fever. Or did she?

7

The Boarded Window

Ambrose Bierce

In 1830, only a few miles away from what is now the great city of Cincinnati, lay an immense and almost unbroken forest. The whole region was sparsely settled by people of the frontier—restless souls who no sooner had hewn fairly habitable homes out of the wilderness and attained to that degree of prosperity which today we should call indigence than, impelled by some mysterious impulse of their nature, they abandoned all and pushed farther westward, to encounter new perils and privations in the effort to regain the meagre comforts which they had voluntarily renounced. Many of them had already forsaken that region for the remoter settlements, but among those remaining was one who had been of those first arriving. He lived alone in a house of logs surrounded on all sides by the great forest, of whose gloom and silence he seemed a part, for no one had ever known him to smile nor speak a needless word. His simple wants were supplied by the sale or barter of skins of wild animals in the river town, for not a thing did he grow upon the land which, if needful, he might have claimed by right of undisturbed possession. There were evidences of "improvement"—a few acres of ground immediately about the house had once been cleared of its trees, the decayed stumps of which were half concealed by the new growth that had been suffered to repair the ravage wrought by the ax. Apparently the man's zeal for agriculture had burned with a failing flame, expiring in penitential ashes.

The little log house, with its chimney of sticks, its roof of warping clapboards weighted with traversing poles and its "chinking" of clay, had a single door and, directly opposite, a window. The latter, however, was boarded up—nobody could remember a time when it was not. And none knew why it was so closed; certainly not because of the occupant's dislike of light and air, for on those rare occasions when a hunter had passed that lonely spot the recluse had commonly been sunning himself on his doorstep if heaven had provided sunshine for his need. I fancy there are few persons living today who ever knew the secret of that window, but I am one, as you shall see.

The man's name was said to be Murlock. He was apparently seventy years old, actually about fifty. Something besides years had had a hand in his aging. His hair and long, full beard were white, his gray, lustreless eyes sunken, his face singularly seamed with wrinkles which appeared to belong to two intersecting systems. In figure he was tall and spare, with a stoop of the shoulders—a burden bearer. I never saw him; these particulars I learned from my grandfather, from whom also I got the man's story when I was a lad. He had known him when living nearby in that early day.

One day Murlock was found in his cabin, dead. It was not a time and place for coroners and newspapers, and I suppose it was agreed that he had died from natural causes or I should have been told and should remember. I know only that with what was probably a sense of the fitness of things the body was buried near the cabin, alongside the grave of his wife, who had preceded him by so many years that local tradition had retained hardly a hint of her existence. That closes the final chapter of this true story—excepting, indeed, the circumstance that many years afterward, in company with an equally intrepid spirit, I penetrated to the place and ventured near enough to the ruined cabin to throw a stone against it and ran away to avoid the ghost which every well-informed boy thereabout knew haunted the spot. But there is an earlier chapter—that supplied by my grandfather.

When Murlock built his cabin and began laying sturdily about with his ax to hew out a farm—the rifle, meanwhile, his means of support—he was young, strong, and full of hope. In that eastern country whence he came he had married, as was the fashion, a young woman in all ways worthy of his honest devotion, who shared the dangers and privations of his lot with a willing spirit and light heart. There is no known record of her name; of her charms of mind and person tradition is silent and the doubter is at liberty to entertain his doubts; but God forbid that I should share it! Of their affection and happiness there is abundant assurance in every added day of the man's widowed life; for what but the magnetism of a blessed memory could have chained that venturesome spirit to a lot like that?

One day Murlock returned from gunning in a distant part of the forest to find his wife prostrate with fever, and delirious. There was no physician within miles, no neighbor; nor was she in a condition to be left, to summon help. So he set about the task of nursing her back to health, but at the end of the third day she fell into unconsciousness and so passed away, apparently, with never a gleam of returning reason.

From what we know of a nature like his we may venture to sketch in some of the details of the outline picture drawn by my grandfather. When convinced that she was dead, Murlock had sense enough to remember that the dead must be prepared for burial. In performance of this sacred duty he blundered now and again, did certain things incorrectly, and others which he did correctly were done over and over. His occasional failures to accomplish some simple and ordinary act filled him with astonishment, like that of a drunken man who wonders at the suspension of familiar natural laws. He was surprised, too, that he did not weep—surprised and a little ashamed; surely it is unkind not to weep for the dead. "Tomorrow," he said aloud, "I shall have to make the coffin and dig the grave; and then I shall miss her, when she is no longer in sight; but now—she is dead, of course, but it is all right—it *must* be all right, somehow. Things cannot be so bad as they seem."

He stood over the body in the fading light, adjusting the hair and putting the finishing touches to the simple toilet, doing all mechanically, with soulless care. And still through his consciousness ran an undersense of conviction that all was right—that he should have her again as before, and everything explained. He had had no experience in grief; his capacity had not been enlarged by use. His heart could not contain it all, nor his imagination rightly conceive it. He did not know he was so hard struck; *that* knowledge would come later, and never go. Grief is an artist of powers as various as the instruments upon which he plays his dirges for the dead, evoking from some the sharpest, shrillest notes, from others the low, grave chords that throb recurrent like the slow beating of a distant drum. Some natures it startles; some it stupefies. To one it comes like the stroke of an arrow, stinging all the sensibilities to a keener life; to another as the blow of a bludgeon, which in crushing benumbs. We may conceive Murlock to have been that way affected, for (and here we are upon surer ground than that of conjecture) no sooner had he finished his pious work than, sinking into a chair by the side of the table upon which the body lay, and noting how white the profile showed in the deepening gloom, he laid his arms upon the table's edge, and dropped his face into them, tearless yet and unutterably weary. At that moment came in through the open window a long, wailing sound like the cry of a lost child in the far deeps of the darkening wood! But the man did not move. Again, and nearer than before, sounded that unearthly cry upon his failing sense. Perhaps it was a wild beast; perhaps it was a dream. For Murlock was asleep.

Some hours later, as it afterward appeared, this unfaithful watcher awoke and lifting his head from his arms intently listened—he knew not why. There in the black darkness by the side of the dead, recalling all without a shock, he strained his eyes to see—he knew not what. His senses were all alert, his breath was suspended, his blood had stilled its tides as if to assist the silence. Who—what had waked him, and where was it?

Suddenly the table shook beneath his arms, and at the same moment he heard, or fancied that he heard, a light, soft step—another—sounds as of bare feet upon the floor!

He was terrified beyond the power to cry out or move. Perforce he waited—waited there in the darkness through seeming centuries of such dread as one may know, yet live to tell. He tried vainly to speak the dead woman's name, vainly to stretch forth his hand across the table to learn if she was there. His throat was powerless, his arms and hands were like lead. Then occurred something most frightful. Some heavy body seemed hurled against the table with an impetus that pushed it against his breast so sharply as nearly to overthrow him, and at the same instant he heard and felt the fall of something upon the floor with so violent a thump that the whole house was shaken by the impact. A scuffling ensued, and a confusion of sounds impossible to describe. Murlock had risen to his feet. Fear had by excess forfeited control of his faculties. He flung his hands upon the table. Nothing was there!

There is a point at which terror may turn to madness; and madness incites to action. With no definite intent, from no motive but the wayward impulse of a madman, Murlock sprang to the wall, with a little groping seized his loaded rifle, and without aim discharged it. By the flash which lit up the room with a vivid illumination, he saw an enormous panther dragging the dead woman toward the window, its teeth fixed in her throat! Then there were darkness blacker than before, and silence; and when he returned to consciousness the sun was high and the wood vocal with songs of birds.

The body lay near the window, where the beast had left

it when frightened away by the flash and report of the rifle. The clothing was deranged, the long hair in disorder, the limbs lay anyhow. From the throat, dreadfully lacerated, had issued a pool of blood not yet entirely coagulated. The ribbon with which he had bound the wrists was broken; the hands were tightly clenched. Between the teeth was a fragment of the animal's ear.

A dark genius of American letters, Ambrose Bierce was born in Ohio in 1842 and served in the Union army during the Civil War. A bitter and fearless man known for his witty writing (in one book review he wrote, "The covers of this book are too far apart"), he had a long, successful journalism career in San Francisco. His life ended with an eerie touch of mystery: he disappeared somewhere in Mexico in 1914.

Hobo Harold Skidmore was very sick, and when Farmer Plone offered Harold use of his old log cabin, Harold eagerly accepted, even if the cabin had this odd habit of disappearing.

8

The Ghosts of Steamboat Coulee

Arthur J. Burks

A heartless brakeman discovered me and kicked me off the train at Palisades. I didn't care greatly. As well be dropped here in Moses Coulee like a bag of spoiled meal as farther up the line. When a man knows he has but a short time to live, what matters it? Had I not been endowed with a large modicum of my beloved father's stubbornness I believe I should, long ere this, have crawled away into some hole, like a mongrel cur, to die. There was no chance to cheat the Grim Reaper. That had been settled long ago, when, without a gas mask, I had gone through a certain little town in Flanders.

My lungs were just about done. Don't think I am making a bid for sympathy. I know a sick man seldom arouses in the breast of strangers any other emotion than disgust.

But I am telling this to explain my actions in those things which came later.

153

After leaving the train at Palisades I looked up and down the coulee. Where to go? I hadn't the slightest idea. Wenatchee lay far behind me, at the edge of the mighty Columbia River. I had found this thriving little city unsympathetic and not particularly hospitable. I couldn't, therefore, retrace my steps. Besides, I never have liked to go back over lost ground. I saw the train which had dropped me crawl like a snake up the steep incline which led out of the coulee. I hadn't the strength to follow. I knew that I could never make the climb.

So, wearily, I trudged out to the road and headed farther into the coulee, to come, some hours later, to another cul-de-sac. It was another (to me impossible) incline, this time a wagon road. I have since learned that this road leads, via a series of three huge terraces bridged by steep incline, out of Moses Coulee. It is called the Three Devils—don't ask me why, for it was named by the Siwash Indians.

At the foot of this road, and some half-mile from where it began to climb, I saw a small farmhouse, from the chimney of which a spiral of blue smoke arose lazily into the air. Here were folks, country folks, upon whose hospitality I had long ago learned to rely. Grimy with the dust of the trail, damp with perspiration, red spots dancing in the air before my eyes because of the unaccustomed exertion to which I had compelled myself, I turned aside and presently knocked at the door of the farmhouse.

A housewife answered my knock and nervously motioned me enter. I was shortly pointed to a seat at the table to partake of the tasty viands brought forth. When I had finished eating I arose from my place and was about to ask her what I might do in payment for the meal, when I was seized with a fit of coughing which left me faint and trembling; and I had barely composed myself when the woman's husband and a half-grown boy entered the house silently and looked at me.

"How come a man as sick as you is out on the road afoot like this?" demanded the man.

I told them my story, and that I had neither friends nor family, nor abode. While I talked they exchanged glances with one another, and when I had finished the husband looked at me steadily for a long moment.

"Is there a chance for you to get well?" he asked finally.

"I am afraid not." I tried to make my voice sound cheerful.

"Would you like to find a place where nobody'd bother you? A place where you could loaf along about as you wished until your time came?"

I nodded in answer to the question. The man strode to the door and pointed.

"See there?" he asked. "That's the road you came here on, against that two hundred foot cliff. Opposite that cliff, back of my house, is another cliff, thirteen hundred feet high. Matter of fact, my place is almost surrounded by cliffs, don't need to build fences, except where the coulee opens away toward Columbia River, which is some lot of miles away from here. Cliffs both sides of it, all the way down. No other exit, except there!"

As he spoke he swung his extended forearm straight toward the cliff to the north.

"See what looks like a great black shadow against the face of the cliff, right where she turns to form the curve of the coulee?"

"Yes, I see it."

"Well, that ain't a shadow. That's the entrance to another and smaller coulee which opens into this one. It is called Steamboat Coulee, and if you look sharp you can see why."

I studied that black shadow as he pointed, carefully, running my eyes over the face of the cliff. Then I exclaimed suddenly, so unexpectedly did I discover the reason for the name. Right at the base of that black shadow was a great pile of stone, its color all but blending with the mother cliff unless one looked closely; and this mass of solid rock, from where we stood in the doorway of the farmhouse, looked like a great steamboat slowly emerging from the cleft in the giant walls!

"Good Lord!" I exclaimed. "If I didn't know better I would swear that was a boat under steam!"

"It's fooled a lot of folks," returned the farmer. "Well,

that coulee entrance is on my land, so I guess I have a right to make this proposition to you. Back inside that coulee about two miles is my old log cabin that could easy be made livable. Just the place for you, and I could send in what little food you would need. It's kind of cool at night, but in the daytime the sun makes the coulee as hot as an oven, and you could loaf all day in the heat. There are plenty of big rocks there to flop on and—who knows—maybe you'd even get well!''

"I thank you, sir," I said, as politely as I could; "you are very kind. I accept your offer with great pleasure. May I know to whom I am indebted for this unusually benevolent service?"

The man hesitated before answering.

"What difference does a name make? We don't go much on last names here. That there is Reuben, my boy, and this is my wife, Hildreth. My own name is Plone. You can tell us what to call you, if you wish, but it don't make much difference if you don't care to."

"My name is Harold Skidmore, late of the U. S. Army. Once more allow me to thank you, then I shall go into my new home before it gets so dark I can't find it."

"That's all right. Reuben will go along and show you the place. Hillie will put up a sack of grub for you—enough to last a couple of days—and tote it in tomorrow. You'll probably be too sore from your walk to come out for a while—and we may be too busy to take any in to you."

The woman dropped her arms to her side and moved into the kitchen to do the bidding of Plone. Plone! What an odd name for a man! I studied him as, apparently having forgotten me, he stared moodily down the haze-filled coulee. I tried to see what his eyes were seeking, but all I could tell was that he watched the road by which I had come to this place—watched it carefully and in silence, as though he expected other visitors to come around the bend which leads to the Three Devils. He did not turn back to me again; and when, ten minutes or so later, Reuben touched my arm and started off in the direction of Steamboat, Plone was still staring down the road.

I studied the territory over which we traveled. Though I knew absolutely nothing about farming, I would have sworn that this ground hadn't been cultivated for many years. It had been plowed once upon a time, but the plowing had been almost obliterated by scattered growths of green sagebrush which had pushed through and begun to thrive, while in the open Reuben and I struggled through regular matted growths of wild hollyhocks, heavy with their fiery blooms. Plone's farm was nothing but a desert on the coulee floor.

We were approaching Steamboat Coulee entrance, and the nearer we strode the less I liked the bargain I had made, for the huge maw looked oddly like a great open mouth that might take one in and leave no trace. But those red spots were dancing before my eyes again and may have helped me to imagine things.

When we reached the gap its mouthlike appearance was not so pronounced, and the rock which had looked like a steamboat did not resemble a steamboat at all. The floor of this coulee was a dry stream-bed which, when the spring freshets came, must have been a roaring torrent.

Before entering I looked back at the house of Plone, and shouted in amazement.

"Reuben! Where is the house? I can see all of that end of the coulee, and your house is not in sight!"

"We come over a rise, a high one, that's all," he replied carelessly; "if we go back a piece we can see the house. Only we ain't got time. I want to show you the cabin and get back before dark. This coulee ain't nice to get caught in after dark."

"It isn't?" I questioned. "Why not?"

But Reuben had begun the entrance to Steamboat Coulee and did not answer. I was very hesitant about following him now, for I knew that he had lied to me. We hadn't come over any rise, and I should have been able to see the farmhouse!

I liked this coulee less and less as we went deeper into it. Walls rose straight on either hand, and they were so close that they seemed to be pressing over upon me. The stream-bed narrowed and deepened. On its banks grew thickets of wild willow, interspersed with clumps of squaw-berry bushes laden with pink fruit. Behind these thickets arose the talus slope of shell-rock.

I studied the slopes for signs of pathways which might lead out in case a heavy rain should fill the stream-bed and cut off my retreat by the usual way, but saw none. I saw instead something that filled me with a sudden feeling of dread, causing a sharp constriction of my throat. It was just a mottled mass on a large rock; but as I looked at it the mass moved, untwisted itself, and a huge snake glided out of sight in the rocks.

"Reuben," I called, "are there many snakes in this coulee?"

"Thousands!" he replied without looking back. "Rattlers, blue racers and bull whips—but mostly rattlers. Keep to your shanty at night and stay in the stream-bed in the daytime and they won't be any danger to you!"

Well, I was terribly tired, else I would have turned around and quitted this place—yes, though I fell dead from exhaustion ten minutes later. As it was I followed Reuben, who turned aside finally and climbed out of the stream-bed. I followed him and stood upon a trail which led down a gloomy aisle into a thicket of willows. Heavy shadows hung in this moody aisle, but through these I could make out the outline of a squatty log cabin.

Ten minutes later I had a fire going in the cracked stove which the house boasted, and its light was driving away the shadows in the walls. The board floor was well laid—no cracks through which venturesome rattlers might smell me out. I made sure of this before I would let Reuben get away, and that the door could be closed and bolted.

"Well," said Reuben, who had stood by while I put the place rapidly to rights, "you'll be all right now. Snug as a bug in a rug—if you ain't afraid of ghosts!"

His hand had dropped to the doorknob as he began to talk, and when he had uttered this last sinister sentence he opened the door and slipped out before I could stop him. Those last six words had sent a chill through my whole body. In a frenzy of fear which I could not explain, I rushed to the door and looked out, intending to call Reuben back.

I swear he hadn't had time to reach that stream-bed and drop into it out of sight; but when I looked out he was nowhere to be seen, and when I shouted his name until the echoes rang to right and left through the coulee, there was no answer! He must have fairly flown out of that thicket!

I closed the door and barred it, placed the chair back under the doorknob, and sat down upon the edge of the bed, gazing into the fire.

What sort of place had I wandered into?

For a time the rustling of the wind through the willows outside the log cabin was my only answer. Then a gritty grating sound beneath the floor, slow and intermittent, told me that a huge snake, sluggish with the coolness of the evening, was crawling there and was at that moment scraping alongside one of the timbers which supported the floor.

I was safe from these, thank God.

The feeling of security which now descended upon me, together with the cheery roaring of the fire in the stove, almost lulled me to sleep as I sat. My eyes were closing wearily and my head was sinking upon my breast. . . .

II

A cry that the wildest imagination would never have expected to hear in this place, came suddenly from somewhere in the darkness outside.

It was a cry as of a little baby that awakes in the night and begs plaintively to be fed. And it came from somewhere out there in the shell-rock of the talus slopes.

Merciful heavens! How did it happen that a wee small child such as I guessed this to be had wandered out into the darkness of the coulee? Whence had it come? Were there other inhabitants in Steamboat? But Plone had not mentioned any. Then how explain that eery cry outside? A possible explanation, inspired by frayed nerves, came to me, and froze the marrow in my bones before I could reason myself out of it.

"If you ain't afraid of ghosts!"

What had Reuben of the unknown surname meant by this remark? And by what means had he so swiftly disappeared after he had quitted my new home?

Just as I asked myself the question, that wailing cry came again, from about the same place, as near as I could judge, on the talus slope in rear of my cabin. Unmistakably the cry of a lost baby, demanding by every means of expression in its power, the attention of its mother. Out there alone and frightened in the darkness, in the heart of Steamboat Coulee, which Reuben had told me was infested by great numbers of snakes, at least one kind of which was venomous enough to slay.

Dread tugged at my throat. My tongue became dry in my mouth, cleaving to the palate. I knew before I opened the door that the coulee was now as dark as Erebus, and that moving about would be like groping in some gigantic pocket. But there was a feeble child out there on the talus slope, lost in the darkness, wailing for its mother. And I prided myself upon being at least the semblance of a man.

Mentally girding myself, I strode to the door and flung it open. A miasmatic mist came in immediately, cold as the breath from a sunless marsh, chilling me anew. Instinctively I closed the door as though to shut out some loathsome presence—I know not what. The heat of the fire absorbed the wisps of vapor that had entered. I leaned against the door, panting with a nameless terror, when, from the talus slope outside, plain through the darkness came again that eery wailing.

Gulping swiftly, swallowing my terrible fear, I closed my eyes and flung the door wide open. Nor did I close it until I stood outside and opened *my* eyes against an opaque blanket of darkness. When Plone had told me the coulee was cold after nightfall, he had not exaggerated. It was as cold as the inside of a tomb.

The crying of the babe came again, from directly behind my cabin. The cliff bulked large there, while above its rim, high up, I made out the soft twinkling of a pale star or two.

Before my courage should fail me and send me back into the cheery cabin, thrice cheery now that I was outside it, I ran swiftly around the cabin, nor stopped until I had begun to clamber up the talus slope, guided by my memory of whence that wailing cry had come. The shell-rock shifted beneath me, and I could hear the shale go clattering down among the brush about the bases of the willows below. I kept on climbing.

Once I almost fell when I stepped upon something round, which writhed beneath my foot, causing me to jump straight into the air with a half-suppressed cry of fear. I was glad now that the coulee was cold after nightfall, else the snake, were it by chance a rattler, could have struck me a death-blow. The cold, however, made the vile creature sluggish.

When I thought I had climbed far enough I bent over and tried to pierce the heavy gloom, searching the talus intently for a glimpse of white—white which should discover to me the clothing of the baby which I sought. Failing in this, I remained quiet, waiting for the cry to come again. I waited amid a silence that could almost be felt, a silence lasting so long that I began to dread a repetition of that cry. What if there were no baby—flesh and blood, that is? Reuben had spoken of ghosts. Utter nonsense! No grown man believes in ghosts! And if I didn't find the child before long the little tot might die of the cold. Where had the child gone? Why this eery silence? Why didn't the child cry again? It was almost as though it had found that which it sought, there in the darkness. That cry had spoken eloquently of a desire for sustenance.

If the child did not cry, what was I to believe? Who, or what, was suckling the baby out on the cold talus slope?

I became as a man turned to stone when the eery cry came again. It was not a baby's whimper, starting low and increasing in volume; it was a full-grown wail as it issued from the unseen mouth. And it came from at least a hundred feet higher up on the talus! I, a grown man, had stumbled heavily in the scramble to reach this height; yet a baby so small that it wailed for its milk had crept a hundred feet farther up the slope! It was beyond all reason; weird beyond the wildest imagination. But undoubtedly the wailing of a babe.

I did not believe in ghosts. I studied the spot whence the wail issued, but could see no blotch of white. Only two lambent dots, set close together, glowing like resting fireflies among the shale. I saw them for but a second only. Undoubtedly mating fireflies, and they had flown.

I began to climb once more, moving steadily toward the spot where I had heard the cry.

I stopped again when the shell-rock above me began to flow downward as though something, or somebody, had started it moving. What, in God's name, was up there at the base of the cliff? Slowly, my heart in my mouth, I climbed on.

There was a rush, as of an unseen body, along the face of the talus. I could hear the contact of light feet on the shale; but the points of contact were unbelievably far apart. No baby in the world could have stepped so far—or jumped. Of course the cry might have come from a half-witted grown person; but I did not believe it.

The cry again, sharp and clear; but at least two hundred yards up the coulee from where I stood, and on about a level with me. Should I follow or not? Did some nocturnal animal carry the babe in its teeth? It might be; I had heard of such things, and had read the myth of Romulus and Remus. Distorted fantasies? Perhaps; but show me a man who can think coolly while standing on the talus slope of Steamboat after dark, and I will show you a man without nerves—and without a soul.

Once more I took up the chase. I had almost reached the spot whence the cry had come last, when I saw again those twin balls of lambent flame. They seemed to blink at me—off and on, off and on.

I bent over to pick up a bit of shale to hurl at the dots, when, almost in my ears, that cry came once more; but this time the cry ended in a spitting snarl as of a tomcat when possession of food is disputed!

With all my might I hurled the bit of shale I had lifted,

straight at those dots of flame. At the same time I gave
utterance to a yell that set the echoes rolling the length and
breadth of the coulee. The echoes had not died away when
the coulee was filled until it rang with that eery wailing—as
though a hundred babies cried for mothers who did not
come!

Then—great God!—I knew!

Bobcats! The coulee was alive with them! I was alone on
the talus, two hundreds yards from the safe haven of my
cabin, and though I knew that one alone would not attack a
man in the open, I had never heard whether they hunted in
groups. For all I knew they might. At imminent risk of
breaking my neck, I hurled myself down the slope and into
the thicket of willows at the base. Through these and into
the dry stream-bed I blundered, still running. I kept this
mad pace until I had reached the approximate point where
the trail led to my cabin, climbed the bank of the dry stream
and sought for the aisle through the willows.

Though I searched carefully for a hundred yards on each
hand I could not find the path. And I feared to enter the
willow thicket and beat about. The ominous wailing had
stopped suddenly, as though at a signal, and I believed that
the bobcats had taken to the trees at the foot of the talus. I
studied the dark shadows for dots of flame in pairs, but
could see none. I knew from reading about them that
bobcats have been known to drop on solitary travelers from
the limbs of trees. Their sudden silence was weighted with
ponderous menace.

I was afraid—*afraid!* Scared as I had never been in my
life before—and I had gone through a certain town in
Flanders without a gas mask.

Why the sudden, eery silence? I would have welcomed
that vast chorus of wailing, had it begun again. But it did
not.

When I crept back to the bank of the stream-bed a pale
moon had come up, partly dispelling the shadows in
Steamboat Coulee. The sand in the stream-bed glistened
frostily in the moonlight, making me think of the blinking
eyes of a multitude of toads.

Where, in Steamboat, was the cabin with its cheery fire? I had closed the door to keep my courage from failing me, and now there was no light to guide me.

It is hell to be alone in such a place, miles from the nearest other human being.

I sat down on the high bank, half sidewise so that I could watch the shadows among the willows, and tried mentally to retrace my steps, hoping that I could reason out the exact location of the cabin in the thicket.

Sitting as I was, I could see for a hundred yards or so down the stream-bed. I studied its almost straight course for a moment or two, for no reason that I can assign. I saw a black shadow dart across the open space, swift as a breath of wind, and disappear in the thicket on the opposite side. It was larger than a cat, smaller than the average dog. A bobcat had changed his base hurriedly, and in silence.

Silence! That was the thing that was now weighing upon me, more even than the thought of my failure to locate the little cabin. Why had the cats stopped their wailing so suddenly, as though they waited for something? This thought deepened the feeling of dread that was upon me. If the cats were waiting, for what were they waiting?

Then I breathed a sigh of relief. For, coming around a bend in the stream-bed, there strode swiftly toward me the figure of a man. He was a big man who looked straight before him. He walked as a country man walks when he hurries home to a late supper. Then there were other people in this coulee, after all!

But what puzzled me about this newcomer was his style of dress. He was garbed after the manner of the first pioneers who had come into this country from the East. From his high-topped boots, into which his trousers were tucked loosely, to his broad-brimmed hat, he was dressed after the manner of those people who had vanished from this country more than a decade before my time. An old prospector evidently, who had clung to the habiliments of his younger days. But he did not walk like an old man; rather he strode, straight-limbed and erect, like a man in his early thirties. There was a homely touch about him, though, picturesque as he was; for he smoked a corncob pipe, from the bowl of which a spiral of blue smoke eddied forth into the chill night air. I knew from this that, did I call to him, his greeting in return would be bluffly friendly.

I waited for him to come closer, hoping that he would notice me first. As he approached I noticed with a start that two huge revolvers, the holsters tied back, swung low upon his hips. People nowadays did not carry firearms openly. In an instant I had decided to let this stranger pass, even though I spent the remainder of the night on the bank of the dry stream. Sight of those savage weapons had filled me with a new and different kind of dread.

Then I started as another figure, also of a man, came around the selfsame bend of the watercourse, for there was something oddly familiar about that other figure. He moved swiftly, his body almost bent double as he hurried forward. As he came around the bend and saw the first man who had come into my range of vision, he bent lower still.

As he did so the moonlight glowed dully on something that he carried in the crook of his arm. I knew instantly that what he carried was a rifle. Once more that chill along my spine, for there was no mistaking his attitude.

He was stalking the first man, furtively, and there was murder in his heart!

It did not take his next action to prove this to me. I knew it, even as the second man knelt swiftly in the sand of the watercourse and flung his rife to his shoulder, its muzzle pointing at the man approaching me.

I cried out with all the power of my shattered lungs. But the man ahead, all unconscious of the impending death at his heels, paid me absolutely no attention. He was no more than twenty yards from me when I shouted, yet he did not turn his head. For all the attention he paid me I might as well have remained silent. It was as though he were stone-deaf.

I shouted again, waving my arms wildly. Perhaps he could not see me because of the shadows at my back. Still he did not see me. I whirled to the kneeling man, just as a sheet of yellow flame leaped from the muzzle of his rifle.

The first man was right in front of me when the bullet struck him. He stopped, dead in his tracks. I guessed that the bullet had struck him at the base of the skull. Even so, he whirled swiftly, and both his guns were out. But he could not raise them to fire. He slumped forward limply, and sprawled in the sand.

I had not heard the report of the rifle, for simultaneously with that spurt of flame the bobcats had begun their wailing once more, drowning out the sound.

With a great cry, whose echoes could be heard in the coulee even through the wailing of the bobcats, I sprang to my feet and ran, staggering, down the watercourse, in the direction of what I thought was Steamboat's entrance.

Long before I had reached it my poor body failed me and I fell to the sandy floor, coughing my lungs away, while scarlet stains wetted the sand near my mouth.

III

When I awoke in the sand the sun was shining. Some sixth sense told me to remain motionless, warning me that all was not well. Without moving my head I rolled my eyes until I could see ahead in the direction I had fallen. In falling my right hand had been flung out full length, fingers extended.

Imagine my fear and horror when I saw, coiled up within six inches of my hand, a huge rattlesnake! His head was poised above the coil, while just behind it, against the other arc of the vicious circle, the tip of the creature's tail, adorned with an inch or more of rattles, hummed its fearful warning.

With all my power I sprang back and upward. At the same time the bullet head, unbelievably swift, flashed toward my hand and—thank God—safely beneath it! Stretched helplessly now to its full length, the creature's mouth, with its forked tongue, had stopped within a scant two inches of where my face had been.

Before the rattler could return and coil again I had stepped upon the bullet head, grinding it deep into the sand, and when the tail whipped frantically against my leg I seized it and hurled the reptile with all my might, out of the stream-bed into the shell-rock. Even as I did it I wondered where I had found the courage; and what had kept me from moving while unconscious. Had I moved I might never again have awakened.

I climbed the bank of the dry stream to look for the entrance to my log cabin which I believed to lay ahead of me, but kept well away from the thickets for fear of snakes. With the sun high in the heavens, turning the coulee into a furnace, the snakes came out by hundreds to bask upon the shale, and as I passed, they coiled and warned me away with myriad warnings. I did not trespass upon their holdings.

After I had plodded along for fully an hour I knew that I must be quite close to the rock which gave Steamboat its name; but still I had not found the pathway leading to the log cabin. Evidently I had already passed it.

Even as I had this thought I came upon a path leading into the shadows of the willow thicket—a path that seemed familiar, even though, from the stream-bed, I could not see the cabin. With a sigh, and much surprised that I had, last night, traveled so far in my hysterical terror, I turned into this path and increased my pace.

I came shortly to pause, chilled even though the sun was shining. For at the end of the mossy trail there was no cabin; but a cleared plot of ground adorned with aged mounds and rough-hewn crosses! Rocks were scattered profusely over the mounds and, I guessed, had been placed to foil the creatures which otherwise would have despoiled the bodies resting there. There was a great hangover of the cliff wall, bulging out over the little graveyard, and from the overhang came a steady drip of moisture. Slimy water lay motionless in a pool in the center of the plot. Mossy green were the stones. Mudpuppies scurried into the deeps as I stopped and stared, turning the water to a pool of slime.

How uneasy I felt in this place! Why had such a remote location been chosen as a cemetery, hidden away here from the brightness of God's sunshine? Nothing but shadow-filled silence, except for the dripping of the water from the overhang.

I hurried back to the stream-bed and continued on my way.

Another hour passed, during which, my body racked with continual coughing, I suffered the torments of the damned. Those red dots were dancing before my eyes again, and nothing looked natural to me. The sunning snakes in the shale seemed to waver grotesquely—twisting, writhing, coiling. Here, on the cliff, was a row of ponderous palisades; but they seemed to be ever buckling and bending, as though shaken by an earthquake.

Then, far ahead, I saw the rock at the entrance. With a sob of joy I began to run—only to stop when I reached the pile, with a cry of hopelessness and despair. For the rock, unscalable even to one who possessed the strength to climb, now filled the coulee from lip to lip, while on my side of the pile there nestled a little lake, clear and pellucid, into which I could look, straight down, for what I guessed must have been all of twenty feet!

Some great shifting of the walls, during the night, had blocked the entrance, entombing me in Steamboat Coulee with all its nameless horrors!

There was no one to see me, so I flung myself down at the edge of the pool and wept weakly, bemoaning my terrible fate.

After a time I regained control of my frayed nerves, arose to my knees and bathed my throbbing temples. Sometime, somehow, I reasoned, Plone would find a way to reach me. There was nothing to do now but return and search again for my cabin. Plone had said that Hildreth would bring supplies to me—and I felt that they would know how to get in by some other way. They had lived in the coulee and should know their way about.

Wearily I began the return march. It never occurred to me to note that the sun went ahead of me on its journey into the west. I can only blame my physical condition for not noting this. Had I done so I would have realized at once that I had gone in the wrong direction, and that straight ahead of me lay freedom. I had gone to the head of the coulee, straight in from Steamboat Rock, and when I found the coulee blocked at the end had thought the entrance closed against me.

But I did not note the sun.

I strode wearily on, and found the cabin with ridiculous ease.

Inside, awaiting my coming, sat Hildreth, the wife of Plone! She said nothing when I opened the door, just sat on the only chair in the house and looked at me. I spoke to her, thanking her for the sack of provisions which I saw on the rickety shelf on the wall beyond the door. Still she said nothing. Just stared at me, unblinking.

I asked her about leaving this place and she shook her head, as though she did not catch my meaning.

"For God's sake, Hildreth!" I cried. "Can't you speak?"

For it had come to me that I had never heard her speak. When I had first entered the farmhouse she had placed a meal for me, and had bidden me eat of it. But I remembered now that she had done so by gestures with her hands.

In answer now to my question she opened her mouth and pointed into it with her forefinger. Hildreth, the wife of Plone, had no tongue!

Did you ever hear a tongueless person try to speak? It is terrible. For after this all-meaning gesture there came a raucous croak from the mouth of Hildreth—wordless, gurgling, altogether meaningless.

I understood no word; but the eyes of the woman, strangely glowing now, were eloquent. She pointed toward the door, trying to warn me of something, and stamped her foot impatiently when I did not understand. I saw her foot move as she stamped it—but failed to notice at the time that the contact of her foot with the board floor made no noise! Later I remembered it.

When I shook my head she arose from her chair and strode to the door, flinging it wide. Then she pointed up the coulee in the direction I had entered originally. Again that raucous croak, still meaningless. Once more I shook my head.

Was there something by the entrance that menaced me? I was filled with dread of the unknown, wished with all my soul that I could understand what this woman was trying to say to me.

I stepped back, to search about the place for paper, so that, with the aid of a pencil which I possessed, she might write what she had to tell me. I found it and turned back to the woman, who had watched me gravely while I searched. Noting the paper she shook her head, telling me mutely that she could not write.

Then Plone, his face as dark as a thundercloud, stood in the doorway! To me he paid no attention. His eyes, glowering below heavy brows, burned as he stared at the woman. In her eyes I could read fright unutterable. She gave one frightened croak and turned to flee. But she could not go far, for she fled toward the bare wall opposite the open door. Plone leaped after her, and when I jumped between them, he flung me to the floor, where I bumped my head and lay stunned for a moment.

In that horrifying instant I realized why the murderer looked familiar last night. It was Plone! I half rose and whirled around to see what aid I could offer Hildreth. But they had vanished just like Reuben had the night before.

Trembling in every fiber of my being I strode to the back wall and ran my hand over the rough logs. They were as solid, almost, as the day the cabin had been built. To me this was a great relief. I was beginning to fear that I had stumbled into a land of wraiths and shadows or was hallucinating and I should not have been surprised if the logs had also proved to be things of shadow-substance, letting me through to stand amazed upon the shell-rock behind the cabin.

But here was one place in the coulee of shadows that was real.

I went to the door, locked and barred it. Then I returned and lighted the stove to disperse the unnatural chill that hovered in the room. After this I searched out my food and wolfed some of it ravenously. Another thought came to me: if Reuben, Plone and Hildreth were nothing but fantasies, where had I procured this food, which was real enough and well cooked? Somewhere in my adventures since being

kicked off the train at Palisades there must be a great gap I
had tried to fill in. What had happened, really, in that blank
space?

Having eaten, I stepped to the door and looked out. If I
again went forth into the stream-bed in any attempt to get
out of the coulee, I should never reach it before dark. What
would it mean to my tired reason to be caught in the open,
in the midst of this coulee, for another terrible night? I could
not do it.

Again I secured the door. Nothing *real* could get in to
bother me—and even now I reasoned myself out of positive
belief in ghosts. The hallucinations which had so terrified
me had undoubtedly been born of my sickness.

Convinced of this at last I lay down on the rough cot and
went to sleep.

IV

When I awoke suddenly in the night, the fire had burned
very low and a heavy chill possessed the cabin. I had a
feeling that I was not the only occupant of my abode; but,
striving to pierce the gloom in the cabin's corners, I could
see nothing.

In the farthest corner I saw the pale, ghostly lineaments of
a woman! Just the face, shimmering there in the gloom,
oddly, but neither body nor substance. The face of Hildreth,
wife of Plone! Then her hands, no arms visible, came up
before her face and began to gesture. Her mouth opened and
I imagined I again heard that raucous croak of the tongueless. Again her eyes were eloquent, mutely giving a warning
which I could not understand.

Fear seizing me in its terrible grip, I leaped from my bed
and threw wood on the fire, hoping to dispel this silent
shadow. When the light flared up the head shimmered
swiftly and began to fade away; but not before I saw a pair
of hands come forth from nowhere and fasten themselves
below that head, about where the neck should have been.
Hands that were gnarled and calloused from toil on an

unproductive farm—the work-torn hands of the killer, Plone!

Then the weird picture vanished and I was alone with my fantasies.

I had scarcely returned to my seat on the bed, sitting well back against the wall so that my back was against something solid, when the wailing of lost babies broke out again on the talus slopes outside. I had expected this to happen after nightfall; but the reality left me weak and shivering, even though I knew that the animals that uttered the mournful wails were flesh and blood. The wailing of bobcats, no matter how often it is heard, always brings a chill that is hard to reason away. Nature certainly prepared weird natural protections for some of her creatures!

Then the wailing stopped suddenly—short off. And the silence was more nerve-devastating than the eery wailing.

Nothing for many minutes. Then the rattle of sliding talus, as the shale glided into the underbrush.

This stopped, and a terrible silence pressed down upon me.

Then my cabin shook with the force of the wind that suddenly swooped through the coulee. It rattled through the eaves, shook the door on its hinges, while the patter-patter on the roof told me of showers of sand which the wind had scooped up from the bed of the dry stream. The wind was terrific, I thought; but ever it increased in power and violence.

The patter on the roof and the rattle in the eaves began to take on a new significance; for the patter sounded like the scamper of baby feet above my head, while the wailing about the eaves sounded like the screaming of people who are tongueless. The door bellied inward against the chair back as though many hands were pressed against it from outside, seeking entrance. Yet I knew that there was no one outside.

Then, faint and feeble through the roaring of the wind, I caught that eery cry in the night. It was the despairing voice of a woman, and she was calling aloud, hopelessly, for help! I shivered and tried not to hear. But the cry came again, farther now, as though the woman was being dragged away from me.

In God's name! What woman could be abroad in such a night?

The cry again. No man, fear the shadows as he might, could ignore that pitiful plea and call himself a man again.

I gritted my teeth and ran to the door, flinging it open. A veritable sea of flying sand swept past me; but through the increased roar came plainly that cry for help. I left the door open this time, so that the light would stream out and guide my return.

On the bank of the dry stream I stopped.

And before and below me I saw Hildreth, wife of Plone, fighting for her very life with her brutal husband! She was groveling on her knees at his feet—his hands were about her throat. As she begged for mercy I could understand her words. She had a tongue, after all! Then Plone, holding Hildreth with his left hand, raised his right and, crooking it like a fearful talon, poised it above the face of Hildreth.

He did a ghastly, unbelievable thing. I can not tell it. But when his hand came away her words were meaningless, gurgling—the raucous croaking of a person who had no tongue.

Frenzied with horror at what Plone had done, I leaped into the dry stream and ran forward—to bring up short in the middle of the sandy open space, staring aghast.

For I was all alone—no Hildreth, the tongueless—no Plone with the calloused hands! Once more a hallucination had betrayed me.

Screaming in fear I sprang out of the stream-bed and rushed toward the cabin, only to dart off the trail as I saw another man walk out of the cabin's light. He was dressed very much as had been the man whom I had seen fall before the murderous rifle of Plone last night. But he was older, stooped slightly under the weight of years. I heard him sigh softly, as a man sighs whose stomach is comfortably filled with food.

He walked toward the stream-bed, following the path through the thicket.

He had passed me when a malevolently leering figure followed him from the cabin—and that figure was Reuben, the feral son of Plone! Reuben, as his father had stalked that other unfortunate, stalked the aged man who preceded him. The latter passed a clump of service berry bushes and paused on the lip of the dry stream. He had scarcely halted when out of the clump of service berries stepped Plone himself, moving stealthily, like a cat that stalks a helpless, unsuspecting bird.

The older man half turned as though he heard some slight sound, when Plone, with the silent fury of the bobcat making a kill, leaped bodily upon his back and bore him to the ground, where the two of them, fighting and clawing, rolled into the sand below.

Reuben began to run when his father closed with the stranger, and I was right at his heels when he leaped over the edge to stop beside the silent combatants. Then he bent to assist his father.

The end was speedy. For what chance has an aged man, taken by surprise, against two determined killers? They slew him there in the sand, while I, my limbs inert because of my fright, looked on, horror holding me mute when I would have screamed aloud.

Their bloody purpose accomplished, Reuben and Plone methodically began to turn the pockets of the dead man inside out. The contents of these they divided between themselves. This finished, in silence, the murderers, taking each an arm of the dead man, began to drag the body up the sandy stretch toward the end of the coulee—the closed end.

Still I stood, as one transfixed.

Then I became conscious of a low, heart-breaking sobbing at my side. Turning, I saw the figure of Hildreth standing there, tragedy easily readable in her eyes, wringing her hands as her eyes followed the figures of her husband and her son. Then she extended her hands in a pleading gesture, calling the two who dragged the body.

She began to follow them along the stream-bed, dodging from thicket to thicket on the bank as though she screened her movements from Plone and Reuben. I watched her until her wraithlike form blended with the shadows in the thickets and disappeared from view.

As I watched her go, and saw the figures of Plone and Reuben passing around a sharp bend in the dry stream, there came back to my memory a mental picture of a graveyard located in perpetual shadow, adorned with rotting crosses upon which no names were written. Slimy stones at the edge of a muddy pool populated by serpentine mudpuppies.

Turning then, I hurried back to the cabin, whose door remained open—to pause aghast at the threshold, staring into the interior.

At a table in the center of the room—a table loaded with things to eat, fresh and steaming from the stove—sat another stranger, this time a man dressed after the manner of city folk. His clothing bespoke wealth and refinement, while his manner of eating told that he was accustomed to choicer food than that of which necessity now compelled him to partake. Daintily he picked over the viands, sorting judiciously, while near the stove stood Hildreth, her eyes wide with fright and wordless entreaty.

Reuben stood in a darkened corner and his eyes never left the figure of the stranger at the table. As he stared at this one I saw his tongue come forth from his mouth and describe a circle, moistening his lips, anticipatorily, like a cat that watches a saucer of cream.

Plone, too, was silently watching, standing just inside the door, with his back toward me. As I watched him he moved slightly, edging toward the table.

Then Plone was upon the stranger, a carving knife, snatched from the table, in his hand.

But why continue? I had seen this same scene, slightly varied, but a few minutes before, in the sand of the dry stream.

Crouching there in the darkness I guessed what the wraith of Hildreth had tried to tell me. Going back in my memory I watched her lips move again. And as they moved I read the words she would have uttered. As plain as though she had spoken I now understood the warning.

"As you value the life God has given you—*do not stay in this cabin tonight!*"

The cabin was a trap! The ghosts of Reuben and Plone—for surely they must be ghosts—knew where it was, and could shimmer through its walls, to slay me at their will. By chance, I had escaped being murdered by going outside both nights. But until I escaped the coulee, I could be found and killed.

For hours I trembled in the shadows, afraid to move, while Reuben and Plone carried forward their ghastly work. Many times during those hours did I see them make their kill. Ever it was Plone who commanded, ever it was Reuben who stood at his father's side to assist. Ever it was Hildreth who raised her hand or her voice in protest.

Then, suddenly, she was back in the cabin with Reuben and Plone. She told the latter something, gesturing vehemently as she spoke. These gestures were simple, easy to understand. For she pointed back down the coulee, in the direction of Steamboat Rock. Somehow I knew that what she tried to tell him was that she had gone forth and told the authorities what he and Reuben had done. Plone's face became black with wrath. Reuben's turned to the pasty gray of fear which is unbounded. Both sprang to the door and stared down the coulee. Then Plone leaped back to Hildreth, striking her in the face with his fist. She fell to the floor, groveling on her knees at his feet. He dragged her forth into the trail, along it to the stream-bed and, as I crept toward the edge, repeated that terrible scene I had witnessed once before.

Reuben advanced to the lip of the dry stream as Plone fought with Reuben's mother. He paid them no heed, however, but shaded his eyes with his hands as he gazed into the west in the direction of Steamboat Rock. Then he gestured excitedly to Plone, pointing down the coulee.

Plone was all activity at once. With Reuben at his heels and Hildreth stumbling farther in the rear, they rushed to the cabin and began to throw rough packs together, one each for Reuben and Plone.

But in the midst of their activities they paused and stared

at the doorway where I stood transfixed. Then, slowly, though no one stood there except myself, they raised their hands above their heads, while Hildreth crouched in a corner, wild-eyed, whimpering.

Plone and Reuben suddenly lurched toward me, haltingly, as though propelled by invisible hands. Their hands were at their sides now as though bound there securely by ropes. Outside they came, walking oddly with their hands still at their sides.

They stopped beneath a tree which had one bare limb, high up from the ground—a strong limb, white as a ghost in the moonlight. Reuben and Plone looked upward at this limb, and both their faces were gray. Hildreth came out and stood nearby, also looking up, wringing her hands, grief marring her face that might once have been beautiful.

Reuben and Plone looked at each other and nodded. Then they looked mutely at Hildreth, as though asking her forgiveness. After this they turned and nodded toward no one that I could see, as though they gestured to unseen hangmen.

I cried aloud, even though I had foreseen what was to come, as both Plone and Reuben sprang straight into the air to an unbelievable height, to pause midway to that bare limb; their necks twisted at odd angles, their bodies writhing grotesquely.

I watched until the writhing stopped. Until the bodies merely swayed, as though played upon by vagrant breezes sweeping in from the sandy dry stream.

Then, for the last time, I heard the piercing, wordless shriek of a tongueless woman. I swerved to look for Hildreth, and saw a misty, wraithlike shadow disappear among the willows, flashing swiftly out of sight up the coulee.

Hildreth had gone, and I was alone, swaying weakly, nauseated, staring crazily up to two bodies which oscillated to and fro as though played upon by vagrant breezes.

Then the bodies faded slowly away as my knees began to buckle under me. I sank to the ground before the cabin, and darkness descended once more.

When I regained consciousness I opened my eyes, expecting to see those swaying bodies in the air above me. There were no bodies. Then I noted that my wrists were close together, held in place by manacles of shining steel.

From the cabin behind me came the sound of voices—voices of men who talked as they ate—noisily. Behind the cabin I could hear the impatient stamping of horses.

I lay there dully, trying to understand it all.

Then two men came out of the cabin toward me. One of them chewed busily upon a bit of wood in lieu of a toothpick. Upon the mottled vest of this one glistened a star, emblem of the sheriff. The second man I knew to be his deputy.

"He's awake, I see, Al," said the first man as he looked at me.

"So I see," said the man addressed as Al.

Then the sheriff bent over me.

"Ready to talk, young man?" he demanded.

It must have mystified this one greatly when I leaped suddenly to my feet and ran my hands over him swiftly. How could they guess what it meant to me to learn that these two were flesh and blood?

"Thank God!" I cried. Then I began to tremble so violently that the man called Al, perforce, supported me with a burly arm about my shoulders. As he did so his eyes met those of the sheriff and a meaningful glance passed between them.

The sheriff passed around the cabin, returning almost at once with three horses, saddled and bridled for the trail. The third horse was for me. Weakly, aided by Al, I mounted.

Then we clambered down into the dry stream and started toward Steamboat Rock.

I found my voice.

"For what am I wanted, sheriff?" I asked.

"For burglarious entry, son," he replied, not unkindly. "You went into a house in Palisades, while the owner and his wife were working in the fields, and stole every bit of food you could lay your hands on. There's no use denying it, for we found the sack you brought it away in, right in that there cabin!''

"But Hildreth, the wife of Plone, gave me that food!" I cried. "I didn't steal it!"

"Hildreth? Plone?" The sheriff fairly shouted the two names.

Then he turned and stared at his deputy—again that meaningful exchange of glances. The sheriff regained control of himself.

"This Hildreth and Plone," he began, hesitating strangely, "did they have a son, a half-grown boy?"

"Yes! Yes!" I cried eagerly. "The boy's name was Reuben! He led me into Steamboat Coulee!"

Then I told them my story, from beginning to end, sparing none of the unbelievable details. When I had finished, the two of them turned in their saddles and looked back into the coulee, toward the now invisible log cabin we had left behind. The deputy shook his head, muttering, while the sheriff removed his hat and scratched his poll. He spat judiciously into the sand of the dry stream before he spoke.

"Son," he said finally, "if I didn't know you was a stranger here I would swear that you was crazy as a loon. There ain't a darn thing real that you saw or heard, except the rattlesnakes and the bobcats!"

I interrupted him eagerly.

"But what about Plone, Hildreth and Reuben?"

"Plone and Reuben," he replied, "were hanged fifteen years ago! Right beside that cabin where we found you! Hildreth went crazy and ran away into the coulee. She was never seen again."

I waited, breathless, for the sheriff to continue.

"Plone and Reuben," he went on, "were the real bogy men of this coulee in the early days. They lived in that log cabin. Reuben used to lure strangers in there, where the two of them murdered the wanderers and robbed their dead bodies, burying them afterward in a gruesome graveyard farther inside Steamboat Coulee. Hildreth, so the story goes, tried to prevent these murders; but was unable to do so.

Finally she reported to the pioneer authorities—and Plone cut her tongue out as punishment for the betrayal. God knows how many unsuspecting travelers the two made away with before they were found out and strung up without trial!''

"But how about Plone's farm in Moses Coulee, outside Steamboat, and the farmhouse where I met the family?"

"It's mine," replied the sheriff. "There's never been a house on it to my knowledge. I foreclosed on it for the taxes, and the blasted land is so poor that even the rattlesnakes starve while they are crawling across it!"

"But I saw it as plainly as I see you!"

"But you're a sick man, ain't you? You never went near the place where you say the house was. We followed your footprints, and they left the main road at the foot of the Three Devils, from which they went straight as a die, to the mouth of Steamboat Coulee! They was easy to follow, and if I hadn't had another case on I'd have picked you up before you ever could have reached the cabin!"

Would to God that he had! It would have saved me many a weird and terrifying nightmare in the nights which have followed.

There the matter ended—seemingly. The sheriff, not a bad fellow at all, put me in the way of work which, keeping me much in the open beneath God's purifying sunshine, is slowly but surely mending my ravished lungs. After a while, there will come a day when I shall no longer be a sick man.

But ever so often, I raise my eyes from my work, allowing them to wander, against my will, in the direction of that shadow against the walls of Moses Coulee—that shadow out of which seems slowly to float the stony likeness of a steamboat under reduced power. And I wonder.

Born on a farm in Washington State in 1898, Arthur J. Burks served in the Marines in World War I. During the 1930s, he began writing for the pulp magazines, becoming so prolific that he became one of the fabulous ''million-

words-a-year writers.'' His novelette, Salute for Sunny, *was the most popular story* Sky Fighters *ever ran. His stories collected in* Black Medicine *(1966) are based on his experiences in the Caribbean as an aide-de-camp to Gen. Smedley Butler. He died in 1974.*

Karl had to take care of his mother—no matter what happened to him.

9

He Walked by Day
Julius Long

Friedenburg, Ohio, sleeps between the muddy waters of the Miami River and the trusty track of a little-used spur of the Big Four. It suddenly became important to us because of its strategic position. It bisected a road which we were to surface with tar. The materials were to come by way of the spur and to be unloaded at the tiny yard.

We began work on a Monday morning. I was watching the tar distributor while it pumped tar from the car, when I felt a tap upon my back. I turned about, and when I beheld the individual who had tapped me, I actually jumped.

I have never, before or since, encountered such a singular figure. He was at least seven feet tall, and he seemed even taller than that because of the uncommon slenderness of his frame. He looked as if he had never been warmed by the rays of the sun, but confined all his life in a dank and dismal cellar. I concluded that he had been the prey of some insidious, etiolating disease. Certainly, I thought, nothing else could account for his ashen complexion. It seemed that not blood, but shadows passed through his veins.

"Do you want to see me?" I asked.

"Are you the road feller?"

"Yes."

"I want a job. My mother's sick. I have her to keep. Won't you please give me a job?"

We really didn't need another man, but I was interested in this pallid giant with his staring, gray eyes. I called to Juggy, my foreman.

"Do you think we can find a place for this fellow?" I asked.

Juggy stared incredulously. "He looks like he'd break in two."

"I'm stronger'n anyone," said the youth.

He looked about, and his eyes fell on the Mack, which had just been loaded with six tons of gravel. He walked over to it, reached down and seized the hub of a front wheel. To our utter amazement, the wheel was slowly lifted from the ground. When it was raised to a height of eight or nine inches, the youth looked inquiringly in our direction. We must have appeared sufficiently awed, for he dropped the wheel with an abruptness that evoked a yell from the driver, who thought his tire would blow out.

"We can certainly use this fellow," I said, and Juggy agreed.

"What's your name, Shadow?" he demanded.

"Karl Rand," said the boy but "Shadow" stuck to him, as far as the crew was concerned.

We put him to work at once, and he slaved all morning, accomplishing tasks that we ordinarily assigned two or three men to do.

We were on the road at lunchtime, some miles from Friedenburg. I recalled that Shadow had not brought his lunch.

"You can take mine," I said. "I'll drive in to the village and eat."

"I never eat none," was Shadow's astonishing remark.

"You never eat!" The crew had heard his assertion, and there was an amused crowd about him at once. I fancied that he was pleased to have an audience.

"No, I never eat," he repeated. "You see"—he lowered his voice—"you see, I'm a ghost!"

We exchanged glances. So Shadow was psychopathic. We shrugged our shoulders.

"Whose ghost are you?" gibed Juggy. "Napoleon's?"

"Oh, no. I'm my own ghost. You see, I'm dead."

"Ah!" This was all Juggy could say. For once, the arch-kidder was nonplussed.

"That's why I'm so strong," added Shadow.

"How long have you been dead?" I asked.

"Six years. I was fifteen years old then."

"Tell us how it happened. Did you die a natural death, or were you killed trying to lift a fast freight off the track?" This question was asked by Juggy, who was slowly recovering.

"It was in the cave," answered Shadow solemnly. "I slipped and fell over a bank. I cracked my head on the floor. I've been a ghost ever since."

"Then why do you walk by day instead of by night?"

"I got to keep my mother."

Shadow looked so sincere, so pathetic when he made this answer, that we left off teasing him. I tried to make him eat my lunch, but he would have none of it. I expected to see him collapse that afternoon, but he worked steadily and showed no sign of tiring. We didn't know what to make of him. I confess that I was a little afraid in his presence. After all, a madman with almost superhuman strength is a dangerous character. But Shadow seemed perfectly harmless and docile.

When we had returned to our boarding-house that night, we plied our landlord with questions about Karl Rand. He drew himself up authoritatively, and lectured for some minutes upon Shadow's idiosyncrasies.

"The boy first started telling that story about six years ago," he said. "He never was right in his head, and nobody paid much attention to him at first. He said he'd fallen and busted his head in a cave, but everybody knows they ain't no caves hereabouts. I don't know what put that idea in his head. But Karl's stuck to it ever since, and I 'spect they's lots of folks round Friedenburg that's growed to believe him—more'n admits they do.''

That evening, I patronized the village barber shop, and was careful to introduce Karl's name into the conversation. ''All I can say is,'' said the barber solemnly, ''that his hair ain't growed any in the last six years, and they was nary a whisker on his chin. No, sir, nary a whisker on his chin.''

This did not strike me as so tremendously odd, for I had previously heard of cases of such arrested growth. However, I went to sleep that night thinking about Shadow.

The next morning, the strange youth appeared on time and rode with the crew to the job.

''Did you eat well?'' Juggy asked him.

Shadow shook his head. ''I never eat none.''

The crew half believed him.

Early in the morning, Steve Bradshaw, the nozzle man on the tar distributor, burned his hand badly. I hurried him in to see the village doctor. When he had dressed Steve's hand, I took advantage of my opportunity and made inquiries about Shadow.

''Karl's got me stumped,'' said the country practitioner. ''I confess I can't understand it. Of course, he won't let me get close enough to him to look at him, but it don't take an examination to tell there's something abnormal about him.''

''I wonder what could have given him the idea that he's his own ghost,'' I said.

''I'm not sure, but I think what put it in his head was the things people used to say to him when he was a kid. He always looked like a ghost, and everybody kidded him about it. I kind of think that's what gave him the notion.''

''Has he changed at all in the last six years?''

''Not a bit. He was as tall six years ago as he is today. I think that his abnormal growth might have had something to do with the stunting of his mind. But I don't know for sure.''

I had to take Steve's place on the tar distributor during the next four days, and I watched Shadow pretty closely. He never ate any lunch, but he would sit with us while we devoured ours. Juggy could not resist the temptation to joke at his expense.

"There was a ghost back in my home town," Juggy once told him. "Mary Jenkens was an awful pretty woman when she was living, and when she was a girl, every fellow in town wanted to marry her. Jim Jenkens finally led her down the aisle, and we was all jealous—especially Joe Garver. He was broke up awful. Mary hadn't no more'n come back from the Falls when Joe was trying to make up to her. She wouldn't have nothing to do with him. Joe was hurt bad.

"A year after she was married, Mary took sick and died. Jim Jenkens was awful put out about it. He didn't act right from then on. He got to imagining things. He got suspicious of Joe.

"'What you got to worry about?' people would ask him. 'Mary's dead. There can't no harm come to her now.'

"But Jim didn't feel that way. Joe heard about it, and he got to teasing Jim.

"'I was out with Mary's ghost last night,' he would say. And Jim got to believing him. One night, he lays low for Joe and shoots him with both barrels. 'He was goin' to meet my wife!' Jim told the judge."

"Did they give him the chair?" I asked.

"No, they gave him life in the state hospital."

Shadow remained impervious to Juggy's yarns, which were told for his special benefit. During this time, I noticed something decidedly strange about the boy, but I kept my own counsel. After all, a contractor can not keep the respect of his men if he appears too credulous.

One day Juggy voiced my suspicions for me. "You know," he said, "I never saw that kid sweat. It's uncanny. It's ninety in the shade today, and Shadow ain't got a drop of perspiration on his face. Look at his shirt. Dry as if he'd just put it on."

Everyone in the crew noticed this. I think we all became uneasy in Shadow's presence.

One morning he didn't show up for work. We waited a

few minutes and left without him. When the trucks came in with their second load of gravel, the drivers told us that Shadow's mother had died during the night. This news cast a gloom over the crew. We all sympathized with the youth.

"I wish I hadn't kidded him," said Juggy.

We all put in an appearance that evening at Shadow's little cottage, and I think he was tremendously gratified. "I won't be working no more," he told me. "There ain't no need for me now."

I couldn't afford to lay off the crew for the funeral, but I did go myself. I even accompanied Shadow to the cemetery.

We watched while the grave was being filled. There were many others there, for one of the chief delights in a rural community is to see how the mourners "take on" at a funeral. Moreover, their interest in Karl Rand was deeper. He had said he was going back to his cave, that he would never again walk by day. The villagers, as well as myself, wanted to see what would happen.

When the grave was filled, Shadow turned to me, eyed me pathetically a moment, then walked from the grave. Silently, we watched him set out across the field. Two mischievous boys disobeyed the entreaties of their parents, and set out after him.

They returned to the village an hour later with a strange and incredible story. They had seen Karl disappear into the ground. The earth had literally swallowed him up. The youngsters were terribly frightened. It was thought that Karl had done something to scare them, and their imaginations had got the better of them.

But the next day they were asked to lead a group of the more curious to the spot where Karl had vanished. He had not returned, and they were worried.

In a ravine two miles from the village, the party discovered a small but penetrable entrance to a cave. Its existence had never been dreamed of by the farmer who owned the land. (He has since then opened it up for tourists, and it is known as Ghost Cave.)

Someone in the party had thoughtfully brought an electric searchlight, and the party squeezed its way into the cave.

Exploration revealed a labyrinth of caverns of exquisite beauty. But the explorers were oblivious to the esthetics of the cave; they thought only of Karl and his weird story.

After circuitous ramblings, they came to a sudden drop in the floor. At the base of this precipice they beheld a skeleton.

The coroner and the sheriff were duly summoned. The sheriff invited me to accompany him.

I regret that I cannot describe the gruesome, awesome feeling that came over me as I made my way through those caverns. Within their chambers the human voice is given a peculiar, sepulchral sound. But perhaps it was the knowledge of Karl's bizarre story, his unaccountable disappearance that inspired me with such awe, such thoughts.

The skeleton gave me a shock, for it was a skeleton of a man *seven feet tall!* There was no mistake about this; the coroner was positive.

The skull had been fractured, apparently by a fall over the bank. It was I who discovered the hat nearby. It was rotted with decay, but in the leather band were plainly discernible the crudely penned initials, ''K.R.''

I felt suddenly weak. The sheriff noticed my nervousness. ''What's the matter, have you seen a ghost?''

I laughed nervously and affected nonchalance. With the best off-hand manner I could command, I told him of Karl Rand. He was not impressed.

''You don't—?'' He did not wish to insult my intelligence by finishing his question.

At this moment, the coroner looked up and commented: ''This skeleton has been here about six years, I'd say.''

I was not courageous enough to acknowledge my suspicions, but the villagers were outspoken. The skeleton, they declared, was that of Karl Rand. The coroner and the sheriff were incredulous, but, politicians both, they displayed some sympathy with this view.

My friend, the sheriff, discussed the matter privately with me some days later. His theory was that Karl had discovered the cave, wandered inside and come upon the corpse of some unfortunate who had preceded him. He had been so excited by his discovery that his hat had fallen down beside the body. Later, aided by the remarks of the villagers about his ghostliness, he had fashioned his own legend.

This, of course, may be true. But the people of Friedenburg are not convinced by this explanation, and neither am I. For the identity of the skeleton has never been determined, and Karl Rand has never since been seen to walk by day.

Lawyer Julius Long took to writing fiction to supplement his income during the Great Depression. Until his death in 1955 at the age of forty-eight, he was a steady contributor of more than two hundred short stories. Nearly all his work was in the detective genre. "He Walked by Day" first appeared in Weird Tales.

*John fell in love with the farmer's daughter, even though
everyone told him that the farmhouse and the family who
lived there had been destroyed years ago.*

10

The Phantom Farmhouse

Seabury Quinn

I had been at the New Briarcliff Sanitarium nearly three
weeks before I actually saw the house.

Every morning, as I lay abed after the nurse had taken my
temperature, I wondered what was beyond the copse of fir
and spruce at the turn of the road. The picture seemed
incomplete without chimneys rising among the evergreens.
I thought about it so much I finally convinced myself there
really was a house in the wood. A house where people lived
and worked and were happy.

All during the long, trying days when I was learning to
navigate a wheelchair, I used to picture the house and the
people who lived in it. There would be a father, I was sure;
a stout, good-natured father, somewhat bald, who sat on the
porch and smoked a cob pipe in the evening. And there was
a mother, too; a waistless, plaid-skirted mother with hair
smoothly parted over her forehead, who sat beside the father

as he rocked and smoked, and who had a brown work-basket in her lap. She spread the stocking feet over her outstretched fingers and her vigilant needle spied out and closed every hole with a cunning no mechanical loom could rival.

Then there was a daughter. I was a little hazy in my conception of her; but I knew she was tall and slender as a hazel wand, and that her eyes were blue and wide and sympathetic.

Picturing the house and its people became a favorite pastime with me during the time I was acquiring the art of walking all over again. By the time I was able to trust my legs on the road I felt I knew my way to my vision-friends' home as well as I knew the byways of my own parish; though I had as yet not set foot outside the sanitarium.

Oddly enough, I chose the evening for my first long stroll. It was unusually warm for September in Maine, and some of the sturdier of the convalescents had been playing tennis during the afternoon. After dinner they sat on the veranda, comparing notes on their respective cases of influenza, or matching experiences in appendicitis operations.

After building the house bit by bit from my imagination, as a child pieces together a picture puzzle, I should have been bitterly disappointed if the woods had proved empty; yet when I reached the turn of the road and found my dream house a reality, I was almost afraid. Bit for bit and part for part, it was as I had visualized it.

A long, rambling, comfortable-looking farmhouse it was, with a wide porch screened by vines, and a whitewashed picket fence about the little clearing before it. There was a tumbledown gate in the fence, one of the kind that is held shut with a weighted chain. Looking closely, I saw the weight was a disused ploughshare. Leading from gate to porch was a path of flat stones, laid unevenly in the short grass and bordered with a double row of clam shells. A lamp burned in the front room, sending out cheerful golden rays to meet the silver moonlight.

A strange, eerie sensation came over me as I stood there.

Somehow, I felt I had seen that house before; many, many times before; yet I had never been in that part of Maine till I came to Briarcliff, nor had anyone ever described the place to me. Indeed, except for my idle dreams, I had had no intimation that there was a house in those pines at all.

"Who lives in the house at the turn of the road?" I asked the fat man who roomed next to me.

He looked at me as blankly as if I had addressed him in Choctaw, then countered, "What road?"

"Why, the south road," I explained. "I mean the house in the pines—just beyond the curve, you know."

If such a thing had not been obviously absurd, I should have thought he looked frightened at my answer. Certainly his already prominent eyes started a bit further from his face.

"Nobody lives there," he assured me. "Nobody's lived there for years. There isn't any house there."

I became angry. What right had this fellow to make my civil question the occasion for an ill-timed jest? "As you please," I replied. "Perhaps there isn't any house there for you; but I saw one there last night."

"My God!" he ejaculated, and hurried away as if I'd just told him I was infected with smallpox.

Later in the day I overheard a snatch of conversation between him and one of his acquaintances in the lounge.

"I tell you it's so," he was saying with great earnestness. "I thought it was a lot of poppycock, myself; but that clergyman saw it last night. I'm going to pack my traps and get back to the city, and not waste any time about it, either."

"Rats!" his companion scoffed. "He must have been stringing you."

Turning to light a cigar, he caught sight of me. "Say, Mr. Weatherby," he called, "you didn't mean to tell my friend here that you really saw a house down by those pines last night, did you?"

"I certainly did," I answered, "and I tell you, too. There's nothing unusual about it, is there?"

"Is there!" he repeated. "*Is* there? Say, what'd it look like?"

I described it to him as well as I could, and his eyes grew as wide as those of a child hearing the story of Bluebeard.

"Well, I'll be a Chinaman's uncle!" he declared as I finished. "I sure will!"

"See here," I demanded. "What's all the mystery about that farmhouse? Why shouldn't I see it? It's there to be seen isn't it?"

He gulped once or twice, as if there were something hot in his mouth, before he answered.

"Look here, Mr. Weatherby, I'm telling you this for your own good. You'd better stay in nights; and you'd better stay away from those pines in particular."

Nonplussed at this unsolicited advice, I was about to ask an explanation, when I detected the after-tang of whisky on his breath. I understood, then. I was being made the butt of a drunken joke by a pair of race course followers.

"I'm very much obliged, I'm sure," I replied with dignity, "but if you don't mind, I'll choose my own comings and goings."

"Oh, go as far as you like"—he waved his arms wide in token of my complete free-agency—"go as far as you like. I'm going to New York."

And he did. The pair of them left the sanitarium that afternoon.

A slight recurrence of my illness held me housebound for several days after my conversation with the two sportively inclined gentlemen, and the next time I ventured out at night the moon had waxed to the full, pouring a flood of light upon the earth that rivaled midday. The minutest objects were as readily distinguished as they would have been before sunset; in fact, I remember comparing the evening to a silver-plated noon.

As I trudged along the road to the pine copse I was busy formulating plans for intruding into the family circle at the farmhouse; devising all manner of pious frauds by which to scrape acquaintance.

"Shall I feign having lost my way, and inquire direction to the sanitarium; or shall I ask if some mythical acquaintance, a John Squires, for instance, lives there?" I asked myself as I neared the turn of the road.

Fortunately for my conscience, all these subterfuges were unnecessary, for as I neared the whitewashed fence, a girl left the porch and walked quickly to the gate, where she stood gazing pensively along the moonlit road. It was almost as if she were coming to meet me, I thought, as I slacked my pace and assumed an air of deliberate casualness.

Almost abreast of her, I lessened my pace still more, and looked directly at her. Then I knew why my conception of the girl who lived in that house had been misty and indistinct. For the same reason the venerable John had faltered in his description of the New Jerusalem until his vision in the Isle of Patmos.

From the smoothly parted hair above her wide, forget-me-not eyes, to the hem of her white cotton frock, she was as slender and lovely as a Rossetti saint; as wonderful to the eye as a medieval poet's vision of his lost love in paradise. Her forehead, evenly framed in the beaten bronze of her hair, was wide and high, and startlingly white, and her brows were delicately penciled as if laid on by an artist with a camel's hair brush. The eyes themselves were sweet and clear as forest pools mirroring the September sky, and lifted a little at the corners, like an Oriental's, giving her face a quaint, exotic look in the midst of these Maine woods.

So slender was her figure that the swell of her bosom was barely perceptible under the light stuff of her dress, and, as she stood immobile in the nimbus of moon rays, the undulation of the line from her shoulders to ankles was what painters call a "curve of motion."

One hand rested lightly on the gate, a hand as finely cut as a bit of Italian sculpture, and scarcely less white than the limed wood supporting it. I noticed idly that the forefinger was somewhat longer than its fellows, and that the nails were almond shaped and very pink—almost red—as if they had been rouged and brightly polished.

No man can take stock of a woman thus, even in a cursory, fleeting glimpse, without her being aware of the inspection, and in the minute my eyes drank up her beauty, our glances crossed and held.

The look she gave back was as calm and unperturbed as though I had been nonexistent; one might have thought I was an invisible wraith of the night; yet the faint suspicion of a flush quickening in her throat and cheeks told me she was neither unaware nor unappreciative of my scrutiny.

Mechanically, I raised my cap, and wholly without conscious volition, I heard my own voice asking:

"May I trouble you for a drink from your well? I'm from the sanitarium—only a few days out of bed, in fact—and I fear I've overdone myself in my walk."

A smile flitted across her rather wide lips, quick and sympathetic as a mother's response to her child's request, as she swung the gate open for me.

"Surely—" she answered, and her voice had all the sweetness of the south wind soughing through her native pines—"surely you may drink at our well, and rest yourself, too—if you wish."

She preceded me up the path, quickening her pace as she neared the house, and running nimbly up the steps to the porch. From where I stood beside the old-fashioned well, fitted with windlass and bucket, I could hear the sound of whispering voices in earnest conversation. Hers I recognized, lowered though it was, by the flutelike purling of its tones; the other two were deeper, and it seemed to me, hoarse and throaty. Somehow, odd as it seemed, there was a queer, canine note in them, dimly reminding me of the muttering of not too friendly dogs—such fractious growls I had heard while doing missionary duty in Alaska, when the savage, half-wolf malemutes were not fed promptly at the relay stations.

Her voice was a trifle higher, as if in argument, and I fancied I heard her whisper, "This one is mine, I tell you; mine. I'll brook no interference. Go to your own hunting."

An instant later there was a reluctant assenting growl from the shadow of the vines curtaining the porch, and a light laugh from the girl as she descended the steps, swinging a bright tin cup in her hand. For a second she looked at me, as she sent the bucket plunging into the stone-curbed well; then she announced, in explanation:

"We're great hunters here, you know. The season is just in, and Dad and I have the worst quarrels about whose game is whose."

She laughed in recollection of their argument, and I laughed with her. I had been quite a Nimrod as a boy, myself, and well I remembered the heated controversies as to whose charge of shot was responsible for some luckless bunny's demise.

The well was very deep, and my breath was coming fast by the time I had helped her wind the bucket-rope upon the windlass; but the water was cold as only spring-fed well water can be. As she poured it from the bucket it shone almost like foam in the moonlight, and seemed to whisper with a half-human voice, instead of gurgling as other water does when poured.

I had drunk water in nearly every quarter of the globe; but never such water as that. Cold as the breath from a glacier, limpid as visualized air, it was yet so light and tasteless in substance that only the chill in my throat and the sight of the liquid in the cup told me that I was doing more than going through the motions of drinking.

"And now, will you rest?" she invited, as I finished my third draught. "We've an extra chair on the porch for you."

Behind the screen of vines I found her father and mother seated in the rays of the big kitchen lamp. They were just as I had expected to find them: plain, homely, sincere country folk, courteous in their reception and anxious to make a sick stranger welcome. Both were stout, with the comfortable stoutness of middle age and good health; but both had surprisingly slender hands. I noticed, too, that the same characteristic of an over-long forefinger was apparent in their hands as in their daughter's, and that both their nails were trimmed to points and stained almost a brilliant red.

"My father, Mr. Squires," the girl introduced, "and my mother, Mrs. Squires."

I could not repress a start. These people bore the very name I had casually thought to use when inquiring for some imaginary person. My lucky stars had surely guided me away from that attempt to scrape an acquaintance. What a figure I should have cut if I had actually asked for Mr. Squires!

Though I was not aware of it, my curious glance must have stayed longer on their reddened nails than I had intended, for Mrs. Squires looked deprecatingly at her hands. ''We've all been turning, putting up fox grapes''— she included her husband and daughter with a comprehensive gesture. ''And the stain won't wash out; has to wear off, you know.''

I spent, perhaps, two hours with my new-found friends, talking of everything from the best methods of potato culture to the surest way of landing a nine-pound bass. All three joined in the conversation and took a lively interest in the topics under discussion. After the vapid talk of the guests at the sanitarium, I found the simple, interested discourse of these country people as stimulating as wine, and when I left them it was with a hearty promise to renew my call at an early date.

''Better wait until after dark,'' Mr. Squires warned. ''We'd be glad to see you any time; but we're so busy these fall days, we haven't much time for company.''

I took the broad hint in the same friendly spirit it was given.

It must have grown chillier than I realized while I sat there, for my new friends' hands were clay-cold when I took them in mine at parting.

Homeward bound, a whimsical thought struck me so suddenly I laughed aloud. There was something suggestive of the dog tribe about the Squires family, though I could not for the life of me say what it was. Even Mildred, the daughter, beautiful as she was, with her light eyes, her rather prominent nose and her somewhat wide mouth, reminded me in some vague way of a lovely silver collie I had owned as a boy.

I struck a tassel of dried leaves from a cluster of weeds with my walking stick as I smiled at the fanciful conceit. The legend of the werewolf—those horrible monsters, formed as men, but capable of assuming bestial shape at will, and killing and eating their fellows—was as old as mankind's fear of the dark, but no mythology I had ever read contained a reference to dog-people.

Strange fancies strike up in the moonlight, sometimes.

September ripened to October, and the moon, which had been as round and bright as an exchange-worn coin when I first visited the Squires house, waned as thin as a shaving from a silversmith's lathe.

I became a regular caller at the house in the pines. Indeed, I grew to look forward to my nightly visits with those homely folk as a welcome relief from the tediously gay companionship of the over-sophisticated people at the sanitarium.

My habit of slipping away shortly after dinner was the cause of considerable comment and no little speculation on the part of my fellow convalescents, some of whom set it down to the eccentricity which, to their minds, was the inevitable concomitant of a minister's vocation, while others were frankly curious. Snatches of conversation I overheard now and then led me to believe that the objective of my strolls was the subject of wagering, and the guarded questions put to me in an effort to solve the mystery became more and more annoying.

I had no intention of taking any of them to the farmhouse with me. The Squires were my friends. Their cheerful talk and unassuming manners were as delightful a contrast to the atmosphere of the sanitarium as a breath of mountain balsam after the fetid air of a hothouse; but to the city-centered crowd at Briarcliff they would have been only the objects of less than half scornful patronage, the source of pitying amusement.

It was Miss Leahy who pushed the impudent curiosity further than any of the rest, however. One evening, as I was setting out, she met me at the gate and announced her intention of going with me.

"You must have found something *dreadfully* attractive to take you off every evening this way, Mr. Weatherby," she hazarded as she pursed her rather pretty, rouged lips at me and caught step with my walk. "We girls really *can't* let some little country lass take you away from us, you know. We simply can't."

I made no reply. It was scarcely possible to tell a pretty girl, even such a vain little flirt as Sara Leahy, to go home and mind her business. Yet that was just what I wanted to do. But I would not take her with me; to that I made up my mind. I would stop at the turn of the road, just out of sight of the farmhouse, and cut across the fields. If she wanted to accompany me on a cross-country hike in high-heeled slippers, she was welcome to do so.

Besides, she would tell the others that my wanderings were nothing more mysterious than nocturnal explorations of the nearby woods; which bit of misinformation would satisfy the busybodies at Briarcliff and relieve me of the espionage to which I was subjected, as well.

I smiled grimly to myself as I pictured her climbing over fences and ditches in her flimsy party frock and beaded pumps, and lengthened my stride toward the woods at the road's turn.

We marched to the limits of the field bordering the Squires' grove in silence, I thinking of the mild revenge I should soon wreak upon the pretty little busybody at my side, Miss Leahy too intent on holding the pace I set to waste breath in conversation.

As we neared the woods she halted, an expression of worry, almost fear, coming over her face.

"I don't believe I'll go any farther," she announced.

"No?" I replied, a trifle sarcastically. "And is your curiosity so easily satisfied?"

"It's not that." She turned half round, as if to retrace her steps. "I'm afraid of those woods."

"Indeed?" I queried. "And what is there to be afraid of? Bears, Indians, or wildcats? I've been through them several times without seeing anything terrifying." Now she had come this far, I was anxious to take her through the fields and underbrush.

"No-o," Miss Leahy answered, a nervous quaver in her

voice, "I'm not afraid of anything like that; but—oh, I don't know what you call it. Pierre told me all about it the other day. Some kind of dreadful thing—loup—loup—something or other. It's a French word, and I can't remember it."

I was puzzled. Pierre Geronte was the ancient French-Canadian gardener at the sanitarium, and, like all doddering old men, would talk for hours to anyone who would listen. Also, like all *habitants,* he was full of wild folklore his ancestors brought overseas with them generations ago.

"What did Pierre tell you?" I asked.

"Why, he said that years ago some terrible people lived in these woods. They had the only house for miles 'round; and travelers stopped there for the night, sometimes. But no stranger was ever seen to leave that place, once he went in. One night the farmers gathered about the house and burned it, with the family that lived there. When the embers had cooled down they made a search, and found nearly a dozen bodies buried in the cellar. That was why no one ever came away from that dreadful place.

"They took the murdered men to the cemetery and buried them; but they dumped the charred bodies of the murderers into graves in the barnyard, without even saying a prayer over them. And Pierre says—Oh, look! *Look!*"

She broke off her recital of the old fellow's story, and pointed a trembling hand across the field to the edge of the woods. A second more and she shrank against me, clutching at my coat with fear-stiffened fingers and crying with excitement and terror.

I looked in the direction she indicated, myself a little startled by the abject fear that had taken such sudden hold on her.

Something white and ungainly was running diagonally across the field from us, skirting the margin of the woods and making for the meadow that adjoined the sanitarium pasture. A second glance told me it was a sheep; probably one of the flock kept to supply our table with fresh meat.

I was laughing at the strength of the superstition that could make a girl see a figure of horror in an innocent mutton that had strayed away from its fellows and was scared out of its silly wits, when something else attracted my attention.

Loping along in the trail of the fleeing sheep, somewhat to the rear and a little to each side, were two other animals. At first glance they appeared to be a pair of large collies; but as I looked more intently, I saw that these animals were like nothing I had ever seen before. They were much larger than any collie—nearly as high as St. Bernards—yet shaped in a general way like Alaskan sledge dogs—huskies.

The farther one was considerably the larger of the two, and ran with a slight limp, as if one of its hind paws had been injured. As nearly as I could tell in the indifferent light, they were a rusty brown color, very thick-haired and unkempt in appearance. But the strangest thing about them was the fact that both were tailless, which gave them a terrifyingly grotesque look.

As they ran, a third form, similar to the other two in shape, but smaller, slender as a greyhound, with much lighter-hued fur, broke from the thicket of short brush edging the wood and took up the chase, emitting a series of short, sharp yelps.

"Sheep-killers," I murmured, half to myself. "Odd. I've never seen dogs like that before."

"They're not dogs," wailed Miss Leahy against my coat. "They're not dogs. Oh, Mr. Weatherby, let's go away. Please, please take me home."

She was rapidly becoming hysterical, and I had a difficult time with her on the trip back. She clung whimpering to me, and I had almost to carry her most of the way. By the time we reached the sanitarium, she was crying bitterly, shivering, as if with a chill, and went in without stopping to thank me for my assistance.

I turned and made for the Squires farm with all possible speed, hoping to get there before the family had gone to bed. But when I arrived the house was in darkness, and my knock at the door received no answer.

As I retraced my steps to the sanitarium I heard faintly, from the fields beyond the woods, the shrill, eerie cry of the sheep-killing dogs.

• • •

A torrent of rain held us marooned the next day. Miss Leahy was confined to her room, with a nurse in constant attendance and the house doctor making hourly calls. She was on the verge of a nervous collapse, he told me, crying with a persistence that bordered on hysteria, and responding to treatment very slowly.

An impromptu dance was organized in the great hall and half a dozen bridge tables set up in the library; but as I was skilled in neither of these rainy day diversions, I put on a waterproof and patrolled the veranda for exercise.

On my third or fourth trip around the house I ran into old Geronte shuffling across the porch, wagging his head and muttering portentously to himself.

"See here, Pierre," I accosted him, "what sort of nonsense have you been telling Miss Leahy about those pine woods down the south road?"

The old fellow regarded me unwinkingly with his beady eyes, wrinkling his age-yellowed forehead for all the world like an elderly baboon inspecting a new sort of edible. "*M'sieur* goes out alone much at nights, *n'est ce pas*?" he asked, at length.

"Yes, Monsieur goes out alone much at night," I echoed, "but what Monsieur particularly desires to know is what sort of tales have you been telling Mademoiselle Leahy. *Comprenez vous*?"

The network of wrinkles about his lips multiplied as he smiled enigmatically, regarding me askance from the corners of his eyes.

"*M'sieur* is *anglais*," he replied. "He would not understand—or believe."

"Never mind what I'd believe," I retorted. "What is this story about murder and robbery being committed in those woods? Who were the murderers, and where did they live? *Hein*?"

For a few seconds he looked fixedly at me, chewing the cud of senility between his toothless gums, then, glancing carefully about, as if he feared being overheard, he tiptoed up to me and whispered:

"*M'sieur* mus' stay indoors these nights. There are evil things abroad at the dark of the moon, *M'sieur*. Even las' night they keel t'ree of my bes' sheep. Remembair, *M'sieur*, the *loup-garou*, he is out when the moon hide her light."

And with that he turned and left me; nor could I get another word from him save his cryptic warning. "Remembair, *M'sieur*; the *loup-garou*. Remembair."

In spite of my annoyance, I could not get rid of the unpleasant sensation the old man's words left with me. The *loup-garou*—werewolf—he had said, and to prove his goblin-wolf's presence, he had cited the death of his three sheep.

As I paced the rain-washed porch I thought of the scene I had witnessed the night before, when the sheep-killers were at their work.

"Well," I reflected, "I've seen the *loup-garou* on his native heath at last. From causes as slight as this, no doubt, the horrible legend of the werewolf had sprung. Time was when all France quaked at the sound of the *loup-garou*'s hunting call and the bravest knights in Christendom trembled in their castles and crossed themselves fearfully because some renegade shepherd dog quested his prey in the night. On such a foundation are the legends of a people built."

Whistling a snatch from *Pinafore* and looking skyward in search of a patch of blue in the clouds, I felt a tug at my raincoat sleeve, such as a neglected terrier might give. It was Geronte again.

"*M'sieur*," he began in the same mysterious whisper, "the *loup-garou* is verity, certainly. I, myself, have nevair seen him"—he paused to bless himself—"but my cousin, Baptiste, was once pursued by him. Yes.

"It was near the shrine of the good Sainte Anne that Baptiste lived. One night he was sent to fetch the curé for a dying woman. They rode fast through the trees, the curé and my cousin Baptiste, for it was at the dark of the moon, and the evil forest folk were abroad. And as they galloped, there came a *loup-garou* from the woods, with eyes as bright as hell fire. It followed hard, this tailless hound from the devil's kennel; but they reached the house before it, and the curé put his book, with the Holy Cross on its cover, at the doorstep. The *loup-garou* wailed under the windows like a child in pain until the sun rose; then it slunk back to the forest.

"When my cousin Baptiste and the curé came out, they found its hand marks in the soft earth around the door. Very like your hand, or mine, they were, *M'sieur,* save that the first finger was longer than the others."

"And did they find the *loup-garou*?" I asked, something of the old man's earnestness communicated to me.

"Yes, *M'sieur*; but of course," he replied gravely. "T'ree weeks before a stranger, drowned in the river, had been buried without the office of the Church. W'en they opened his grave they found his fingernails as red as blood, and sharp. Then they knew. The good curé read the burial office over him, and the poor soul that had been snatched away in sin slept peacefully at last."

He looked quizzically at me, as if speculating whether to tell me more; then, apparently fearing I would laugh at his outburst of confidence, started away toward the kitchen.

"Well, what else, Pierre?" I asked, feeling he had more to say.

"*Non, non, non,*" he replied. "There is nothing more, *M'sieur*. I did but want *M'sieur* should know my own cousin, Baptiste Geronte, had seen the *loup-garou* with his very eyes."

"Hearsay evidence," I commented, as I went in to dinner.

During the rainy week that followed I chafed at my confinement like a privileged convict suddenly deprived of his liberties, and looked as wistfully down the south road as any prisoned gypsy ever gazed upon the open trail.

The quiet home circle at the farmhouse, the unforced conversation of the old folks, Mildred's sweet companionship, all beckoned me with an almost irresistible force. For in this period of enforced separation I discovered what I had dimly suspected for some time. I loved Mildred Squires. And, loving her, I longed to tell her of it.

No lad intent on visiting his first sweetheart ever urged his feet more eagerly than I when, the curtains of rain at last drawn up, I hastened toward the house at the turn of the road.

As I hoped, yet hardly dared expect, Mildred was standing at the gate to meet me as I rounded the curve, and I yearned toward her like a hummingbird seeking its nest.

She must have read my heart in my eyes, for her greeting smile was as tender as a mother's as she bends over her babe.

"At last you have come, my friend," she said, putting out both hands in welcome. "I am very glad."

We walked silently up the path, her fingers still resting in mine, her face averted. At the steps she paused, a little embarrassment in her voice as she explained, "Father and Mother are out; they have gone to a—meeting. But you will stay?"

"Surely," I acquiesced. And to myself I admitted my gratitude for this chance of Mildred's unalloyed company.

We talked but little that night. Mildred was strangely distrait, and, much as I longed to, I could not force a confession of my love from my lips. Once, in the midst of a long pause between our words, the cry of the sheep-killers came faintly to us, echoed across the fields and woods, and as the weird, shrill sound fell on our ears, she threw back her head, with something of the gesture of a hunting dog scenting its quarry.

Toward midnight she turned to me, a panic of fear having apparently laid hold of her.

"You must go!" she exclaimed, rising and laying her hand on my shoulder.

"But your father and mother have not returned," I objected. "Won't you let me stay until they get back?"

"Oh, no, no," she answered, her agitation increasing. "You must go at once—please." She increased her pressure on my shoulder, almost as if to shove me from the porch.

Taken aback by her sudden desire to be rid of me, I was

picking up my hat, when she uttered a stifled little scream and ran quickly to the edge of the porch, interposing herself between me and the yard. At the same moment, I heard a muffled sound from the direction of the front gate, a sound like a growling and snarling of savage dogs.

I leaped forward, my first thought being that the sheep-killers I had seen the other night had strayed to the Squires place. Crazed with blood, I knew, they would be almost as dangerous to men as to sheep, and every nerve in my sickness-weakened body cried out to protect Mildred.

To my blank amazement, as I looked from the porch I beheld Mr. and Mrs. Squires walking sedately up the path, talking composedly together. There was no sign of the dogs or any other animals about.

As the elderly couple neared the porch I noticed that Mr. Squires walked with a pronounced limp, and that both their eyes shone very brightly in the moonlight, as though they were suffused with tears.

They greeted me pleasantly enough; but Mildred's anxiety seemed increased, rather than diminished, by their presence, and I took my leave after a brief exchange of civilities.

On my way back I looked intently in the woods bordering the road for some sign of the house of which Pierre had told Miss Leahy; but everywhere the pines grew so thickly as though neither axe nor fire had ever disturbed them.

"Geronte is in his second childhood," I reflected, "and like an elder child, he loves to terrify his juniors with fearsome witch-tales."

Yet an uncomfortable feeling was with me till I saw the gleam of the sanitarium's lights across the fields; and as I walked toward them it seemed to me that more than once I heard the baying of the sheep-killers in the woods behind me.

A buzz of conversation, like the sibilant arguments of a cloud of swarming bees, greeted me as I descended the stairs to breakfast next morning.

It appeared that Ned, one of the pair of great mastiffs attached to the sanitarium, had been found dead before his kennel, his throat and brisket torn open and several gaping wounds in his flanks. Boris, his fellow, had been discovered whimpering and trembling in the extreme corner of the doghouse, the embodiment of canine terror.

Speculation as to the animal responsible for the outrage was rife, and, as usual, it ran the gamut of possible and impossible surmises. Every sort of beast from a grizzly bear to a lion escaped from the circus was in turn indicted for the crime, only to have a complete alibi straightaway established.

The only one having no suggestion to offer was old Geronte, who stood Sphinx-like in the outskirts of the crowd, smiling sardonically to himself and wagging his head sagely. As he caught sight of me he nodded, sapiently, as if to include me in the joint tenancy to some weighty secret.

Presently he worked his way through the chattering group and whispered, "*M'sieur*, he was here last night—and with him was the other tailless one. Come and see."

Plucking me by the sleeve, he led me to the rear of the kennels, and, stooping, pointed to something in the moist earth. "You see?" he asked, as if a printed volume lay for my reading in the mud.

"I see that someone has been on his hands and knees here," I answered, inspecting the hand prints he indicated.

"*Something,*" he corrected, as if reasoning with an obstinate child. "Does not *M'sieur* behol' that the first finger is the longest?"

"Which proves nothing," I defended. "There are many hands like that."

"Oh—yes?" he replied with that queer upward accent of his. "And where has *M'sieur* seen hands like that before?"

"Oh, many times," I assured him somewhat vaguely, for there was a catch at the back of my throat as I spoke. Try as I would, I could recall only three pairs of hands with that peculiarity.

His little black eyes rested steadily on me in an unwinking stare, and the corners of his mouth curved upward in a malicious grin. It seemed, almost, as if he found a grim pleasure in thus driving me into a corner.

"See here, Pierre," I began testily, equally annoyed at myself and him, "you know as well as I that the *loup-garou* is an old woman's tale. Someone was looking here for tracks, and left his own while doing it. If we look among the patients here we shall undoubtedly find a pair of hands to match these prints."

"God forbid!" he exclaimed, crossing himself. "That would be an evil day for us, *M'sieur*. Here, Bor-ees," he snapped his fingers to the surviving mastiff, "come and eat."

The huge beast came wallowing over to him with the ungainly gait of all heavily muscled animals, stopping on his way to make a nasal investigation of my knees. Scarcely had his nose come into contact with my trousers when he leaned back, every hair in his mane and along his spine stiffly erect, every tooth in his great mouth bared in a savage snarl. But instead of the mastiff's fighting growl, he emitted only a low, frightened whine, as though he were facing some animal of greater power than himself, and knew his own weakness.

"Good heavens!" I cried, thoroughly terrified at the friendly brute's sudden hostility.

"Yes, *M'sieur*," Geronte cut in quickly, putting his hand on the dog's collar and leading him a few paces away. "It is well you should call upon the heavenly ones; for surely you have the odor of hell upon your clothes."

"What do you mean?" I demanded angrily. "How dare you—?"

He raised a thin hand deprecatingly. "*M'sieur* knows what he knows," he replied evenly; "and what I also know."

And leading Boris by the collar, he shuffled to the house.

Mildred was waiting for me at the gate that evening, and again her father and mother were absent at one of their meetings.

We walked silently up the path and seated ourselves on the porch steps where the waning moon cast oblique rays through the pine branches.

I think Mildred felt the tension I was drawn to, for she talked trivialities with an almost feverish earnestness, stringing her sentences together, and changing her subjects as a Navajo rug weaver twists and breaks her threads.

At last I found an opening in the abatis of her small talk.

"Mildred," I said, very simply, for great emotions tear the ornaments from our speech, "I love you, and I want you for my wife. Will you marry me, Mildred?" I laid my hand on hers. It was cold as lifeless flesh, and seemed to shrink beneath my touch.

"Surely, dear, you must have read the love in my eyes," I urged, as she averted her face in silence. "Almost from the night I first saw you, I've loved you! I—"

"O-o-h, don't!" Her interruption was a strangled moan, as if wrung from her by my words.

I leaned nearer her. "Don't you love me, Mildred?" I asked. As yet she had not denied it.

For a moment she trembled, as if a sudden chill had come on her, then, leaning to me, she clasped my shoulders in her arms, hiding her face against my jacket.

"John, John, you don't know what you say," she whispered disjointedly, as though a sob had torn the words before they left her lips. Her breath was on my cheek, moist and cold as air from a vault.

I could feel the litheness of her through the thin stuff of her gown, and her body was as devoid of warmth as a dead thing.

"You're cold," I told her, putting my arms shieldingly about her. "The night has chilled you."

A convulsive sob was her only answer.

"Mildred," I began again, putting my hand beneath her chin and lifting her face to mine, "tell me, dear, what is the matter?" I lowered my lips to hers.

With a cry that was half scream, half weeping, she thrust me suddenly from her, pressing her hands against my breast and lowering her head until her face was hidden between her outstretched arms. I, too, started back, for in the instant our lips were about to meet, hers had writhed back from her teeth, like a dog's when he is about to spring, and a low, harsh noise, almost a growl, had risen in her throat.

"For God's sake," she whispered hoarsely, agony in every note of her shaking voice, "never do that again! Oh, my dear, dear love, you don't know how near to a horror worse than death you were."

"A—horror—worse—than—death?" I echoed dully, pressing her cold little hands in mine. "What do you mean, Mildred?"

"Loose my hands," she commanded with a quaint reversion to the speech of our ancestors, "and hear me. I do love you. I love you better than life. Better than death. I love you so I have overcome something stronger than the walls of the grave for your sake, but John, my very love, this is our last night together. We can never meet again. You must go, now, and not come back until tomorrow morning."

"Tomorrow morning?" I repeated blankly. What wild talk was this?

Heedless of my interruption, she hurried on. "Tomorrow morning, just before the sun rises over those trees, you must be here, and have your prayer book with you."

I listened speechless, wondering which of us was mad.

"By that corncrib there"—she waved a directing hand— "you will find three mounds. Stand beside them and read the office for the burial of the dead. Come quickly, and pause for nothing on the way. Look back for nothing; heed no sound from behind you. And for your own safety, come no sooner than to allow yourself the barest time to read your office."

Bewildered, I attempted to reason with the mad woman; begged her to explain this folly; but she refused all answer to my fervid queries, nor would she suffer me to touch her.

Finally, I rose to go. "You will do what I ask?" she implored.

"Certainly not," I answered firmly.

"John, John, have pity!" she cried, flinging herself to the earth before me and clasping my knees. "You say you love me. I only ask this one favor of you; only this. Please, for my sake, for the peace of the dead and the safety of the living, promise you will do this thing for me."

Shaken by her abject supplication, I promised, though I felt myself a figure in some grotesque nightmare as I did it.

"Oh, my love, my precious love," she wept, rising and taking both my hands. "At last I shall have peace, and you shall bring it to me. No," she forbade me as I made to take her in my arms at parting. "The most I can give you, dear, is this." She held her icy hands against my lips. "It seems so little, dear, but oh! it is so much."

Like a drunkard in his cups I staggered along the south road, my thoughts gone wild with the strangeness of the play I had just acted.

Across the clearing came the howls of the sheep-killers, a sound I had grown used to of late. But tonight there was a deeper, fiercer *timbre* in their bay; a note that boded ill for man as well as beast. Louder and louder it swelled; it was rising from the field itself, now, drawing nearer and nearer the road.

I turned and looked. The great beasts I had seen pursuing the luckless sheep the other night were galloping toward me. A cold finger seemed traced down my spine; the scalp crept and tingled beneath my cap. There was no other object of their quest in sight. I was their elected prey.

My first thought was to turn and run; but a second's reasoning told me this was worse than useless. Weakened with long illness, with an uphill road to the nearest shelter, I should soon be run down.

No friendly tree offered asylum; my only hope was to stand and fight. Grasping my stick, I spread my feet, bracing myself against their charge.

And as I waited their onslaught, there came from the shadow of the pines the shriller, sharper cry of the third beast. Like the crest of a flying, wind-lashed wave, the slighter, silver-furred brute came speeding across the meadow, its ears laid back, its slender paws spurning the sod daintily. Almost, it seemed as if the pale shadow of a cloud were racing toward me.

The thing dashed slantwise across the field, its flight

converging on the line of the other two's attack. Midway between me and them it paused; hairs bristling, limbs bent for a spring.

All the savageness of the larger beasts' hunting cry was echoed in the smaller creature's bay, and with it a defiance that needed no interpretation.

The attackers paused in their rush; halted, and looked speculatively at my ally. They took a few tentative steps in my direction; and a fierce whine, almost an articulate curse, went up from the silver-haired beast. Slowly the tawny pair circled and trotted back to the woods.

I hurried toward the sanitarium, grasping my stick firmly in readiness for another attack.

But no further cries came from the woods, and once, as I glanced back, I saw the light-haired beast trotting slowly in my wake, looking from right to left, as if to ward off danger.

Half an hour later I looked from my window toward the house in the pines. Far down the south road, its muzzle pointed to the moon, the bright-furred animal crouched and poured out a lament to the night. And its cry was like the wail of a child in pain.

Far into the night I paced my room, like a condemned convict when the vigil of the death watch is on him. Reason and memory struggled for the mastery; one urging me to give over my wild act, the other bidding me obey my promise to Mildred.

Toward morning I dropped into a chair, exhausted with my objectless marching. I must have fallen asleep, for when I started up the stars were dimming in the zenith, and bands of slate, shading to amethyst, slanted across the horizon.

A moment I paused, laughing cynically at my fool's errand, then, seizing cap and book, I bolted down the stairs, and ran through the paling dawn to the house in the pines.

There was something ominous and terrifying in the two-toned pastel of the house that morning. Its windows stared at me with blank malevolence, like the half-closed eyes of one stricken dead in mortal sin. The little patches of hoarfrost on the lawn were like leprous spots on some unclean thing. From the trees behind the clearing an owl hooted mournfully, as if to say, "Beware! beware!" and the wind soughing through the black pine boughs echoed the refrain ceaselessly.

Three mounds, sunken and weed-grown, lay in the unkempt thicket behind the corncrib. I paused beside them, throwing off my cap and adjusting my stole hastily. Thumbing the pages to the committal service, I held the book close, that I might see the print through the morning shadows, and commenced: "I know that my redeemer liveth—"

Almost beside me, under the branches of the pines, there rose such a chorus of howls and yelps I nearly dropped my book. Like all the hounds in the kennels of hell, the sheep-killers clamored at me, rage and fear and mortal hatred in their cries. Through the bestial cadences, too, there seemed to run a human note; the sound of voices heard before beneath these very trees. Deep and throaty, and raging mad, two of the voices came to me, and, like the tremolo of a violin lightly played in an orchestra of brass, the shriller cry of a third beast sounded.

As the infernal hubbub rose at my back, I half turned to fly. Next instant I grasped my book more firmly and resumed my office, for like a beacon in the dark, Mildred's words flashed on my memory: *"Look back for nothing; heed no sound behind you."*

Strangely, too, the din approached no nearer; but as though held by an invisible bar, stayed at the boundary of the clearing.

"Man that is born of a woman hath but a short time to live and is full of misery—deliver us from all our offenses—O, Lord, deliver us not into the bitter pains of eternal death—" and to such an accompaniment, surely, as no priest ever before chanted the office, I pressed through the brief service to the final *Amen*.

Tiny grouts of moisture stood out on my forehead, my breath struggled in my throat as I gasped out the last word. My nerves were frayed to shreds and my strength nearly gone as I let fall my book, and turned upon the beasts among the trees.

They were gone. Abruptly as it had begun, their clamor

stopped, and only the rotting pine needles, lightly gilded by the morning sun, met my gaze. A light touch fell in the palm of my open hand, as if a pair of cool, sweet lips had laid a kiss there.

A vaporlike swamp-fog enveloped me. The outbuildings, the old stone-curbed well where I had drunk the night I first saw Mildred, the house itself—all seemed fading into mist and swirling away in the morning breeze.

"Eh, eh, eh; but *M'sieur* will do himself an injury, sleeping on the wet earth!" Old Geronte bent over me, his arm beneath my shoulders. Behind him, great Boris, the mastiff, stood wagging his tail, regarding me with doggish good humor.

"Pierre," I muttered thickly, "how came you here?"

"This morning, going to my tasks, I saw *M'sieur* run down the road like a thing pursued. I followed quickly, for the woods hold terrors in the dark, *M'sieur*."

I looked toward the farmhouse. Only a pair of chimneys, rising stark and bare from a crumbling foundation, were there. Fence, well, barn—all were gone, and in their place a thicket of sumac and briars, tangled and overgrown as though undisturbed for thirty years.

"The house, Pierre! Where is the house?" I croaked, sinking my fingers into his withered arm.

"'Ouse?" he echoed. "Oh, but of course. There is no 'ouse here, *M'sieur*; nor has there been for years. This is an evil place, *M'sieur*; it is best we quit it, and that quickly. There be evil things that run by night—"

"No more," I answered, staggering toward the road, leaning heavily on him. "I brought them peace, Pierre."

He looked dubiously at the English prayer book I held. A Protestant clergyman is a thing of doubtful usefulness to the orthodox French-Canadian. Something of the heartsick misery in my face must have touched his kind old heart, for at last he relented, shaking his head pityingly and patting my shoulder gently, as one would soothe a sorrowing child.

"Per'aps, *M'sieur*," he conceded. "Per'aps; who shall say no? Love and sorrow are the purchase price of peace. Yes. Did not *le bon Dieu* so buy the peace of the world?"

The creator of one of the most famous of all occult detectives, Dr. Jules de Grandin, Seabury Quinn was born in Washington, D.C., in 1889. A man of several careers, Quinn was a lawyer, editor of trade journals for funeral directors, and was an expert on mortuary science. Most of his more than 160 stories appeared in Weird Tales, _and many of his de Grandin tales have been collected in six volumes, beginning with_ The Adventures of Jules de Grandin. _The best of his non–de Grandin works are collected in_ Is the Devil a Gentleman?

John Jeremy could recover any body from the river, but he kept his methods secret. Twelve-year-old Peter was determined to find out why.

11

Stillwater, 1896

Michael Cassutt

They are big families up here on the St. Croix. I myself am the second of eight, and ours was the smallest family of any on Chestnut Street. You might think we were all hard-breeding Papists passing as Lutherans, but I have since learned that it is due to the long winters. For fifty years I have been hearing that Science will take care of winters just like we took care of the river, with our steel high bridge and diesel-powered barges that go the size of a football field. But every damn November the snow falls again and in spring the river swells from bluff to bluff. The loggers can be heard cursing all the way from Superior. I alone know that this is because of what we done to John Jeremy.

I was just a boy then, short of twelve, that would be in 1896, and by mutual agreement of little use to anyone, not my father nor my brothers nor my departed mother. I knew my letters, to be sure, and could be trusted to appear at

Church in a clean collar, but my primary achievement at that age was to be known as the best junior logroller in the county, a title I had won the previous Fourth of July, beating boys from as far away as Rice Lake and Taylors Falls. In truth, I tended to lollygag when sent to Kinnick's Store, never failing to take a detour down to the riverfront, where a Mississippi excursion boat like the *Verne Swain* or the *Kalitan*, up from St. Louis or New Orleans, would be pulled in. I had the habit of getting into snowball fights on my way to school and was notorious for one whole winter as the boy who almost put out Oscar Tolz's eye with a missile into which I had embedded a small pebble. (Oscar Tolz was a God damned Swede and a bully to boot.) Often I would not get to school at all. This did not vex my father to any great degree, as he had only a year of schooling himself. It mightily vexed my elder brother, Dolph. I can still recall him appearing like an avenging angel wherever I went, it seemed, saying, "Peter, what in God's name are you doing there? Get away from there!" Dolph was all of fourteen at the time and ambitious, having been promised a job at the Hersey Bean Lumberyard when the Panic ended. He was also suspicious of my frivolous associates, particularly one named John Jeremy.

I now know that John Jeremy was the sort of man you meet on the river—bearded, unkempt, prone to sudden, mystifying exclamations and gestures. The better folk got no further with him, while curious boys found him somewhat more interesting, perhaps because of his profession. "I'm descended from the line of St. Peter himself," he told me once. "Do you know why?"

I drew the question because my given name is Peter. "Because you are a fisher of men," I told him.

Truth, in the form of hard liquor, was upon John Jeremy that day. He amended my phrase: "A fisher of dead men." John Jeremy fished for corpses.

He had been brought up from Chicago, they said, in 1885 by the Hersey family itself. Whether motivated by a series of personal losses or by some philanthropic spasm I do not know, having been otherwise occupied at the time. I found few who were able or willing to discuss the subject when at last I sprouted interest. I do know that a year did not pass then that the St. Croix did not take at least half a dozen people to its shallow bottom. This in a town of less than six hundred, though that figure was subject to constant change due to riverboats and loggers who, I think, made up a disproportionate amount of the tribute. You can not imagine the distress a drowning caused in those days. Now part of this was normal human grief (most of the victims were children), but much of it, I have come to believe, was a deep revulsion in the knowledge that the source of our drinking water, the heart of our livelihood—the river!—was fouled by the bloating, gassy corpse of someone we all knew. There was nothing rational about it, but the fear was real nonetheless: when the whistle at the courthouse blew, you ran for it, for either the town was on fire, or somebody was breathing river.

Out would go the rowboats, no matter what the weather or time of night, filled with farmers unused to water with their weights, poles, nets, and hopes. It was tedious, sad, and unrewarding work . . . except for a specialist like John Jeremy.

"You stay the hell away from that man," Dolph hissed at me one day. "I've seen you hanging around down there with him. He's the Devil himself."

Normally, a statement like this from Dolph would have served only to encourage further illicit association, but none was actually needed. I had come across John Jeremy for the first time that spring, idly fishing at a spot south of town near the lumberyard. It was not the best fishing hole, if you used worms or other unimaginative bait, for the St. Croix was low that year, as it had been for ten years, and the fish were fat with bugs easily caught in the shallows. I had picked up a marvelous invention known as the casting fly and had applied it that spring with great success. And I was only too happy to share the secret with a thin, pale, scruffy fellow who looked as if he had skipped meals of late. We introduced ourselves and proceeded to take a goodly number of crappies and sunfish during the afternoon. "That's quite a trick you got there," John Jeremy told me. "You make that up all by yourself?"

I confessed that I had read about it in a dime novel, though if Oscar Tolz had asked me, I would have lied. John Jeremy laughed, showing that his teeth were a match for the rest of his ragged appearance.

"Well, it works good enough. Almost makes me wish I'd learned how to read."

By this point, as I remember it, we had hiked up to the Afton Road and were headed back to Stillwater. As we walked, I was struck by John Jeremy's thinness and apparent ill health, and in a fit of Christian charity—I was just twelve—I offered him some of my catch, which was far larger than his.

John Jeremy regarded me for a moment. I think he was amused. "Aren't you a rascal, Peter Gollwitzer. Thank you, but no. In spite of the fact that it's been a long dry spell, I'm still able to feed myself, though it don't show. I'll grant you that. In fact, in exchange for your kindness"—his voice took on a conspiratorial tone—"I shall reward you with this." And into my hand he pressed a five-dollar gold piece. "For the secret of the fly, eh? Now run along home."

My father was unamused by my sudden wealth, especially when he learned the source. "That man is worse than a grave robber. He profits through the misfortune of others." It was then that I learned John Jeremy's true profession, and that he had been known to charge as much as *five hundred dollars* for a single "recovery," as it was called. "One time, I swear by the Lord," my father continued, "he *refused* to turn over a body he had recovered because the payment wasn't immediately forthcoming! A man like that is unfit for human company." I reserved judgment, clutching the eagle in my sweaty palm, happier than I would have been with a chestful of pirate treasure.

June is a month to be remembered for tornados, with the wind screaming and trees falling and the river churning. In this instance there was a riverboat, the *Sidney*, taking a side trip from St. Paul—and regretting it—putting into town just as one of those big blowers hit. One of her deckhands, a Negro, was knocked into the water. Of course, none of those people can swim, and in truth I doubt Jonah himself could have got out of those waters that day. The courthouse whistle blew, though it was hard to hear over the roar of the wind, and Dolph (who had been sent home from the yard) grabbed my arm and tugged me toward the docks.

The crowd there was bigger than you'd expect, given the weather—not only townspeople, but many from the *Sidney,* who were quite vocal in their concern about the unfortunate blackamoor. Into our midst came John Jeremy, black gunnysack—he referred to it as his "bag of tricks"—over his shoulder. People stepped aside, the way they do for the sheriff, letting him pass. He sought out the *Sidney*'s captain. I took it that they were haggling over the price, since the captain's voice presently rose above the storm: "I've never heard such an outrage in my life!" But an agreement was reached and soon, in the middle of the storm, we saw John Jeremy put out in his skiff. It was almost dark by then and the corpse fisher, floating with the wind-whipped water with all the seeming determination of a falling leaf, disappeared from our sight.

The onlookers began to drift home then while the passengers from the *Sidney* headed up the street in search of a warm, dry tavern. Dolph and I and the younger ones— including Oscar Tolz—stayed behind. Because of my familiarity with the corpse fisher I was thought to have intimate and detailed knowledge of his techniques, which, they say, he refused to discuss. "I bet he uses loaves of bread," one boy said. "Like in Mark Twain."

"Don't be a dope," Oscar Tolz said. "Books are not real. My old man says he's got animals in that sack. Some kind of trained rats—maybe muskrats."

"Like hell," said a third. "I saw that sack and there was nothing alive in it. Muskrats would be squirming to beat the band."

"Maybe they're *drowned* muskrats," I offered, earning a cuff from Dolph. Normally, that would have been my signal to shut my mouth, as Dolph's sense of humor—never notable—was not presently on duty. But that evening, for some reason, I felt immune. I asked him, "Okay, Dolph, what do *you* think he uses?"

One thing Dolph always liked was a technical question. He immediately forgot that he was annoyed with me. "I think," he said after a moment, "that John Jeremy's got some sort of compass." Before anyone could laugh, he raised his hand. "Now just you remember this: all the strange machines people got nowadays. If they got a machine that can make pictures move and another one can say words, how hard can it be to make a compass that instead of finding north finds dead people?"

This sounded so eminently reasonable to all of us that we promptly clasped the idea to us with a fervor of which our parents—having seen us bored in Church—thought us incapable. The boy who knew Mark Twain's stories suggested that this compass must have been invented by Thomas Edison, and who was to dispute that? Oscar Tolz announced that John Jeremy—who was known to have traveled a bit—might have busted Tom Edison in the noggin and stolen the compass away, which was why he had it and no one else did. "Especially since Edison's been suffering from amnesia ever since," I said. I confess that we grew so riotous that we did not notice how late it had gotten and that John Jeremy's laden skiff was putting in to the dock. We took one good look at the hulking and lifeless cargo coming toward us and scurried away like mice. Later I felt ashamed, because of what John Jeremy must have wondered, and because there was no real reason for us to run. A body drowned, at most, three hours could not have transformed into one of those horrors we had all heard about. It was merely the body of a poor dead black man.

I learned that John Jeremy had earned one hundred dollars for his work that afternoon, plus a free dinner with the captain of the *Sidney*. Feelings in Stillwater ran quite hot against this for some days, since one hundred dollars was the amount Reverend Bickell earned in a year for saving souls.

Over the Fourth I successfully defended my junior

logrolling title; that, combined with other distractions, prevented me from seeing John Jeremy until one afternoon in early August. He was balancing unsteadily on the end of the dock, obviously drunk, occasionally cupping his hand to his ear as if listening to some faroff voice, flapping his arms to right himself.

He did not strike me as a mean or dangerous drunk (such a drinker was my father, rest his soul), just unhappy. "Florida!" he announced abruptly. "Florida, Alabama, Mississippi, Missouri, Illinois, Michigan, Wisconsin, here." He counted the states on his hand. "And never welcome anywhere for long, Peter. Except Stillwater. Why do you suppose that is?"

"Maybe it is better here."

John Jeremy laughed loudly. "I wouldn't have thought to say that, but maybe it is, by God." He coughed. "Maybe it's because I've kept the river quiet . . . and folks appreciate it." He saw none-too-fleeting disdain on my face. "True! By God, when was the last time the St. Croix went over its banks? Tell me when! Eighteen eighty-four is when! One year before the disreputable John Jeremy showed his ugly face in the quiet town of Stillwater. Not one flood in that time, sir! I stand on my record." He almost fell on it, as he was seized with another wheezing cough.

"Then the city should honor you," I said helpfully. "You should be the mayor."

"Huh! You're too innocent, Peter. A corpse fisher for mayor. No, sir, the Christian folk will not have *that*. Better a brewer, or a usurer—or the undertaker!"

He had gotten quite loud, and much as I secretly enjoyed my friendship with him, I recognized truth in what he said.

"You wouldn't want to be mayor, anyway."

He shook his head, grinning. "No. After all, what mayor can do what *I* do, eh? Who speaks to the river like I do? No one." He paused and was quiet, then added, "No one else is strong enough to pay the price."

Though I was far from tired of this conversation, I knew, from extensive experience with my father, that John Jeremy would likely grow steadily less coherent. I tried to help him to his feet, quite an achievement given my stature at the time, and, as he lapsed into what seemed to be a sullen silence, guided him toward his shack.

I was rewarded with a look inside. In the dark, I confess, I expected a magic compass, or muskrat cages, but all that I beheld were the possessions of a drifter: a gunnysack, a pole, some weights, and a net. I left John Jeremy among them, passed out on his well-worn cot.

Four days later, on a Saturday afternoon, in the thick, muggy heat of August, the courthouse whistle blew. I was on my way home from Kinnick's, having run an errand for my father, and made a quick detour downtown. Oscar Tolz was already there, shouting, ''Someone's drowned at the lumberyard!'' I was halfway there before I remembered that Dolph was working.

The sawmill at the Hersey Bean Lumberyard sat on pilings well into the St. Croix, the better to deal with the river of wood that floated its way every spring and summer. It was a God damned treacherous place, especially when huge timbers were being pulled in and swung to face the blades. Dolph had been knocked off because he had not ducked in time.

The water was churning that day beneath the mill in spite of the lack of wind and current. I suspect it had to do with the peculiar set of the pilings and the movements of the big logs. At any rate, Dolph, a strong swimmer, had been hurled into an obstruction, possibly striking his head, so observers said. He had gone under the water then, not to be seen again.

The shoreline just to the south of the yard was rugged and overgrown. It was possible that Dolph, knocked senseless for a moment, had been carried that way where, revived, he could swim to safety, unbeknownst to the rest of us. Some men went to search there.

I was told there was nothing I could do, and to tell the truth, I was glad. My father arrived and without saying a word to me went off with the searchers. He had lost a wife and child already.

John Jeremy arrived. He had his gunnysack over his

shoulder and an oar in his hand. Behind him two men hauled his skiff. I stood up to meet him, I'm ashamed to say, wiping tears on my pantaloons. I had the presence of mind to know that there was business to be conducted.

"This is all I have," I told him, holding out the five-dollar gold piece I had carried for weeks.

I saw real pain in his eyes. The breath itself seemed to seep out of him. "This will be on the house," he said finally. He patted me on the shoulder with a hand that was glazed and hard and went down to the river.

My father's friends took me away then and put some food in me and made me look after the other children. I fell asleep early that warm evening and, not surprisingly, woke while it was still dark, frightened and confused. Had they found him? I wanted to know, and with my father still not home, I had no one to ask.

Dressing, I sneaked out and walked down to the lumber-yard. The air was hot and heavy even though dawn was not far off . . . so hot that even the bugs were quiet. I made my way to the dock and sat there, listening to the lazy slap of the water.

There was a slice of moon in the sky, and by its light it seemed that I could see a skiff slowly crossing back and forth, back and forth, between two prominent coves to the south. A breeze came up all of a sudden, a breeze that chilled but did not cool, hissing in the reeds like a faraway voice. I fell forward on my hands and shouted into the darkness: "Who's there?"

No one answered. Perhaps it was all a dream. I do know that eventually the sky reddened on the Wisconsin side and I was able to clearly see John Jeremy's distant skiff.

Hungry now and deadly sure of my own uselessness in the affair, I drifted home and got something to eat. It was very quiet in the house. My father was home, but tired, and he offered nothing. I went out to Church voluntarily, and prayed for once, alone.

Almost hourly during that Sunday I went down to the St. Croix. Each time, I was able to spot John Jeremy, infinitely patient in his search.

It finally occurred to me about mid-afternoon that I had to do something to help, even if it came to naught. Leaving the house again, I walked past the lumberyard toward the brushy shallows where John Jeremy was, hoping that in some way my sorry presence would encourage a merciful God to end this. I was frankly terrified of what I would see—a body drowned a goodly time and in August heat at that—yet anxious to confront it, to move *past* it and get on with other business.

Two hours of beating through the underbrush, occasionally stepping into the green scum at water's edge, exhausted me. I believe I sat down for a while and cried, and presently I felt better—better enough to continue.

It was almost sunset. The sun had crossed to the Minnesota side and dipped toward the trees on the higher western bluffs, casting eerie shadows in the coves. Perhaps that is why I did not see them until I was almost upon them.

There, in the shallow water, among the cattails and scum, was John Jeremy's skiff. In it was a huge white thing that once was my brother Dolph. The sight was every bit as horrific as I had imagined, and even across an expanse of water the smell rivaled the pits of Hell . . . but that alone, I can honestly say, did not make me scream. It was another thing that made me call out, an image I will carry to my grave, of John Jeremy pressing his ear to the greenish lips of my brother's corpse.

My scream startled him. "Peter!" he yelled. I was as incapable of locomotion as the cattails that separated us. John Jeremy raised himself and began to pole toward me. "Peter, wait for me."

I found my voice, weak though it was. "What are you doing to my brother?"

He beached his nightmare cargo and stumbled out of the skiff. He was frantic, pleading, out of breath. "Don't run. Peter, hear me out."

I managed to back up, putting some distance between us. "Stay away!"

"I told you, Peter, I talk to the river. I *listen* to it, too." He nodded toward Dolph's body. "They tell me where the next one will be found, Peter, so I can get them out, because the river doesn't want them for long—''

I clapped my hands over my ears and screamed again, backing away as fast as I could. The slope was against me, though, and I fell.

John Jeremy held out his hand. "I could teach you the secret, Peter. You have the gift. You could learn it easy."

For a long second, perhaps a heartbeat and a half, I stared at his grimy hand. But a gentle wave lapped at the skiff and the God-awful creaking broke his spell. I turned and scurried up the hill. Reaching the top, I remembered the gold piece in my pocket. I took it out and threw it at him.

At twelve your secrets do not keep. Eventually, some version of what I'd seen and told got around town, and it went hard with John Jeremy. Stillwater's version of tar-and-feathering was to gang up on a man, kick the hell out of him, and drag him as far south as he could be dragged, possessions be damned. I was not there. Sometimes, as I think back, I fool myself into believing that I was . . . that John Jeremy forgave me, like Christ forgave his tormentors. But that did not happen.

Eventually, we learned that John Jeremy's "secret" was actually a special three-pronged hook attached to a weight that could be trolled on a river bottom. Any fool could find a body, they said. Maybe so.

But the flood of '97 damned near killed Stillwater and things haven't improved since then. A day don't go by now that I don't think of John Jeremy's secret and wish I'd said yes. Especially when I go down to the river and hear the water rustling in the reeds, making that awful sound, the sound I keep telling myself is not the voices of the dead.

——————

A new writer whose stories are few but carefully crafted, Michael Cassutt is a California native who works for a television network. His first published story, "The Streak" (1977), is about murder on a baseball diamond; his later tales, nearly all science fiction, have appeared in Omni *and* Isaac Asimov's Science Fiction.

Although Joe Indian believed he didn't believe the Indian religion he was brought up to respect, he had to prove it to himself. . . .

12

Ride the Thunder

Jack Cady

A lot of people who claim not to believe in ghosts will not drive 150 above Mount Vernon. They are wrong. There is nothing there. Nothing with eyes gleaming from the roadside, or flickering as it smoothly glides not quite discernible along the fence rows. I know. I pull it now, although the Lexington route is better with the new sections of interstate complete. I do it because it makes me feel good to know that the going-to-hell old road that carried so many billion tons of trucking is once more clean. The macabre presence that surrounded the road is gone, perhaps fleeing back into smoky valleys in some lost part of the Blue Ridge where haunted fires are said to gleam in great tribal circles and the forest is so thick that no man can make his way through.

Whatever, the road is clean. It can fall into respectable

decay under the wheels of farmers bumbling along at 35 in their '53 Chevies.

Or have you driven Kentucky? Have you driven that land that was known as a dark and bloody ground. Because, otherwise you will not know about the mystery that sometimes surrounds those hills, where a mist edges the distant mountain ridges like a memory.

And, you will not know about Joe Indian who used to ride those hills like a curse, booming down out of Indiana or Southern Illinois and bound to Knoxville in an old B-61 that was probably only running because it was a Mack. You would see the rig first on 150 around Vincennes in Indiana. Or, below Louisville on 64, crying its stuttering wail into the wind and lightning of a river valley storm as it ran under the darkness of electricity-charged air. A picture of desolation riding a road between battered fields, the exhaust shooting coal into the fluttering white load that looked like windswept rags. Joe hauled turkeys. Always turkeys and always white ones. When he was downgrade he rode them at seventy plus. Uphill he rode them at whatever speed the Mack would fetch.

That part was all right. Anyone who has pulled poultry will tell you that you have to ride them. They are packed so tight. You always lose a few. The job is to keep an air stream moving through the cages so they will not suffocate.

But the rest of what Joe Indian did was wrong. He was worse than trash. Men can get used to trash, but Joe bothered guys you would swear could not be bothered by anything in the world. Guys who had seen everything. Twenty years on the road, maybe. Twenty years of seeing people broken up by stupidness. Crazy people, torn-up people, drunks. But Joe Indian even bothered guys who had seen all of that. One of the reasons might be that he never drank or did anything. He never cared about anything. He just blew heavy black exhaust into load after load of white turkeys.

The rest of what he did was worse. He hated the load. Not the way any man might want to swear over some particular load. No. He hated every one of those turkeys on every load. Hated it personally the way one man might hate another man. He treated the load in a way that showed how much he despised the easy death that was coming to most of those turkeys—the quick needle thrust up the beak into the brain the way poultry is killed commercially. Fast. Painless. The night I saw him close was only a week before the trouble started.

He came into a stop in Harrodsburg. I was out of Tennessee loaded with a special order of upholstered furniture to way and gone up in Michigan and wondering how the factory had ever caught that order. The boss had looked sad when I left. That made me feel better. If I had to fight tourists all the way up to the lake instead of my usual Cincinnati run, at least he had to stay behind and build sick furniture. When I came into the stop I noticed a North Carolina job, one of those straight thirty or thirty-five footers with the attic. He was out of Hickory. Maybe one of the reasons I stopped was because there would be someone there who had about the same kind of trouble. He turned out to be a dark-haired and serious man, one who was very quiet. He had a load of couches on that were made to sell but never, never to use. We compared junk for a while, then looked through the window to see Joe Indian pull in with a truck that looked like a disease.

The Mack sounded sick, but from the appearance of the load it must have found seventy on the downgrades. The load looked terrible at close hand. Joe had cages that were homemade, built from siding of coal company houses when the mines closed down. They had horizontal slats instead of the vertical dowel rod. All you could say of them was that they were sturdy, because you can see the kind of trouble that sort of cage would cause. A bird would shift a little, get a wing-tip through the slat and the air stream would do the rest. The Mack came in with between seventy-five and a hundred broken wings fluttering along the sides of the crates. I figured that Joe must own the birds. No one was going to ship like that. When the rig stopped, the wings drooped like dead banners. It was hard to take.

"I know him," the driver who was sitting with me said.

"I know of him," I told the guy, "but, nothing good."

"There isn't any, any more," he said quietly and turned from the window. His face seemed tense. He shifted his chair so that he could see both the door and the restaurant counter. "My cousin," he told me.

I was surprised. The conversation kind of ran out of gas. We did not say anything because we seemed waiting for something. It did not happen.

All that happened was that Joe came in looking like his name.

"Is he really Indian?" I asked.

"Half," his cousin said. "The best half if there is any." Then he stopped talking and I watched Joe. He was dressed like anybody else and needed a haircut. His nose had been broken at one time. His knuckles were enlarged and beat-up. He was tall and rough-looking, but there was nothing that you could pin down as unusual in a tough guy except that he wore a hunting knife sheathed and hung on his belt. The bottom of the sheath rode in his back pocket. The hilt was horn. The knife pushed away from his body when he sat at the counter.

He was quiet. The waitress must have known him from before. She just sat coffee in front of him and moved away. If Joe had seen the driver beside me he gave no indication. Instead he sat rigid, tensed like a man being chased by something. He looked all set to hit, or yell, or kill if anyone had been stupid enough to slap him on the back and say hello. Like an explosion on a hair-trigger. The restaurant was too quiet. I put a dime in the juke and pressed something just for the sound. Outside came the sound of another rig pulling in. Joe Indian finished his coffee, gulping it. Then he started out and stopped before us. He stared down at the guy beside me.

"Why?" the man said. Joe said nothing. "Because a man may come with thunder does not mean that he can ride the thunder," the driver told him. It made no sense. "A man is the thunder," Joe said. His voice sounded like the knife looked. He paused for a moment, then went out. His rig did not pull away for nearly ten minutes. About the time it was in the roadway another driver came in angry and half-scared. He headed for the counter. We waved him over. He came, glad for some attention.

"Jesus," he said.

"An old trick," the guy beside me told him.

"What?" I asked.

"Who is he?" The driver was shaking his head.

"Not a truck driver. Just a guy who happens to own a truck."

"But, how come he did that." The driver's voice sounded shaky.

"Did what?" I asked. They were talking around me.

The first guy, Joe's cousin, turned to me. "Didn't you ever see him trim a load?"

"What!"

"Truck's messy," the other driver said. "That's what he was saying. Messy. Messy." The man looked half sick.

I looked at them still wanting explanation. His cousin told me. "Claims he likes neat cages. Takes that knife and goes around the truck cutting the wings he can reach . . . just enough. Never cuts them off, just enough so they rip off in the air stream."

"Those are live," I said.

"Uh huh."

It made me mad. "One of these days he'll find somebody with about thirty-eight calibers of questions."

"Be shooting around that knife," his cousin told me. "He probably throws better than you could handle a rifle."

"But why . . ." It made no sense.

"A long story," his cousin said, "and I've got to be going." He stood up. "Raised in a coal camp," he told us. "That isn't his real name but his mother was full Indian. His daddy shot coal. Good money. So when Joe was a kid he was raised Indian, trees, plants, animals, mountains, flowers, men . . . all brothers. His ma was religious. When he became 16 he was raised coal miner white. Figure it out." He turned to go.

"Drive careful," I told him, but he was already on his way. Before the summer was out Joe Indian was dead. But by then all of the truck traffic was gone from 150. The guys were routing through Lexington. I did not know at first because of trouble on the Michigan run. Wheel bearings in Sault Ste. Marie to help out the worn compressor in Grand Rapids. Furniture manufacturers run their lousy equipment to death. They expect every cube to run on bicycle maintenance. I damned the rig, but the woods up there were nice with stands of birch that jumped up white and luminous in the headlights. The lake and straits were good. Above Traverse City there were not as many tourists. But, enough. In the end I was pushing hard to get back. When I hit 150 it took me about twenty minutes to realize that I was the only truck on the road. There were cars. I learned later that the thing did not seem to work on cars. By then it had worked on me well enough that I could not have cared less.

Because I started hitting animals. Lots of animals. Possum, cat, rabbit, coon, skunk, mice, even birds and snakes . . . at night . . . with the moon tacked up there behind a thin and swirling cloud cover. The animals started marching, looking up off the road into my lights and running right under the wheels.

Not one of them thumped!

I rode into pack after pack and there was no thump, no crunch, no feeling of the soft body being pressed and torn under the drive axle. They marched from the shoulder into the lights, disappeared under the wheels and it was like running through smoke. At the roadside, even crowding the shoulder, larger eyes gleamed from nebulous shapes that moved slowly back. Not frightened; just like they were letting you through. And you knew that none of them were real. And you knew that your eyes told you they were there. It *was* like running through smoke, but the smoke was in dozens of familiar and now horrible forms. I tried not to look. It did not work. Then I tried looking hard. That worked too well, especially when I cut on the spot to cover the shoulder and saw forms that were not men and were not animals but seemed something of both. Alien. Alien. I was afraid to slow. Things flew at the windshields and bounced off without a splat. It lasted for ten miles. Ordinarily it takes about seventeen minutes to do those ten miles. I did it in eleven or twelve. It seemed like a year. The stop was closed in Harrodsburg. I found an all night diner, played the juke, drank coffee, talked to a waitress who acted like I was trying to pick her up, which would have been a compliment . . . just anything to feel normal. When I went back to the truck I locked the doors and climbed into the sleeper. The truth is I was afraid to go back on that road.

So I tried to sleep instead and lay there seeing that road stretching out like an avenue to nowhere, flanked on each side by trees so that a man thought of a high speed tunnel. Then somewhere between dream and imagination I began to wonder if that road really did end at night. For me. For anybody. I could see in my mind how a man might drive that road and finally come into something like a tunnel, high beams rocketing along walls that first were smooth then changed like the pillared walls of a mine with timber shoring on the sides. But not in the middle. I could see a man driving down, down at sixty or seventy, driving deep towards the center of the earth and knowing that it was a mine. Knowing that there was a rock face at the end of the road but the man unable to get his foot off the pedal. And then the thoughts connected and I knew that Joe Indian was the trouble with the road, but I did not know why or how. I was shaking and cold. In the morning it was not all bad. The movement was still there but it was dimmed out in daylight. You caught it in flashes. I barely made Mount Vernon, where I connected with 25. The trouble stopped there. When I got home I told some lies and took a week off. My place is out beyond LaFollette, where you can live with a little air and woods around you. For a while I was nearly afraid to go into those woods.

When I returned to the road it was the Cincinnati run all over with an occasional turn to Indianapolis. I used the Lexington route and watched the other guys. They were all keeping quiet. The only people who were talking were the police who were trying to figure out the sudden shift in traffic. Everybody who had been the route figured if they talked about it, everyone else would think they were crazy.

You would see a driver you knew and say hello. Then the two of you would sit and talk about the weather. When truckers stop talking about trucks and the road something is wrong.

I saw Joe once below Livingston on 25. His rig looked the same as always. He was driving full out like he was asking to be pulled over. You could run at speed on 150. Not on 25. Maybe he *was* asking for it, kind of hoping it would happen so that he would be pulled off the road for a while. Because a week after that and a month after the trouble started I heard on the grapevine that Joe was dead.

Killed, the word had it, by ramming over a bank on 150 into a stream. Half of his load had drowned. The other half suffocated. Cars had driven past the scene for two or three days, the drivers staring straight down the road like always. No one paid enough attention to see wheel marks that left the road and over the bank.

What else the story said was not good and maybe not true. I tried to dismiss it and kept running 25. The summer was dwindling away into fall, the oak and maple on those hills were beginning to change. I was up from Knoxville one night and saw the North Carolina job sitting in front of a stop. No schedule would have kept me from pulling over. I climbed down and went inside.

For a moment I did not see anyone I recognized, then I looked a second time and saw Joe's cousin. He was changed. He sat at a booth. Alone. He was slumped like an old man. When I walked up he looked at me with eyes that seemed to see past or through me. He motioned me to the other side of the booth. I saw that his hands were shaking.

"What?" I asked him, figuring that he was sick or had just had a close one.

"Do you remember that night?" he asked me. No lead up. Talking like a man who had only one thing on his mind. Like a man who could only talk about one thing.

"Yes," I told him, "and I've heard about Joe." I tried to lie. I could not really say that I was sorry.

"Came With Thunder," his cousin told me. "That was

his other name, the one his mother had for him. He was born during an August storm.''

I looked at the guy to see if he was kidding. Then I remembered that Joe was killed in August. It made me uneasy.

"I found him," Joe's cousin told me. "Took my car and went looking after he was three days overdue. Because . . . I knew he was driving that road . . . trying to prove something in spite of Hell."

"What? Prove what?"

"Hard to say. I found him hidden half by water, half by trees and the brush that grows up around here. He might have stayed on into the winter if someone hadn't looked." The man's hands were shaking. I told him to wait, walked over and brought back two coffees. When I sat back down he continued.

"It's what I told you. But, it has to be more than that. I've been studying and studying. Something like this . . . always is." He paused and drank the coffee, holding the mug in both hands.

"When we were kids," the driver said, "we practically lived at each other's house. I liked his best. The place was a shack. Hell, my place was a shack. Miners made money then, but it was all scrip. They spent it for everything but what they needed." He paused, thoughtful. Now that he was telling the story he did not seem so nervous.

"Because of his mother," he continued. "She was Indian. Creek maybe but west of Creek country. Or maybe from a northern tribe that drifted down. Not Cherokee because their clans haven't any turkeys for totems or names that I know of . . .''

I was startled. I started to say something.

"Kids don't think to ask about stuff like that," he said. His voice was an apology as if he were wrong for not knowing the name of a tribe.

"Makes no difference anyway," he said. "She was Indian religious and she brought Joe up that way because his old man was either working or drinking. We all three spent a lot of time in the hills talking to the animals, talking to flowers . . .''

"What?"

"They do that. Indians do. They think that life is round like a flower. They think animals are not just animals. They are brothers. Everything is separate like people."

I still could not believe that he was serious. He saw my look and seemed discouraged, like he had tried to get through to people before and had not had any luck.

"You don't understand," he said. "I mean that dogs are not people, they are dogs. But each dog is important because he has a dog personality as same as a man has a man personality."

"That makes sense," I told him. "I've owned dogs. Some silly. Some serious. Some good. Some bad."

"Yes," he said. "But, most important. When he dies a dog has a dog spirit the same way a man would have a man spirit. That's what Joe was brought up to believe."

"But they kill animals for food," I told him.

"That's true. It's one of the reasons for being an animal . . . or maybe, even a man. When you kill an animal you are supposed to apologize to the animal's spirit and explain you needed meat."

"Oh."

"You don't get it," he said. "I'm not sure I do either but there was a time . . . anyway, it's not such a bad way to think if you look at it close. But the point is Joe believed it all his life. When he got out on his own and saw the world he couldn't believe it anymore. You know? A guy acting like that. People cause a lot of trouble being stupid and mean."

"I know."

"But he couldn't quite not believe it either. He had been trained every day since he was born, and I do mean every day."

"Are they that religious?"

"More than any white man I ever knew. Because they live it instead of just believe it. You can see what could happen to a man?"

"Not quite."

"Sure you can. He couldn't live in the camp anymore because the camp was dead when the mines died through this whole region. He had to live outside so he had to change, but a part of him couldn't change . . . Then his mother died. Tuberculosis. She tried Indian remedies and died. But I think she would have anyway."

"And that turned him against it." I could see what the guy was driving at.

"He was proving something," the man told me. "Started buying and hauling the birds. Living hand to mouth. But, I guess everytime he tore one up it was just a little more hate working out of his system."

"A hell of a way to do it."

"That's the worst part. He turned his back on the whole thing, getting revenge. But always, down underneath, he was afraid."

"Why be afraid?" I checked the clock. Then I looked at the man. There was a fine tremble returning to his hands.

"Don't you see," he told me. "He still halfway believed. And if a man could take revenge, animals could take revenge. He was afraid of the animals helping out their brothers." The guy was sweating. He looked at me and there was fear in his eyes. "They do, you know. I'm honest-to-God afraid that they do."

"Why?"

"When he checked out missing I called the seller, then called the process outfit where he sold. He was three days out on a one day run. So I went looking and found him." He watched me. "The guys aren't driving that road."

"Neither am I," I told him. "For that matter, neither are you."

"It's all right now," he said. "There's nothing left on that road. Right outside of Harrodsburg, down that little grade and then take a hook left up the hill, and right after you top it . . ."

"I've driven it."

"Then you begin to meet the start of the hill country. Down around the creek I found him. Fifty feet of truck laid over in the creek and not an ounce of metal showing to the road. Water washing through the cab. Load tipped but a lot of it still tied down. All dead of course.''

''A mess.''

''Poultry rots quick,'' was all he said.

''How did it happen?''

''Big animal,'' he told me. ''Big like a cow or a bull or a bear . . . There wasn't any animal around. You know what a front end looks like. Metal to metal doesn't make that kind of dent. Flesh.''

''The stream washed it away.''

''I doubt. It eddies further down. There hasn't been that much rain. But he hit something . . .''

I was feeling funny. ''Listen, I'll tell you the truth. On that road I hit everything. If a cow had shown up I'd have run through it, I guess. Afraid to stop. There wouldn't have been a bump.''

''I know,'' he told me. ''But Joe bumped. That's the truth. Hard enough to take him off the road. I've been scared. Wondering. Because what he could not believe I can't believe either. It does not make sense, it does not . . .'' He looked at me. His hands were trembling hard.

''I waded to the cab,'' he said. ''Waded out there. Careful of sinks. The smell of the load was terrible. Waded out to the cab hoping it was empty and knowing damned well that it wasn't. And I found him.''

''How?''

''Sitting up in the cab sideways with the water swirling around about shoulder height and . . . Listen, maybe you'd better not hear. Maybe you don't want to.''

''I didn't wait this long not to hear,'' I told him.

''Sitting there with the bone handle of the knife tacked to his front where he had found his heart . . . or something, and put it in. Not in time though. Not in time.''

''You mean he was hurt and afraid of drowning?''

''Not a mark on his body except for the knife. Not a break anywhere, but his face . . . sitting there, leaning into that knife and hair all gone, chewed away. Face mostly gone, lips, ears, eyelids all gone. Chewed away, scratched away.

I looked, and in the opening that had been his mouth something moved like disappearing down a hole . . . but, in the part of the cab that wasn't submerged there was a thousand footprints, maybe a thousand different animals . . ."

His voice broke. I reached over and steadied him by the shoulder. "What was he stabbing?" the man asked. "I can't figure. Himself, or . . ."

I went to get more coffee for us and tried to make up something that would help him out. One thing I agreed with that he had said. I agreed that I wished he had not told me.

Ohio-born Jack Cady has enjoyed a wide and varied literary career. Newspaper editor and owner, university teacher and visiting professor of English are among his accomplishments. He has won such writing awards as a "First" from the Atlantic Monthly *for his short story, "The Burning" (which also received the Governor's Award and the Iowa Award in 1972) and the National Literary Award for his short story "The Shark" (1971). Much of his work has supernatural themes, such as the ghost novel* The Jonah Watch *(1982) and* The Man Who Could Make Things Vanish *(1983).*

Sometimes an archaeologist finds more than pot shards and arrowheads.

13

The Resting Place
Oliver La Farge

The possibility that Dr. Hillebrand was developing kleptomania caused a good deal of pleasure among his younger colleagues—that is, the entire personnel of the Department of Anthropology, including its director, Walter Klibben. It was not that anybody really disliked the old boy. That would have been hard to do, for he was co-operative and gentle, and his humor was mild; he was perhaps the greatest living authority on Southwestern archaeology, and broadly learned in the general science of anthropology; and he was a man who delighted in the success of others.

Dr. Hillebrand was the last surviving member of a group of men who had made the Department of Anthropology famous in the earlier part of the twentieth century. His ideas were old-fashioned; to Walter Klibben, who at forty was very much the young comer, and to the men he had gathered about him, Dr. Hillebrand's presence, clothed with author-

243

ity, was as incongruous as that of a small, mild brontosaurus would be in a modern farmyard.

On the other hand, no one living had a finer archaeological technique. Added to this was a curious intuition, which caused him to dig in unexpected places and come up with striking finds—the kind of thing that delights donors and trustees, such as the largest unbroken Mesa Verde black-on-white jar known up to that time, the famous Biltabito Cache of turquoise and shell objects, discovered two years before and not yet on exhibition, and, only the previous year, the mural decorations at Painted Mask Ruin. The mural, of which as yet only a small part had been uncovered, compared favorably with the murals found at Awatovi and Kawaika-a by the Peabody Museum, but was several centuries older. Moreover, in the part already exposed there was an identifiable katchina mask, unique and conclusive evidence that the katchina cult dated back to long before the white man came. This meant, Dr. Klibben foresaw gloomily, that once again all available funds for publication would be tied up by the old coot's material.

The trustees loved him. Several years ago, he had reached the age of retirement and they had waived the usual limitation in his case. He was curator of the museum, a position only slightly less important than that of director, and he occupied the Kleinman Chair in American Archaeology. This was an endowed position paying several thousand a year more than Klibben's own professorship.

Dr. Hillebrand's occupancy of these positions, on top of his near monopoly of publication money, was the rub. He blocked everything. If only the old relic would become emeritus, the younger men could move up. Klibben had it all worked out. There would be the Kleinman Chair for himself, and McDonnell could accede to his professorship. He would leave Steinberg an associate, but make him curator. Thus, Steinberg and McDonnell would have it in mind that the curatorship always might be transferred to McDonnell as the man with senior status, which would keep them both on their toes. At least one assistant professor could, in due course, be made an associate, and young George Franklin, Klibben's own prized student, could be promoted from instructor to assistant. It all fitted together and reinforced his own position. Then, given free access to funds for monographs and papers. . . .

But Dr. Hillebrand showed no signs of retiring. It was not that he needed the money from his two positions; he was a bachelor and something of an ascetic, and much of his salary he put into his own expeditions. He loved to teach, he said—and his students liked him. He loved his museum; in fact, he was daffy about it, pottering around in it until late at night. Well, let him retire, and he could still teach a course or two if he wanted; he could still potter, but Klibben could run his Department as he wished, as it ought to be run.

Since there seemed no hope that the old man would give out physically in the near future, Klibben had begun looking for symptoms of mental failure. There was, for instance, the illogical way in which Dr. Hillebrand often decided just where to run a trench or dig a posthole. As Steinberg once remarked, it was as if he were guided by a ouija board. Unfortunately, his eccentricity produced splendid results.

Then, sometimes Hillebrand would say to his students, "Now, let us imagine—" and proceed to indulge in surprising reconstructions of the daily life and religion of the ancient cliff dwellers, going far beyond the available evidence. The director had put Franklin onto that, because the young man had worked on Hopi and Zuñi ceremonials. Franklin reported that the old boy always made it clear that these reconstructions were not science, and further, Franklin said that they were remarkably shrewd and had given him some helpful new insights into aspects of the modern Indians' religion.

The possibility of kleptomania was something else again. The evidence—insufficient so far—concerned the rich Bilt-abito Cache, which Dr. Hillebrand himself was enumerating, cataloguing, and describing, mostly evenings, when the museum was closed. He was the only one who knew exactly how many objects had been in the find, but it did look as if some of it might now be missing. There was also what the night watchman thought he had seen. And then there was that one turquoise bead—but no proof it had come from that source, of course—that McDonnell had found on the floor near the cast of the Quiriguá stela, just inside the entrance to the museum.

The thefts—if there had been any—had taken place in April and early May, when everyone was thinking of the end of the college year and the summer's field trips. A short time later, and quite by accident, Klibben learned from an associate professor of ornithology that old Hillebrand had obtained from him a number of feathers, which he said he wanted for repairing his collection of katchina dolls. Among them were parrot and macaw feathers, and the fluffy feathers from the breast of an eagle.

Klibben's field was not the American Southwest, but any American anthropologist would have been able to draw an obvious conclusion: turquoise, shell, and feathers of those sorts were components of ritual offerings among the modern Hopis and Zuñis, and possibly their ancestors, whose remains Dr. Hillebrand had carried on his lifework. Dr. Klibben began to suspect—or hope—that the old man was succumbing to a mental weakness far more serious than would be evidenced by the mere stealing of a few bits of turquoise and shell.

The director made tactful inquiries at the genetics field laboratory to see if the old man had been seeking corn pollen, another component of the ritual offerings, and found that there the question of the evolution of *Zea maiz* in the Southwest was related to the larger and much vexed question of the origin and domestication of that important New World plant, so interesting to archaeologists, botanists, and geneticists. Dr. Hillebrand had been collecting specimens of ancient corn from archaeological sites for a long time—ears, cobs, and grains extending over two millenniums or more, and other parts of the plant, including some fragments of tassels. It was, Klibben thought, the kind of niggling little detail you would expect to find Hillebrand spending good time on. Dr. Hillebrand had been turning his specimens over to the plant and heredity boys, who were delighted to have them. They, in turn, had followed this up by obtaining—for comparison—seed of modern Pueblo Indian, Navajo, and Hopi corn, and planting it. It was natural enough, then, that from time to time Dr. Hillebrand should take specimens of seed and pollen home to study on his own. It might be clear as day to Klibben that the old boy had gone gaga to the point of making ritual offerings to the gods of the cliff dwellings; he still had nothing that would convince a strongly pro-Hillebrand board of trustees.

Even so, the situation was hopeful. Klibben suggested to the night watchman that, out of concern for Professor Hillebrand's health, he keep a special eye on the Professor's after-hours activities in the museum. Come June, he would arrange for Franklin—with his Southwestern interests, Franklin was the logical choice—to go along on Hillebrand's expedition and see what he could see.

Franklin took the assignment willingly, by no means unaware of the possible advantages to himself should the old man be retired. The archaeologist accepted this addition to his staff with equanimity. He remarked that Franklin's knowledge of Pueblo daily life would be helpful in interpreting what might be uncovered, while a better grounding in Southwestern prehistory would add depth to the young man's ethnographic perceptions. Right after commencement, they set out for the Navajo country of Arizona, accompanied by two undergraduate and four graduate students.

At Farmington, in New Mexico, they picked up the university's truck and station wagon and Hillebrand's own field car, a Model A Ford as archaic as its owner. In view of the man's income, Franklin thought, his hanging on to the thing was one more oddity, an item that could be added to many others to help prove Klibben's case. At Farmington, too, they took on a cook and general helper. Dr. Hillebrand's work was generously financed, quite apart from what went into it from his own earnings.

The party bounced over the horrifying road past the Four

Corners and around the north end of Beautiful Mountain, into the Chinlee Valley, then southward and westward until, after having taken a day and a half to drive about two hundred miles, they reached the cliffs against which stood Painted Mask Ruin. The principal aim of the current summer's work was to excavate the decorated kiva in detail, test another kiva, and make further, standard excavations in the ruin as a whole.

By the end of a week, the work was going nicely. Dr. Hillebrand put Franklin, as the senior scientist under him, in charge of the work in the painted kiva. Franklin knew perfectly well that he was deficient in the required techniques; he would, in fact, be dependent upon his first assistant, Philip Fleming, who was just short of his Ph.D. Fleming had worked in that kiva the previous season, had spent three earlier seasons with Dr. Hillebrand, and was regarded by him as the most promising of the many who had worked under him. There was real affection between the two men.

Two of the other graduate students were well qualified to run a simple dig for themselves. One was put in charge of the untouched second kiva, the other of a trench cutting into the general mass of the ruin from the north. Franklin felt uncomfortably supernumerary, but he recognized that that was an advantage in pursuing his main purpose of keeping a close watch on the expedition's director.

After supper on the evening of the eighth day, Dr. Hillebrand announced rather shyly that he would be gone for about four days, "to follow an old custom you all know about." The younger men smiled. Franklin kept a blank face to cover his quickened interest.

This was a famous, or notorious, eccentricity of the old man's, and one in which Drs. Klibben, McDonnell, and the rest put great hope. Every year, early in the season, Dr. Hillebrand went alone to a ruin he had excavated early in his career. There was some uncertainty as to just where the ruin was; it was believed to be one known to the Navajos as Tsekaiye Kin. No one knew what he did there. He said he found the surroundings and the solitude invaluable for thinking out the task in hand. It was usually not long after his return from it that he would announce his decision to dig in such-and-such a spot and proceed to uncover the painted kiva, or the Kettle Cave fetishes, or the Kin Hatsosi blanket, or some other notable find.

If Franklin could slip away in the station wagon and follow the old man, he might get just the information he wanted. So far, Dr. Hillebrand's activities on the expedition had evidenced nothing but his great competence. If the old man ever performed mad antique rites with stolen specimens, it would be at his secret place of meditation. Perhaps he got up and danced to the ancient gods. One might be able to sneak a photo. . . .

Dr. Hillebrand said, "I shan't be gone long. Meantime, of course, Dr. Franklin will be in charge." He turned directly to his junior. "George, there are several things on which you must keep a close watch. If you will look at these diagrams—and you, too, Phil. . . ."

Franklin and Fleming sat down beside him. Dr. Hillebrand expounded. Whether the ancient devil had done it intentionally or not, Franklin saw that he was neatly hooked. In the face of the delicacy and the probable outcome of the next few days' work, he could not possibly make an excuse for absenting himself when the head of the expedition was also absent.

Dr. Hillebrand took off early the next morning in his throbbing Model A. He carried with him a Spartan minimum of food and bedding. It was good to be alone once more in the long-loved reaches of the Navajo country. The car drove well. He still used it because, short of a jeep, nothing newer had the clearance to take him where he wanted to go.

He drove slowly, for he was at the age when knowledge and skill must replace strength, and getting stuck would be serious. When he was fifty, he reflected, he would have reached T'iiz Hatsosi Canyon from this year's camp in under four hours; when he was thirty, if it had been possible then to travel this country in a car, he would have made even greater speed, and as like as not ended by getting lost. He reached the open farming area outside the place where T'iiz Hatsosi sliced into the great mesa to the south. There were nearly twice as many hogans to be seen as when he had first come here; several of them were square and equipped with windows, and by some of them cars were parked. Everything was changing, but these were good people still, although not as genial and hospitable as their grandparents had been when he first packed in.

He entered the narrow mouth of T'iiz Hatsosi Canyon in the late afternoon, and by the exercise of consummate skill drove some four miles up it. At that point, it was somewhat wider than elsewhere, slightly under two hundred feet across the bottom. The heavy grazing that had so damaged all the Navajos' land had had some effect here. There was less grass than there used to be—but then, he reflected, he had no horses to pasture—and the bed of the wash was more deeply eroded, and here and there sharp gullies led into it from the sides.

Still the cottonwoods grew between the occasional stream and the high, warmly golden-bluff cliffs. Except at noon, there was shade, and the quality of privacy, almost of secrecy, remained. In the west wall was the wide strip of white rock from which the little ruin took its name, Tsekaiye Kin, leading the eye to the long ledge above which the cliff arched like a scallop shell, and upon which stood the ancient habitations. The lip of the ledge was about twenty feet above the level of the canyon, and approachable by a talus slope that was not too hard to negotiate. Some small evergreens grew at the corners of the ledge. From the ground, the settlement did not seem as if it had been empty for centuries, but rather as if its occupants at the moment happened not to be visible. The small black rectangles of doorways and three tiny squares of windows made him feel, as they had done over forty years ago, as if the little settlement were watching him.

South of the far end of the ledge, and at the level of the

canyon floor, was the spring. Water seeped richly through a crack in the rock a few feet above the ground and flowed down over rock to form a pool at the base. The wet golden-brown stone glistened; small water growths clung to the crevices. In the pool itself, there was cress, and around it moss and grass rich enough to make a few feet of turf.

Here Dr. Hillebrand deposited his bedroll and his food. He estimated that he had better than two hours of daylight left. He cut himself a supply of firewood. Then he took a package out of his coffeepot. The package was wrapped in an old piece of buckskin. With this in hand, he climbed up the slope to the ruin.

The sense of peace had begun once he was out of sight of the camp at Painted Mask Ruin. It had grown when he entered T'iiz Hatsosi Canyon; it had become stronger when he stepped out of the car and glimpsed through the cottonwoods his little village, with its fourteen rooms. By the spring, it had become stronger yet, and mixed with a nostalgia of past times that was sweetly painful, like a memory of an old and good lost love. These feelings were set aside as he addressed himself to the task of climbing, which was not entirely simple; then they returned fourfold when he was in the ruin. Here he had worked alone, a green young man with a shiny new Doctor's degree, a boy-man not unlike young Fleming. Here he had discovered what it was like to step into a room that still had its roof intact, and see the marks of the smoke from the household fire, the loom ties still in place in the ceiling and floor, the broken cooking pots still in the corner.

He paid his respects to that chamber—Room 4-B; stood in the small, open central area; then went to the roofless, irregular oval of the kiva. All by himself he had dug it out.

Could Dr. Franklin have been there, spying unseen, he would have been most happy. From under a stone that appeared firmly embedded in the clay flooring Dr. Hillebrand took an ancient, crude stone pipe fitted with a recent willow stem. He filled it with tobacco, performed curious motions as he lit it, and puffed smoke in the six directions.

Then he climbed out of the kiva on the inner side and went behind the double row of habitations, to the darker area under the convex curve of the wall at the back of the cave, the floor of which was a mixture of earth and rubbish. Two smallish, rounded stones about three feet apart inconspicuously marked a place. Sitting by it on a convenient ledge of rock, he puffed at the pipe again; then he opened the buckskin package and proceeded to make an offering of ancient turquoise beads, white and red shell, black stone, feathers and down, and corn pollen.

Sitting back comfortably, he said, "Well, here I am again."

The answer did not come from the ground, in which the bones of the speaker reposed, but from a point in space, as if he were sitting opposite Dr. Hillebrand. "Welcome, old friend. Thank you for the gifts; their smell is pleasing to us all."

"I don't know whether I can bring you any more," the archaeologist said. "I can buy new things, of course, but getting the old ones is becoming difficult. They are watching me."

"It is not necessary," the voice answered. "We are rich in the spirits of things such as these, and our grandchildren on earth still offer them to us. It has been rather for your benefit that I have had you bringing them, and I think that that training has served its purpose."

"You relieve me." Then, with a note of anxiety, "That doesn't mean that I have to stop visiting you?"

"Not at all. And, by the way, there is a very handsome jar with a quantity of beans of an early variety in it where you are digging now. It was left behind by accident when the people before the ones who built the painted kiva moved out. It belonged to a woman called Bluebird Tailfeather. Her small child ran off and was lost just as they were moving, and by the time she found him, the war chief was impatient. However, we can come back to that later, I can see that you have something on your mind."

"I'm lonely," Dr. Hillebrand said simply. "My real

friends are all gone. There are a lot of people I get on nicely with, but no one left I love—that is, above the ground—and you are the only one below the ground I seem to be able to reach. I—I'd like to take your remains back with me, and then we could talk again.''

"I would not like that.''

"Then of course I won't.''

"I was sure of that. Your country is strange to me, and traveling back and forth would be a lot of effort. What I saw that time I visited you was alien to me; it would be to you, too, I think. It won't be long, I believe, before I am relieved of attachment to my bones entirely, but if you moved them now, it would be annoying. You take that burial you carried home ten years ago—old Rabbit Stick. He says you treat him well and have given him the smell of ceremonial jewels whenever you could, but sometimes he arrives quite worn out from his journey.''

"Rabbit Stick,'' Dr. Hillebrand mused. "I wondered if there were not someone there. He has never spoken to me.''

"He couldn't. He was just an ordinary Reed Clan man. But he is grateful to you for the offerings, because they have given him the strength he needed. As you know, I can speak with you because I was the Sun's Forehead, and there was the good luck that you were thinking and feeling in the right way when you approached me. But tell me, don't the young men who learn from you keep you company?''

"Yes. There is one now who is like a son to me. But then they have learned, and they go away. The men in between, who have become chiefs, you might say, in my Department, have no use for me. They want to make me emeritus—that is, put me on a pension, take over my authority and my rewards, and set me where I could give advice and they could ignore it. They have new ways, and they despise mine. So now they are watching me. They have sent a young man out this time just to watch me. They call him a student of the ways of your grandchildren; he spent six weeks at Zuñi once, and when even he could see that the people didn't like him, he went and put in the rest of the summer at Oraibi.''

"New Oraibi or Old Oraibi?" the Sun's Forehead asked.

"New Oraibi."

The chief snorted.

"So, having also read some books, he thinks he is an ethnographer, only he calls himself a cultural anthropologist. And he is out here to try to find proof that my mind is failing." He smiled. "They'd certainly think so if they saw me sitting here talking to empty air."

The Sun's Forehead chuckled. "They certainly would. They wouldn't be able to hear me, you know." Then his voice became serious again. "That always happens, I think. It happened to me. They wanted to do things differently, when I had at last come to the point at which an Old Man talked to me. I reached it in old age—not young, as you did. They could not take my title, but they wanted to handle my duties for me, bring me enough food to live on, hear my advice and not listen to it. Struggling against them became wearying and distasteful, so finally I decided to go under. At the age I reached—about your age—it is easy to do."

"And now you say that you are about to be detached from your bones entirely? You are reaching the next stage?"

"Let us say that I begin to hope. Our life is beautiful, but for a hundred years or so now I have been longing for the next, and I begin to hope."

"How does it happen? Or is it wrong for me to know?"

"You may know. You are good, and you keep your secrets, as our wise men always did. You will see a man who has become young, handsome, and full of light. When we dance, he dances with great beauty; his singing is beautiful, and you feel as if it were creating life. Then one time when the katchinas themselves are dancing before us—not masks, you understand, the katchinas themselves—you can't find him among the watchers. Then you seem to recognize him, there among the sacred people, dancing like them. Then you think that the next time our grandchildren on the earth put on the masks and dance, that one, whom you knew as a spirit striving to purify himself, who used to tell you about his days on earth, will be there. With his own eyes he will see our grandchildren and bless them." The chief's voice trailed off, as though the longing for what he was describing deprived him of words.

"To see the katchinas themselves dancing," Dr. Hillebrand mused. "Not the masks, but what the masks stand for. . . . That would keep me happy for centuries. But then, I could not join your people. I was never initiated. I'd be plain silly trying to dance with them. It's not for me."

"For over forty years I have been initiating you," the Sun's Forehead said. "As for dancing—you will no longer be in that old body. You will not be dancing with those fragile, rheumatic bones. There is room for you in our country. Why don't you come over? Just lie down in that crevice back there and make up your mind."

"You know," Dr. Hillebrand said, "I think I will."

Both the Kleinman Professor of American Archaeology and the spirit who once had been the Sun's Forehead for the settlements in the neighborhood of T'iiz Hatsosi were thoroughly unworldly. It had not occurred to either of them that within six days after Dr. Hillebrand had left camp Dr. George Franklin would organize a search for him, and four days later his body would be found where he had died of, apparently, heart failure. Above all, it had not occurred to them that his body would be taken home and buried with proper pomp and ceremony in the appropriate cemetery. (But Philip Fleming, close to tears, resolutely overlooked the scattering of turquoise and shell in the rubbish between the crevice and the kiva.)

Dr. Hillebrand found himself among people as alien to him as they had been to the Sun's Forehead. They seemed to be gaunt from the total lack of offerings, and the means by which they should purify and advance themselves to where they could leave this life for the next, which he believed to be the final one, were confused. He realized that his spirit was burdened with much dross, and that it would be a long time before he could gather the strength to attempt a journey to the country of his friend.

His portrait, in academic gown and hood, was painted posthumously and hung in the entrance of the museum, to one side of the stela from Quiriguá and facing the reproduction of the famous Painted Kiva mural. Dr. Klibben adroitly handled the promotions and emoluments that fell under his control. Philip Fleming won his Ph.D. with honors, and was promptly offered a splendid position at Harvard. Moved by he knew not what drive, and following one or two other actions he had performed to his own surprise, Fleming went to Dr. Hillebrand's grave, for a gesture of respect and thanks.

It had seemed to him inappropriate to bring any flowers. Instead, as he sat by the grave, with small motions of his hands he sprinkled over it some bits of turquoise and shell he had held out from a necklace he had unearthed, and followed them with a pinch of pollen given him by a Navajo. Suddenly his face registered utter astonishment; then careful listening.

The following season, Fleming returned to Painted Mask Ruin by agreement with Dr. Klibben, who was delighted to get his Department entirely out of Southwestern archaeology. There he ran a trench that led right into a magnificent polychrome pot containing a store of beans of high botanical interest.

Within a few years, he stopped visiting the grave, but he was sentimentalist enough to make a pilgrimage all alone to Tsekaiye Kin at the beginning of each field season. It was jokingly said among his confreres that there he communed with the spirit of old Hillebrand. Certainly he seemed to have inherited that legendary figure's gift for making spectacular finds.

Winner of the Pulitzer prize (1929) for his Laughing Boy, *a novel of Navajo Indian life, Oliver La Farge was born in New York in 1901, educated at Groton and Harvard, and became a distinguished anthropologist and fiction writer. Serving as president of the Association on American Indian Affairs from 1933 on, he was known as an able advocate for Indian rights. Several of his best works are collected in* The Door in the Wall *(1969). He died in 1963.*

Acknowledgments

"Night-Side" by Joyce Carol Oates. Copyright © 1990 by the Ontario Review, Inc. Reprinted by permission of the author.

"Drawer 14"—Copyright © 1965 by H.S.D. Publications. Reprinted by permission of the author.

"The Jest of Warburg Tantavul" by Seabury Quinn. Copyright © 1934 by *Weird Tales*. Reprinted by permission of the agents for the author's Estate, the Scott Meredith Literary Agency, Inc., 845 Third Avenue, New York, NY 10022.

"One of the Dead"—Copyright © 1964 by William Wood. Reprinted by permission of the author.

"Emmett" by Dahlov Ipcar. Copyright © 1990 by Dahlov Ipcar. Published in *The Nightmare and Her Foal and Other Stories* by Dahlov Ipcar; North Country Press, P. O. Box 641, Unity, Maine 04988.

"Night Court"—Copyright © 1958 by Mary Elizabeth Counselman. Reprinted by permission of the author.

"The Ghosts of Steamboat Coulee"—Copyright © 1926 by *Weird Tales*. Reprinted by arrangement with Forrest J. Ackerman, 2495 Glendower Avenue, Los Angeles, CA 90027.

"He Walked by Day"—Copyright © 1934 by *Weird Tales*. Reprinted by permission of Weird Tales, Ltd.

"The Phantom Farmhouse" by Seabury Quinn. Copyright © 1923 by *Weird Tales*. Reprinted by permission of the agents for the author's estate, the Scott Meredith Literary Agency, Inc., 845 Third Avenue, New York, NY 10022.

"Stillwater, 1896"—Copyright © 1984 by Michael Cassutt. Reprinted by permission of the author.

"Ride the Thunder"—Copyright © 1972 by Jack Cady. Reprinted by permission of the author.

"The Resting Place"—Copyright © 1954 by Oliver La Farge. Copyright © renewed 1982 by John Pendaries La Farge. Reprinted by permission of Marie Rodell–Frances Collin Literary Agency.